The Nordic Translation Series

Sponsored by the Nordic Council of
the governments of Denmark,
Finland, Iceland, Norway, and Sweden
Advisory Committee:
Einar Haugen, Harald S. Næss, and
Richard B. Vowles, Chairman

The Great Cycle

The Great Cycle

by Tarjei Vesaas

Det store spelet   Translated from the
Norwegian by Elizabeth Rokkan
with an Introduction by Harald S. Næss
The University of Wisconsin Press
Madison, Milwaukee, and London, 1967

Published by the University of Wisconsin Press
Madison, Milwaukee, and London
U.S.A.: Box 1379, Madison, Wisconsin 53701
U.K.: 26–28 Hallam Street, London, W.1

English translation copyright © 1967
by the Regents of the University of Wisconsin
Originally published by Olaf Norlis Forlag
Oslo, Norway
Copyright © 1934 by Olaf Norlis Forlag
Printed in the United States of America
by The Colonial Press Inc.,
Clinton, Massachusetts
Library of Congress Catalog Card
Number 67–26629

Introduction

Tarjei Vesaas enjoys the paradoxical privilege of being at the same time Norway's most provincial and most cosmopolitan writer. He has spent practically all of his life in relative seclusion among the Telemark farmers whose dialect he speaks and writes, yet he has also travelled widely abroad, and his contact with foreign literature has helped develop his personal style, the most modern and most European in Norway. Vesaas uses Norway's second language, *nynorsk*, which has somewhat restricted his Norwegian popularity; on the other hand he has won many admirers in the neighboring countries and in recent years has seen his books appear simultaneously in *nynorsk*, Danish, and Swedish. His position in Norwegian letters is comparable to that of Pär Lagerkvist in Sweden and Martin A. Hansen in Denmark.

Tarjei Vesaas was born in 1897 at Vinje in Telemark, a district known for its great traditions in rustic arts, folk music, and medieval ballads. Telemark is the home of the fourteenth-century visionary poem *Draumkvædet* as well as of a number of modern poets, notably Aasmund Vinje (1818–70) whose outlook, like that of Vesaas, was European, though he wrote in *nynorsk*. Among contemporary Telemark artists sculptor Dyre Vaa, poetess Aslaug Vaa, and composer Eyvind Groven are second cousins of Vesaas; the *rosemaling* specialist Øystein Vesaas is his uncle.

Vesaas' teens fell in the years of the First World War. He was a lonely and sensitive boy who felt as his own the suffering and broken hopes of youth on the battlefields of Europe. Being the oldest son, he was expected to take over the family farm, even though working with the soil did not satisfy his ambitions; he was a good student and wanted to go on studying. Instead he had to leave school at the age of fourteen, and with the exception of a year at Voss Folk High School, never continued his formal training. For all that he remained a great reader, and the books of Knut Hamsun, Rudyard Kipling, Selma Lagerlöf, and Tagore set him dreaming of a new world, more colorful than Vinje parish, which he now wanted to explore. In 1917 he spent the winter at Voss near Bergen; in 1919 he served seven months with the Royal Guards in Oslo. He went abroad for the first time in 1926 and in the following ten years visited a number of European countries: Sweden, Denmark, Germany, Italy, France, England, Belgium, Czechoslovakia, Switzerland, Austria. In 1934 he married Halldis Moren, a well-known poetess, and settled in Vinje on the farm Midtbø, which he had bought from an uncle. Since 1947 Vesaas has received a yearly stipend from the Norwegian State. He won the 1952 Venice Triennale Prize for the best European prose work of that year, and in 1964 he was awarded the Nordic Council Prize for Literature.

Travelling still excites this writer. He sets out on his journeys with all the intellectual curiosity of a bright school boy unspoiled by inverted snobbery or by cultural pessimism. He relaxes completely on a crowded ocean beach, and has no objections to juke boxes or to electric power plants, even when they threaten to impinge upon the rustic idylls of Telemark. Vesaas can accept the spirit of modern times more easily than many of his restless and disillusioned colleagues because, unlike them, he is still firmly anchored in the old culture of his inland home. His frequent jaunts abroad do not inspire him directly, but act as a catalyst for his only true inspiration, the everyday miracles of Vinje parish. He writes of what are, socially and intellectually speaking, very ordinary people. He is not concerned with analyzing them as products of a Norwegian rural community; rather he wishes to interpret their conduct in terms of the surrounding landscape. Hence he uses a language laden with images of the mountains, waterways, and pine forests of Vinje, and he believes that such images or symbols disclose secrets about his characters which conventional language cannot convey. In this sense Vesaas belongs to the modernist movement in European literature, standing somewhere between Kafka and Robbe-Grillet, but mainly he belongs to Telemark, whose ballad poetry from *Draumkvædet* to modern *nystev* shows an unbroken tradition of symbolic language.

Vesaas' first novel, *Children of Man* (*Menneskebonn,* 1923), is the melancholy story of a boy who loses his parents and later his sweetheart under tragic circumstances, yet who for all his misfortune still retains a naïve faith in the importance of good deeds. The novel has some wonderfully sensitive landscapes, but parts of the plot are not very believable, and the rhetorical style might conceivably produce laughter sometimes where tears were intended. Excessively sweet, though nevertheless attractive to many specialists, is Vesaas' next book *Huskuld the Herald* (*Sendemann Huskuld,* 1924), which tells of a lonely old village eccentric, a local St. Francis of the Birds, whose last years are blessed with the companionship of an adopted child. Most of Vesaas' writing, even his best, is colored by the author's sentimentality and love of melodrama. In these early works, however, the emotional style is carried to extreme limits by exaggerated use of expletives, rhetorical questions, repetitions, and unusual syntax. Such is also the style of the play *God's Abodes* (*Guds bustader,* 1925) and the two-part novel *Grinde Farm* and *Evening at Grinde* (*Grindegard,* 1925; *Grinde-kveld,* 1926). None of these works are important except insofar as they contain the crude beginnings of certain motifs which Vesaas later handled with great skill, *e.g.* the lack of communication between parents and its effect upon a sensitive child. This subject is treated with a rather lively and colorful realism in *The Black Horses* (*Dei svarte hestane,* 1928), Vesaas' first successful novel.

Usually classified as a romantic, Vesaas with some justice could also be termed a realist, not only because he can render details of reality with the penetrating precision of a Dürer drawing, but also because of his ability to express himself convincingly within the framework of complete, realistic actions and situations. This he has done most often in his short stories, a genre well suited to his talents and one in which he achieved early greatness. Already a story like "Signe Ton," from *The Bell in the Mound* (*Klokka i haugen,* 1929), shows a complete integration of plot, character, atmosphere into one bold image; on the other hand such integration is totally lacking in the four novels about Klas Dyregodt: *Father's Journey, Sigrid Stallbrokk, The Unknown Men,* and *The Heart Hears Its Native Music* (*Fars reise,* 1930; *Sigrid Stallbrokk,* 1931; *Dei ukjende mennene,* 1932; *Hjarta høyrer sine heimlandsto-nar,* 1938). Ever since *Children of Man* Vesaas has applied dramatic techniques in much of his prose. His descriptive passages are usually written in a lapidary style, with verbs frequently left out, as in stage directions. Dialogues without *inquit* ("said he") are common, as are long soliloquies which are straight monologues rather than dreamlike streams of consciousness. Of special interest, and difficult to reproduce in English translation, is Vesaas' extensive use of the imper-sonal pronoun *ein* ("one," here normally rendered as "they" or "you") in so-called *erlebte Rede, e.g.* "one was always alone" instead of "'I am always alone,' he thought." Unfortunately Vesaas' prose did not at first have the richness, tempo, and concentration needed for a successful application of such techniques. A case in point is the Dyregodt tetralogy men-tioned above: fine details notwithstanding, the melodrama and forced psychology of these novels as well as the repetitive and drawn-out action make the reading of them unrewarding. Very different is *The Sandalwood* (*Sandeltreet,* 1933), a story about the fears and expectations of a pregnant woman and her relationship with an understanding husband and with her children. The novel is tightly composed, free from exaggerated sentimentality, and on the whole closer to life than Vesaas' earlier works: from this time on a deeper awareness of social and political conditions determines the subject matter of his writing. Thus the play *Ultimatum* (1934; written in Strass-bourg, 1932) shows Vesaas' early reaction to the European arms race and points forward to *House in Darkness* and to other great novels of commitment. Also to this trend belong the present novel about life on a farm, *The Great Cycle* (*Det store spelet*, 1934), and its sequel, *The Women Call: Come Home* (*Kvinnor ropar heim*, 1935). Though perhaps not the chief merit of these books, their picture of peaceful productivity can well be seen as a warning to Norwegian readers that the dissatisfaction, restlessness, and aggressive tendencies in the world might soon invade their own community. This argument is taken up once more in *The Clay and the Wheel* (*Leiret og hjulet*, 1936), a substantial collection of stories, which includes such masterpieces as "Twenty-One" and "Bread."

In the sixteen years between 1923 and 1938 Vesaas published sixteen books, all of them, with the notable exception of *The Great Cycle* and half a dozen stories, the works of a learner experimenting with a new narrative style. Vesaas' first books are filled with conventional imagery: the sun and the moon are personified; gold and silver metaphors are used to indicate beauty, wealth, happiness. Much more interesting is another type of imagery based upon observations of nature and everyday life in Vinje: pine trees are likened to candles burning in the night, the life of a modest man is described as a rustle in the fallen leaves, true love as the filling of hollow hands. The wind and the earth are personified, also the mountains (symbolizing a man's conscience); later the farm, the house, the home, take on personality, and finally abstract ideas like speed, murder, the cry. Vesaas' novels from the 1930's document his efforts to integrate these various symbolic elements, but not until *The Seed* (*Kimen*, 1940; Eng. tr., 1964) did he write a book in which his intentions were fully realized. It tells of a happy island community suddenly stirred up by the news of a murder among them. An insane stranger has killed a young girl, and carried away by excitement that gradually grows into fury, they all join in the pursuit and execution of the "criminal." Then, as their passions subside, they perceive their guilt and need for atonement, and peace is once again restored to the island. Essentially this story of mass hysteria is a reversal of the biblical myth in Luke 8: "Then went the devils out of the man, and entered into the swine." The first part of the book opens with a description of the two sows: "Long naked tusks protruded all too plainly from ugly jaws, vicious teeth rooted in flesh—beneath the pitted, narrowed, overhanging brows." With this background Vesaas is able to use the pitted brow as a symbol of a downfall, of man's inherent evil, his violence, fear, and lack of judgment. The constructive forces, on the other hand, are symbolized by "the seed in the dust" (also from Luke 8), the motto which heads the second part of the book.

House in Darkness (*Huset i mørkret*, 1945) is one of the most significant of several Norwegian novels treating the German occupation of Norway, 1940–45. Its allegorical style is highly imaginative; the occupied country is presented in the form of a bewitched house, constantly creaking, and steeped in darkness except for certain corridors lit by shining arrows that signify the Nazi ideology. The man hired to polish the arrows is a collaborator and later a traitor, yet he is drawn with great sympathy, one of the poor of spirit who always fascinate the author. Vesaas cannot save him from liquidation by the underground, but in a very moving chapter he shows how his innocent children have their honor restored to them. Much more realistic, and hence symbolic rather than allegorical, is the novel *The Bleaching Place* (*Bleikeplassen*, 1946), which was first written as a play. It has retained a number of the qualities of drama—unity of place, a well-developed plot, suspense, and a beautiful white and black atmosphere which suits a drama of sin and atonement. The book calls to mind the biblical story of David and Bathsheba as well as King David's psalms of penitence.

The Norwegian resistance movement is the subject of several Vesaas poems from this period, and also of a play, *Morning Wind* (*Morgonvinden*, 1947), which was produced with some success at the Norwegian Theater in Oslo. While in *The Bleaching Place* atmosphere is evoked through visual imagery, in *Morning Wind* special emphasis is placed on the uses of sound, a technique further developed by Vesaas in his radio plays. In the novel *The Tower* (*Tårnet*, 1948) Vesaas has re-shaped and extended his first important symbol, the mountain peak in *Children of Man*. Jorunn and Randolv, a scrap iron dealer, lose their young baby when he cuts himself on the jagged, rusty iron and then develops blood poisoning. The image of the jagged barb is now used to illustrate the destructive powers of a sick conscience throughout the novel. Conscience is also portrayed, however, as a positive force, and is seen as a shining tower by Randolv's young son Nils. That he, who had been jealous of his new little brother, is finally able to overcome the crippling effects of his conscience, is an example of Vesaas' cautious optimism. Such optimism is present even in the gloomy novel *The Signal* (*Signalet*, 1950), of all Vesaas' novels probably the one most consistently allegoric. The situation is surrealistic rather than realistic: a train full of people stands ready to leave the station, but the signal of departure is not given, and never will be. Vesaas at this time had not studied Kafka, and though many critics have pointed out the similarity between *The Signal* and works by the German modernist, the novel in most of its striking qualities is still entirely typical of Vesaas. The positive note—that Jens is somehow able to make himself at home amid all this meaninglessness—is what set Vesaas most apart from other writers of *romans nouveaux*. In 1952 Vesaas published a collection of short stories, *The Winds* (*Vindane*, 1952), which later appeared in several other languages and won for its author the Venice prize mentioned above. Better than other collections of Vesaas' stories, *The Winds* illustrates his ability to create atmosphere by the simplest of means; typically, three of these thirteen stories have been turned into successful radio plays, and, in fact, Vesaas' rich, evocative language lends itself particularly well to oral presentation.

On the subject of symbolic language, Jacques Maritain writes in one of his English essays: "There is a curious—and tragic—phenomenon, where something great and invaluable is looked for, and missed (namely the dignity of words, which refers to truth, not power), and where by dint of refinement the civilized mind retrogresses to that magical notion of the sign which was normal in the childlike state of mankind, yet is for mankind in its adult stage but a pathological symptom." There is no such retrogression in Vesaas; his style is not the result of refinement and decadence, but of an organic development. As for the adjectives *childlike* and *pathological,* Vesaas' sense of realism has made him choose characters who have these very qualities; that is, characters for whom even in the adult state of mankind symbolic language is natural language. A special Telemark word is the adjective *næpen,* usually used of scales and other weighing instruments to indicate that they are very sensitive. Vesaas uses the word of some of his characters to show how they are weighed down by an abnormal sense of guilt, by feelings of persecution often combined with stubborn pride. They are the people in the Grinde and Dyregodt books, or in books such as *The Sandalwood, The Seed, The Bleaching Place,* and *The Tower.* Especially interesting among Vesaas' sensitive characters are his children and adolescents; they are the most important personalities in his short stories and in many of his novels, such as *Spring Night* (*Vårnatt,* 1954; Eng. tr., 1964). This novel, like *The Signal,* has a simplified plot. A rather neurotic family of five, travelling across the moorland, have to seek refuge in a lonely house after their car breaks down. In this house there are only a young boy and his sister at home; they and each of the five intruders get involved in a curious pattern of events: an old woman dies, a child is born, there is a series of love adventures and as many disenchantments. All action is concentrated within one night and seen through the eyes of the fourteen-year-old boy Hallstein, to whom these hours become a fearful initiation into adult life. In spite of its strained use of the unities, in its details *Spring Night* is more realistic than *The Signal.* This development away from allegory toward a subtly organized symbolic novel is seen more clearly in *The Birds* (*Fuglane,* 1957), one of Vesaas' two or three best novels. Of all Vesaas' characters who express themselves in images, few seem dearer to the author than the village simpleton, people such as Huskuld the Herald or the arrow polisher. In *The Winds,* an entire story, "Tusten," is devoted to him; in *The Birds* he is the novel's "hero," and his name is Mattis. He lives happily in the house of his sister Hege until, one day, she loses her heart to another man, leaving no room for Mattis. *The Birds* is a book about loneliness, but also about the moments full of joy and beauty which may come to a retarded mind. It is a very moving book, sometimes sentimental, yet always tempered with sparkling humor, a rare thing in Vesaas' works.

A Lovely Day (Ein vakker dag, 1959) is Vesaas' most recent collection of stories. These all deal with everyday events in the lives of animals, children, people young and old, but the form ranges from straight realistic description to symbolic-allegorical presentation. Again, the sense of atmosphere in several stories is extraordinary, and some of them have been given as radio plays. *The Fire (Brannen,* 1961) is a novel which suggests both the fearful Kafkaesque world of *The Signal* and Vesaas' Norwegian background: like Olav Aasteson in *Draumkvædet,* Jon in *The Fire* is called upon to wander through a modern inferno. The fire raging in men is a destructive one, yet it also purifies and helps each individual in his search for self. "Have you seen the mirrors turn, so you know who you are? What you are?" Vesaas' answer, even though this is his darkest novel, is not without a faint light: "A speck of dust in an infinite vault. And yet——." *The Ice Palace (Isslottet,* 1963; Eng. tr., 1966) is a novel about young people's withdrawal into intellectual or aesthetic isolation, a common enough theme in Scandinavian literature. Ibsen's use of it comes to mind (*e.g.* Gerd and the Ice Church in *Brand*), or, since in Vesaas' novel it is a question of children, Hans Andersen's "Ice Queen." The treatment, though, is typical only of Vesaas. Central among his visual images is the huge frozen waterfall—the Ice Palace, a beautiful structure of dazzling mazes—where Unn finally loses all sense of direction and freezes to death. Nowhere in Vesaas' work is the problem of a person's identity presented more strikingly than in *The Ice Palace.* Furthermore this book represents a new departure in form: the chapters have headings (used earlier in some novels, *e.g. House in Darkness* and *The Tower*); they are often short, usually lyric in quality, and, sometimes, take the form of poems. One such poem, "Dream of Snow-covered Bridges," describes the snow falling on the arms of two people holding each other's hands:

> As we stand the snow falls thicker.
> Your sleeve turns white.
> My sleeve turns white.
> They rest between us like
> snow-covered bridges.
>
> But snow-covered bridges are frozen.
> In here is living warmth.
> Your arm is warm beneath the snow, and
> a welcome weight on mine.
>
> It snows and snows
> upon silent bridges.
> Bridges unknown to all.

This same problem of human contact is the subject of Vesaas' most recent novel which bears the symbolic title *The Bridges* (*Bruene*, 1966). Two teenage friends, the girl Aud and the boy Torvil, who live near a bridge, discover the corpse of a newly born baby killed and abandoned in the woods by its young mother. Later they have secret meetings with the young woman, whom they wish to protect, but this new contact threatens to destroy the old relationship between Aud and Torvil. In the end Vesaas lets each of the three characters gain a deeper understanding of his or her personality, so that they are able to accept life as it is lived by the bridge. Here, as in other Vesaas novels, the "story" is radically simplified to allow readers to achieve the immediacy of experience (of anguish, sorrow, pride, hope) which is normal in the visual arts.

Although even in the 1930's Vesaas was nationally known as a novelist and writer of short stories and plays, most of his great novels and stories have appeared since the war. During these years he has also established himself as one of Norway's leading poets. Five collections of poetry have appeared: *Kjeldene* (*The Springs*), 1946; *Leiken og lynet* (*The Game and the Lightning*), 1947; *Lykka for ferdesmenn* (*Wanderers' Happiness*), 1949; *Løynde eldars land* (*Land of Hidden Fires*), 1953; and *Ver ny, vår draum* (*May Our Dream Stay New*), 1956. Certain general characteristics of Vesaas' style— its impressionism, symbolism, and lapidary syntax—are naturally less striking in a verse context than in prose. Nevertheless Vesaas' poetry has contributed significantly to the liberation of Norwegian poetry from conventional patterns. His form is modern and international, free from the musical regularity of the popular ballad, and though his themes are mostly the old things which gladden his inland heart—the mountain, the snow, and the trees—he also writes of the wandering tower, the way of a serpent upon the rock, and the anxiety of young people parting:

> Your knees and mine
> and the warm moss
> and our young years
> Your thirsty fear
> like mine
> And heavy like mine
> God's eye in a sun
> ablaze
> Your own confusion
> joins mine:
> Farewell.

The Great Cycle, though it is not always judged to be Vesaas' best novel, is commonly singled out as a classic among his works, possibly because its language is free from the excesses of his experimentation: the monumental simplicity of its Old Testament style has given the book a prominent place in the well-established tradition of Norwegian rustic novels. These novels normally have for their subject the development of a young farm boy under adverse circumstances. In Bjørnstjerne Bjørnson's *Sunny Hill* (1857) the boy is a headstrong descendant of the Vikings who finally learns to behave in society; in Arne Garborg's *Peace* (1892) he is torn between loyalty to his psychotic father (the main character of the novel) and a wish to get away from the farm; in Sigurd Hoel's *The Road to World's End* (1933) he is seen more in Freudian terms as a child reacting against an environment full of falsehood and authority. *The Great Cycle* has a number of points in common with all these books, also with Hamsun's *Growth of the Soil*, whose back-to-nature message reverberates through the pages of Vesaas' novel. Still, while Hamsun gives his hero mythical dimensions, making Isak into a demigod who rides triumphant through all his battles, Vesaas places his people in a real world; *his* Norwegian farm is a typical small holding with no end of hard work, little encouragement for its owner, and no spectacular rewards. Also, instead of pitting a simpleminded superman against nature, Vesaas places the drama inside his protagonist, whose search for meaning in life now makes up the chief subject matter of the book. Thus the story of Per Eilevson Bufast from his sixth to his twenty-first year becomes a modern Norwegian *Entwicklungsroman* in rustic setting.

The great cycle of the earth and the seasons, of which Per himself will ultimately be a part, is a pageant or mystery play with Life and Death as central characters. They make their appearance together at the beginning of the book where the cow calves and the prospect of pancakes and beestings pudding gives the boy a wonderful sense of security which will never quite leave him; but at the same time he must think of the little bull-calves fated to die the minute they are born. Neither Per's mother, with her frothing buckets full of first milk, nor Auntie, who carries around in herself all the rawness and strength that the earth was smelling of, can dispel the fear of death and danger which appears to the boy in many disguises—the big bull in heavy iron bands, the river current which pulls and wills, the ever-present risk of fire—and the word *death* itself, with its hard, dry sound, "so very far away from Sunday," reminds him of the scythed stubble in the field. Not until the end of the book, when Per takes over after his father and, almost in the manner of some ancient high priest, slaughters Goldie, does he see how Life and Death are only different manifestations of one personality.

At the center of Per's cycle is Bufast. The rather unusual name (from the adjective *bufast*, "permanently resident") indicates that though this is a new farm, the owner hopes to honor the Norwegian tradition and have his family live here for generations. Except for the seasonal changes, life on the farm is entirely uneventful. But farther away things are happening, automobiles and summer guests appear on the roads, newspapers tell of fires, naval disasters, wars abroad; and it is toward these more exciting regions that Per directs his yearnings. Once in the city he is struck by the beauty of trees illuminated by lamplight, but his dreams are not otherwise well-defined. Really he only wants to leave Bufast and will do so in the way most common for Norwegian farm boys of his generation: he will be brighter than all the rest at school; then his parents will have to let him study for the ministry. His conscience, however, immediately rises high as mountains: "You are only doing it to get away from Bufast," says the hill, and he is reminded of what sin is: "a polluted well in the yard of a derelict farm; the well had been half dry and full of mud, and smelled rotten."

Per's conscience and his feeling of sin are reflected in nature. There are no people to tell him about right and wrong, for he is an independent boy who has difficulties with his human contacts. He never understands his brother Botolv, and he is hardly aware of little Åsmund until it is too late. To Auntie he is drawn from his earliest years, but he soon becomes ashamed of her caresses. All the more does he welcome the relationship with Olav Bringa, a friendship so pure and poetic that (as also with Auntie) biblical language is needed to describe its temporary close: "he went out and wept bitterly." The account of Olav's, Per's, and Åsne's tacit rivalry contains a number of beautifully sensitive passages, but even more moving is the story of Åsmund's loneliness. Time and again he is described, in Vesaas' symbolic language, as wandering about in the painful fields of thistles; and when he finds himself a companion in little Knut Prikken with the strange, bird-like face, their attachment is of a very special kind. After Knut's death Per reflects that his own friendship with Olav must have been poor by comparison. Although Åsmund is only a minor character, his tragedy is important for an understanding of the book's argument. The Norwegian rural community is peculiar for its so-called alodial rights (*odelsrett*), a form of property ownership acquired by a family to a farm held for at least twenty years, whereby members of this family have the right to redeem it within up to five years of selling. This right falls to the oldest son (*odelsgutt*) as a privilege, though often also as an obligation which he would gladly have taken away from him. In Vesaas' story most of Per's difficulties stem from his conflict with those in power—with father and God, that is—who have scared him too much, saddled him with burdens and judgments, writing the commandments for him, setting flaming texts on his head: "You will stay at Bufast to the end of your days." But as he grows up Per understands that Åsmund's loneliness is much more hopeless than his because Åsmund is cut off from Bufast and the great cycle. Like Hagar's son Ismael he will have to wander into the desert, while Per stays behind to begin a new life as master of the farm.

Most impressive in Vesaas' art are the remarkably delicate lines of his human portraits, particularly his pictures of adolescence. But there are also grown men in his novels, and though they are placed less centrally in the plot than Vesaas' more sensitive characters, they are often made to carry the author's message. "Grown-up" is in itself a word which commands the greatest respect in Vesaas; it signifies justice, compassion, heroism, and instead of young people's morbid self-preoccupation, a strong sense of social obligation. Typically, *The Great Cycle* ends with Per's coming of age and finding his way to a woman with whom he will share his whole adult life. Some readers may feel that blood and milk flow so freely in this novel as to suggest a form of *Blut und Boden* mysticism. They should be reminded that few Norwegian writers have taken their role as spiritual freedom fighters more seriously than Vesaas. In the fall of 1939, when Hitler invaded Poland and Stalin Finland, he gave a lecture, "Poetry and Hard Times," in which he used Edith Södergran's words, "whoever wishes to kill the sun will fail," to sum up his own conviction. The sun and the seasons, he said, could not be controlled by dictatorships, neither could men who were part of nature's rich cycle of birth, love, death, and new birth. This cycle he considered to be the basis of poetry, which is men's longing for the mysterious, the fleeting, the fearful. And because he found it impossible to imagine that men should ever cease to be moved by the miracles of life and death, he believed there would always be poets to interpret men's dreams and to speak out against whoever wished to stop them. To Vesaas, therefore, the ever-rising sun is not only a symbol of nature's regulating forces, but a guarantee that sound individualism will ultimately prevail.

Harald S. Næss

Madison, Wisconsin
June 1967

Bibliography

Works by Tarjei Vesaas

IN THE ORIGINAL LANGUAGE

Menneskebonn (*Children of Man*). Oslo, 1923.
Sendemann Huskuld (*Huskuld the Herald*). Oslo, 1924.
Guds bustader (*God's Abodes*). Oslo, 1925.
Grindegard: Morgonen (*Grinde Farm*). Oslo, 1925.
Grinde-kveld, eller Den gode engelen (*Evening at Grinde*). Oslo, 1926.
Dei svarte hestane (*The Black Horses*). Oslo, 1928.
Klokka i haugen (*The Bell in the Mound*). Oslo, 1929.
Fars reise (*Father's Journey*). Oslo, 1930.
Sigrid Stallbrokk. Oslo, 1931.
Dei ukjende mennene (*The Unknown Men*). Oslo, 1932.
Sandeltreet (*The Sandalwood*). Oslo, 1933.
Det store spelet (*The Great Cycle*). Oslo, 1934.
Ultimatum. Oslo, 1934.
Kvinnor ropar heim (*The Women Call: Come Home*). Oslo, 1935.
Leiret og hjulet (*The Clay and the Wheel*). Oslo, 1936.
Hjarta høyrer sine heimlandstonar (*The Heart Hears Its Native Music*). Oslo, 1938.
Kimen (*The Seed*). Oslo, 1940.
Huset i mørkret (*House in Darkness*). Oslo, 1945.
Kjeldene (*The Springs*). Oslo, 1946.
Bleikeplassen (*The Bleaching Place*). Oslo, 1946.
Morgonvinden (*Morning Wind*). Oslo, 1947.
Leiken og lynet (*The Game and the Lightning*). Oslo, 1947.
Tårnet (*The Tower*). Oslo, 1948.
Lykka for ferdesmenn (*Wanderers' Happiness*). Oslo, 1949.
Signalet (*The Signal*). Oslo, 1950.
Vindane (*The Winds*). Oslo, 1952.

Løynde eldars land (*Land of Hidden Fires*). Oslo, 1953.
Vårnatt (*Spring Night*). Oslo, 1954.
Ver ny, vår draum (*May Our Dream Stay New*). Oslo, 1956.
Fuglane (*The Birds*). Oslo, 1957.
Ein vakker dag (*A Lovely Day*). Oslo, 1959.
Brannen (*The Fire*). Oslo, 1961.
Is-slottet (*The Ice Palace*). Oslo, 1963.
Bruene (*The Bridges*). Oslo, 1966.

IN ENGLISH TRANSLATION

"Exoneration," trans. Sølvi Bateson, in *Life and Letters*, 65: 136–43. New York, 1950. [Excerpt from *Huset i mørkret*.]

The Ice Palace, trans. Elizabeth Rokkan. London, 1966. [*Is-slottet*.]

"Initiation," trans. Kenneth Chapman, in *American-Scandinavian Review*, 52:67. New York, 1964. [Poem "Innbying," from *Løynde eldars land*.]

"Never Tell It," trans. Kenneth Chapman, in *American-Scandinavian Review*, 47:166–71. New York, 1959. [Story "Aldri fortelje det," from *Leiret og hjulet*.]

"Once Upon a Time," trans. Martin and Inga Allwood, in *Twentieth Century Scandinavian Poetry*, pp. 171–72. Oslo, 1950. [Poem "Det var eingong . . . ," from *Leiken og lynet*.]

The Seed, trans. Kenneth Chapman. Oslo, 1965. [*Kimen*.]

"Snow and Fir Forests," trans. Martin and Inga Allwood, in *Twentieth Century Scandinavian Poetry*, pp. 170–71. Oslo, 1950. [Poem "Snø og granskog," from *Kjeldene*.]

Spring Night, trans. Kenneth Chapman. Oslo, 1965. [*Vårnatt*.]

"Twenty-One," trans. Kenneth Chapman, in *New World Writing*, 14:269–80. New York, 1958. [Story "21 år," from *Leiret og hjulet*.]

"Wonder," in *Norseman*, 11:194–204. London, 1953. [Story "Det rare," from *Vindane*.]

Literature on Tarjei Vesaas

Brostrøm, Torben. "Tarjei Vesaas's symbolverden belyst ud fra hans prosaværker 1940–1950," in *Edda*, 55:28–105. Oslo, 1955.

Cederblad-Bengtsson, Tone. "Fågelns outsägliga budskap: Om Vesaas' *Fuglane*," in *Ord och Bild*, 67:533–39. Stockholm, 1963.

Dagerman, Stig. "Regnbågen över snön," in *Vårt behov av tröst*, pp. 277–80. Stockholm, 1955.

Dale, Johannes A. "Tarjei Vesaas," in *Nordisk tidskrift*, 40: 185–94. Stockholm, 1964.

———. "Tarjei Vesaas," in *American-Scandinavian Review*, 54:369–74. New York, 1966.

Hansen, Martin A. "Bygd og dikter," in *Tanker i en skorsten*, pp. 201–21. Oslo, 1952.

Hellesnes, Nils. "Tarjei Vesaas," in *Syn og Segn*, 50:257–65. Oslo, 1944.

Houm, Philip. "Tarjei Vesaas," in Bull, Paasche, *et al., Norsk litteraturhistorie*, 6:246–70. Olso, 1955.

Jarl, Knut Coucheron. "Tarjei Vesaas," in *Mennesker og bøker*, pp. 130–48. Oslo, 1942.

Jensen, Brikt. "Is-slottet," in *Syn og Segn*, 69:445–48. Oslo, 1963.

McFarlane, James W. "Tarjei Vesaas," in *Ibsen and the Temper of Norwegian Literature*, pp. 182–87. London, 1960.

Maehle, Leiv. "Brannen og dei brende: Ny roman av Tarjei Vesaas," in *Syn og Segn*, 67:467–73. Oslo, 1961.

———, ed. *Ei bok om Tarjei Vesaas*. Oslo, 1964. [Essays by ten Scandinavian students.]

Mannsåker, Jørund. "Lykka for ferdesmenn," in *Syn og Segn*, 55:426–31. Oslo, 1949.

Midttun, Olav, ed. *Syn og Segn*, 53:225–96. Oslo, 1947. [Special Vesaas issue.]

Næss, Harald. "Et forsøk over Vesaas' prosastil," in *Edda*, 62; 148–75. Oslo, 1962.

Nordland, Odd. "Tid og ferd i Vesaas' symboldikting," in *Syn og Segn*, 63:337–49. Oslo, 1957.

Øverland, Arnulf. "Tarjei Vesaas," in *I beundring og forargelse*, pp. 100–18. Oslo, 1954. [On *Huset i mørkret* and *Bleikeplassen.*]

Prytz, Carl Fredrik. "Tarjei Vesaas," in *13 norske lyrikere*, pp. 138–52. Oslo, 1956.

Schanche, Angelique. "Bleikeplassen," in *Syn og Segn*, 69:84–97. Oslo, 1963.

Skrede, Ragnvald. *Tarjei Vesaas*. Oslo, 1947.

———. "Tarjei Vesaas," in *Norseman*, 11:206–9. London, 1953.

Stang, Nicolai. "En stor samtidsdikter," in *Vinduet*, 2:739–44. Oslo, 1948.

Steen, Ellisiv. "Tarjei Vesaas," in *Samtiden*, 55:590–600. Oslo, 1946.

———. "Tarjei Vesaas: Is-slottet," in *Edda*, 51:117–28. Oslo, 1964.

Thesen, Rolv. "Midt i en jerntid," in *Mennesket i oss*, pp. 136–39. Oslo, 1951. [On *Kimen.*]

Vesaas, Halldis Moren. "Tarjei Vesaas," in *Vinduet*, 15:9–12. Oslo, 1961.

Vold, Jan Erik, ed. *Tarjei Vesaas*. Oslo, 1964. [Collection of essays, greetings, and reviews published by the Norwegian Students' Association.]

The Great Cycle

You will stay at Bufast to the end of your days.

1

At Bufast farm a little boy awoke at the sound of a door. It was Per, the eldest child. He woke up at once when anything creaked or made a noise in the early morning. But it was *not* morning yet, for it was dark, and the spring had come, when the mornings are light.

Per could hear the clock on the wall; otherwise everything was quiet again. At his side he could feel his younger brother, Botolv. Botolv was put to sleep in Per's little bed now that Mother had an even smaller child sleeping with her. Botolv was sleeping just as soundly as before, his knee sticking into Per's stomach. Per pinched it, and it was gone.

Through the open door to the bedroom came the whimpering of something very new and weak, the voice of the baby— and then immediately afterwards another sound, a deep voice muttering something, half asleep. That was Father's voice, for it sounded as if it came up out of the earth in which he dug so constantly.

So it was probably Mother who had gone out. And Per knew where she had gone; she had gone to the barn to look at the cow whose calf they were expecting.

The room was made gray and chilly by the light coming in through the windowpanes. It was completely quiet. Per listened, straining his ears. Now he could hear Mother's footsteps, a staccato tapping on the frozen spring mud between the house and the barn. What was the matter? Mother didn't come in, but hurried up the outside staircase, jerked open the door on the landing as if to wake someone, and called in to her sister who slept up there: "Are you awake, Anne? Come down. The calf will soon be here."

"Oh—" said Auntie's voice, heavy with sleep. Auntie was only a girl, young and plump, and she slept well.

"Put on the water and then come along!" called Mother,

and went away again at once, hurrying down the stairs and out.

Per tingled with excitement. The calf would soon be here. . . .

The first thing to come into his mind was pancakes. . . . And then beestings pudding.*

When a cow calved, Mother always made pancakes for breakfast out of the first milk. Perhaps she would make them this very morning, even though it was only now, in the small hours, that the strange first milk was to be had. And the following day she always made beestings pudding.

Then he thought about the calf, whether it would be a bull or a heifer. If it was a bull-calf it would be slaughtered, but if it was a heifer it would be fattened up and grow into a cow who would have calves herself.

Auntie had dressed now and come downstairs and indoors. She lighted the lamp and began building up the fire in the stove. She worked fast, without even glancing over at the corner where Per and Botolv were lying. They slept in the living room, an old-fashioned living room which was the kitchen as well. Auntie was vigorous and got things done in a jiffy. She had not had time to put anything on her feet; only when the fire was going and the kettle on did she put on her stockings.

Per watched her round, strong legs enviously, thinking of his own small, stumpy ones.

"What are you doing?" he asked, although he had heard everything and knew she was going to the barn to help.

"The calf's coming," she answered gravely, and put her shoes on and hurried out.

The earthy voice mumbled again out there in the bedroom. Father was still half asleep and thought he was talking sense.

But Per was wide awake now. He gazed at the room, at cupboards and tables and benches, at the hearth and the

* A custard-like dessert, similar to British junket, made from colostrum.

6

cooking-stove. The windowpanes were black and gaping again. A moment before, when no lamp was burning, they had been the lightest thing in the room. Botolv was sleeping with his mouth open. Per quickly looked him up and down: Botolv had dark, soft hair, and his body felt feverish. Botolv was three years old now but very small; he never grew and was never cross. And he had eyes which sometimes made Per feel *he* was the smaller and younger one. Botolv had eyes like the grown-ups. Per disliked them.

Per was six years old.

He gave Botolv a shove. Only the tiniest shove. But Botolv woke up just the same and began to cry. At once the earthy voice in the bedroom woke up as well and asked sharply what Per was up to.

"I only gave Botolv a little push."

"Yes, yes," said his father, dozing off. "Be quiet, can't you?"

Botolv fell silent.

Then Per remembered the calf.

"Father! The calf will be here soon."

"Yes, yes," said his father, already asleep.

Per remembered that Father was tired yesterday evening when he came home from work. He had been working on the cleared land. He always did; he had done so ever since the world began, and every year there was a different place called the cleared land. It moved. This year he was working on it already, even before starting on the spring plowing. He was usually silent in the evenings when he came home. He was in any case so silent as to be unlike everyone else, whatever the time of day.

"The calf," babbled Botolv, blinking those over-shrewd eyes of his.

The stove was roaring; the water began to steam. But Auntie did not come back for it.

Per suddenly jumped out of bed and reached for his trousers. He would go to the barn and see if it was a bull-calf or a heifer! Fumbling, he got his trousers on and slipped barefoot into his shoes. Botolv did nothing; he did not even ask to come too. Botolv rarely spoke.

Father was asleep. Nobody stopped Per.

He went outdoors. It was a bitter spring night, with crackling mud and patches of snow-free earth dotted over the fields. A small murmur was alive up on the hillside, and a stronger murmur rose up from the river Tvinna below. Per was not properly dressed, and he hurried across to the warm barn.

A lamp was burning there, and the fumes met him as he opened the door. Mother and Aunt Anne were standing beside the cow, waiting.

"There, there," said Mother to the cow. The cow was lowing painfully, shifting constantly from one foot to the other.

"What in the world are you doing here?" said Auntie to Per.

"Nothing," said Per.

"Go indoors at once. What in the world are you doing here in the middle of the night?"

It was not said very severely—nor did Per think of obeying her. He stood still between the two women. The cow that was about to calve was making painful lowing sounds, and Mother and Aunt Anne were so strangely a part of it. There were several more cows there and a big bull over in one corner. He was the father of all the calves. Two of the cows had got to their feet and were moving about restlessly in their stalls. The others lay placidly as if nothing was happening. The cow that was about to calve went on lowing and lowing.

"There, there," said Mother to her.

Per had seen calves being born before. He knew all about it.

Mother was not so plump as Aunt Anne and not so red-cheeked either. But they were the same height. Auntie was quicker to smile, but Mother smiled more beautifully when she finally did so.

"There, there," said Mother.

The cow lay down

Then the calf came, head and forelegs first as it should. It lay there wet and dark, sniffing and blowing down its nose.

"Is it a bull-calf?" asked Per watchfully.

"Yes, it is," said Auntie.

"Yes, no more cows this time either," said Mother, and sounded disappointed.

"But this one can live just the same, can't he?" asked Per anxiously. This ugly, wet little creature was already an individual. "Can't he?"

"No," said Auntie curtly.

Per stared at her angrily.

Mother was silent.

"Mother?"

"No, he's not worth keeping," she said.

There he lay, fated to die. It was decided the minute he was born. He would have fine red flanks, they said, but— They carried him away into an empty stall and scrubbed him with a handful of straw to dry him a bit.

The cow watched in surprise as they carried the calf away. But then she turned to the wall and did not bother to look again. It was like this each time. She just stood facing the wall.

Auntie went in to fetch the hot water. Mother began milking. The cow's udder was full to bursting, and the teats bristled. Mother sat close to the cow with her bucket and milked. The jets of milk sang at the bottom of the bucket, different sounds according to whether Mother squeezed hard or not. The cow stood hanging her head with exhaustion.

When Auntie came back, she had made some warm wet mash out of meal. The cow drank it greedily. Afterwards she was given some good hay. The other cows stood tugging crossly at the rope that bound them fast to the wall. Each of them was given a bite of hay to keep the peace.

Mother went on milking. Now there was no song from the bucket: the milk streamed down into a frosting of yellow foam and disappeared into it with a dull sound. Mother was wearing a dress with elbow-length sleeves, and her arms handled the cow's teats rapidly and skillfully. Aunt Anne's sleeves were short too, and suddenly she put her plump arm around Per's neck as he stood waiting for Mother to finish milking. The arm was comforting; it would have been best to let it stay there, and Per pressed close to her skin—but he was too big to stand like that, he thought, and pinched the arm with his nails.

"You lemming!" she said, and removed the comforting arm, leaving his neck naked and cold.

It was quiet now. Only a slow sound of contented munching and then the yellow stream of milk falling into the bucket. It sounded weaker; the bucket would soon be full. Mother squeezed the teats abruptly a few times. Then she had finished. The cow stood still, no longer surprised, merely tired, and went on munching.

And everything here seemed safe. Per felt it strongly. Mother, Auntie, and the cows—it was safe. The big bull stood in heavy iron bands and was never let loose. He bellowed sometimes during the day and was noisy when cows from the neighboring farm were brought to him. But now he was sleeping over there in the corner, breathing deeply and groaning. It was safe here.

Some of the first milk was for the calf, and they struggled to get a little of it into him. He sucked at their fingers and tried to stagger to his feet, thinking he could stand already on those long shanks. But he just fell back in a heap. Then he drank more of the first milk and got it up his nose and let it run out of the corners of his mouth and had big round marbles for eyes. It was a shame he was a bull and had only two weeks to live.

There was still a good deal of milk left after they had poured some of it into the calf's bucket, and Per was so glad that he forgot to be sorry for the calf. He did not need to ask what the beestings would be used for.

Outside it had become much lighter by the time they went back to the house. But the gray dawn came early. Mother sniffed the air and said that it was milder. Per could not tell the difference. On the other hand he smelled something that had not been there during the day. He flared his nostrils towards it.

"What's that smell, do you think?"

Mother said it was the wet earth. It smelled like that early in the morning when people were asleep.

Why?

He did not say it out loud. He had asked why so constantly and received so few replies that he had almost given up.

Why does the wet earth smell like that when people are asleep?

He walked between the two grown-ups without asking them. If he looked around him, he would see only the things he knew from the daytime.

Bufast lay on the slope above the river Tvinna. There was plenty of space around the farm. On the other side of the river were the woods. Through the woods a narrow swath had been cut: the telephone posts followed it. You could see a farm or two some distance away, but behind the hills there were plenty of farms. There they were busy with their own affairs, and at Bufast they were busy with theirs. That was what Mother had replied once. Strangers did not come often; those who did were mainly people who came bringing cows to the big bull. The big bull was the finest one for miles around.

On the slope above the farm was the main road; you could see it from the Bufast yard. A great many carts and carriages rolled past with strangers in them and people on their way to the storekeeper. Up there in the gravel pits beside the road worked a man called Jens. Per knew Jens all right. But now everything was silent and dead except for the river. Not a cheep from the woods, even though the thrush had arrived. They went indoors.

Botolv had fallen asleep. Father slept, and so did the baby. Per too felt very tired when he came in to all this sleeping.

He snuggled down and was asleep before Mother and Aunt Anne had washed themselves and gone to bed.

. . . He awoke into a marvellous spluttering and a marvellous smell. You could not mistake it; you could doze off and still know it was pancakes frying.

Mother and Aunt Anne were already up, for now it really was morning, and they were preparing breakfast as it *should* be today. Mother was standing at the cooking-stove, and Auntie had a pan on a trivet on the hearth and was frying over the open fire. Both of them were flushed. When they put a fresh spoonful of the batter into the pan, it spat and spluttered. There was a little pile of finished pancakes on the dish already.

Per felt very peaceful, and hungry. It was wonderful to have beestings in the house. Botolv was awake and lay blinking straight up at the ceiling. Father's voice came from the bedroom: "Come and take the baby, Ingjerd. I must get up."

He had probably heard the tempting spluttering too. And he had to go out to his digging. Now he was lying out there in the bedroom with the baby.

Mother went out quickly.

Per watched the glow from the hearth shining on Auntie's face. It was strange that she, who was so attractive to look at, was so stubborn that she couldn't let a little bull-calf live.

"Give me a pancake!" he whispered from the bed in the corner.

"Yes, when you're up and properly dressed. Only lazybones eat in bed."

She *was* stubborn. But he had no desire to quarrel with her when she was frying pancakes, so he began slipping into his clothes.

Mother came back, carrying the baby. The baby was cross, flailing his arms and whimpering. Mother knew what to do about that. She sat down in front of the stove and the frying pan, emptied fresh, spluttering pancake batter into the pan, and then opened her bodice and gave the baby the breast.

Per had come over to the stove now to find his stockings, but he paused to watch the baby sucking. Mother is full of milk too, he thought. She was leaning forward, manipulating the frying pan with her right hand and holding the baby to her with her left. The baby had stopped whimpering; he lay with eyes round as saucers, and drank and drank. The corners of his mouth were running with milk, like the calf last night. Mother was smiling. With her right hand she swung the pan, and the pancake turned a somersault in the air and slapped down into the frying pan again. Per watched his mother proudly and happily. The baby sucked. Mother was full of milk.

"What are you standing like that for, Per?" she asked, teasing him good-humoredly.

He blushed around the eyes and began putting on his stockings. Auntie looked at him and laughed.

Father had come in. He was tall and strongly built and had his earthy clothes on. When he went past and out, there was a smell of earth and gravel. He took long, slow steps. He did not say a word. Eilev was his name. He must have been pleased about the calf and the beestings and the pancakes, but there was no sign of it.

Botolv lay blinking. Of course *he* couldn't dress himself; he had to wait until the pancakes were ready. He was incredibly good and almost never complained. But he was not left out of things; Mother looked after Botolv and the baby most of the time. Per was very much aware of it. She had so much to do for them that she seemed to forget about him. You're big, she said; you must look after yourself. And that was how he had gone over to Auntie, in a way.

The baby had fallen asleep with the nipple in his mouth; he was eased away from it and put to bed. Put to bed again. He drank and slept, in turns; that was his life.

Per was dressed and ready and about to help himself to the pancakes on the dish. But no! Mother was watching him.

"Per, have you washed?"

He went sleepily over to the corner and washed. And then,

at last! And they *were* good! Calves ought to be born every day, he thought. Auntie was red in the face now from the open fire. She sat down and ate, hurrying in order to go out to the barn. Today too there would be the first milk from the cow for pancakes and beestings pudding.

Father came in, the earth smell about him, sat down next to Per, and ate his pancakes.

"Did you go to see the calf?" asked Per between mouthfuls.

"Yes."

"Can't he stay alive?"

"No."

Father was like that. He said little besides yes and no. They fell silent and ate in competition. Mother dressed Botolv before coming to the table herself. Botolv was put beside her and given a small piece of pancake to play with. He sat eating the pancake, looking as if he were in church, thought Per. He would never understand Botolv. Sitting there playing with such marvellous food.

"Are you going to make beestings pudding today?"

"Oh, yes, Per," answered Mother, a little tired.

"Per thinks of nothing but food," Auntie told them. He let her say so. She would be surprised if she knew about all the things he *did* think about. She got up and fetched the milk pails.

Father had finished his pancakes too. Before he got up he rested his hands on the table for a moment: big, big hands. He went, and the earth smell left the room. He would go to the cleared land and dig: dig until there was a rim of sweat and dust on his lips. It was no work for a sissy.

Mother remained sitting with Botolv. Botolv had fine hair and sat silently, bolt upright. Suddenly Mother smiled a wonderful smile at him. At Botolv. Per went out.

He hurried into the barn, hurried as fast as his stomach would allow. He was full, but it didn't hurt. He just had to walk a little carefully.

Auntie had begun milking. Her arms moved rapidly. And there was the calf, *standing* in the stall, and staggering towards the rail when Per paused there. It stretched out its muzzle and opened its mouth and nuzzled Per's fingers helplessly. Auntie brought it some of the milk, and the calf blew bubbles and drank.

Per stood beside Auntie. "Couldn't *this* calf stay alive?"

"Do you think he's worth it, when he can't have any calves himself?"

"N-no—?" said Per uncertainly.

The calf stared at them. They stood watching it for a while. The bull over in the corner began to bellow. Then Auntie had to go; she had a lot to do. Per was left alone. The calf sucked at his fingers, looking for milk. The farm seemed to be overflowing with milk. But now the last cow had calved, and it would be a long time before there were any more newborn calves and beestings.

2

Everything happened outside Bufast, and much happened within the boundaries of the farm as well. The sun shone and the rain fell. And people worked. And the river murmured. All night long, continually and evenly it murmured.

On the nearest farms there were only big children, so they did not come to Bufast to play with Per. He had heard of a little girl called Åsne, who was said to be the same age as himself. But she lived many farms away, and Mother and Father never went there. They never went to the other farms; they stayed at Bufast or went to the storekeeper. Per often thought about Åsne, who would have been just right for playing with, but he never asked to be allowed to look for her.

Surely she couldn't be as good to be with as Auntie?

He longed for Åsne all the same, longed for her intensely. They always stayed in the same place.

Up along the road hurried the strangers, summer and winter, but mostly in summer. They came and hurried away again. Tramps called at Bufast to beg; then they went away. On some of the farms townspeople lived for a few weeks during the summer; then they went away again. Carriages drawn by tired post-horses rattled past. Per was given plenty to think about as he sat in the yard at Bufast and watched all this coming and going.

Mother and Aunt Anne and Father never travelled. It was strange how some people travelled about and some stayed in the same place.

The little bull-calf had been dead for a long time. He had lived a bare two weeks. Now his hide was hanging stretched out on the wall of the barn, and the titmice came and pecked at it now and then. Per had been shut indoors when they killed the calf. It was dreadful to be shut indoors and know about something you were not allowed to see.

The spring plowing and all that goes with it had come and gone. Father had not dug new fields then, but had driven manure to the old ones, and plowed and harrowed and sowed. He drove with Brownie. Father had no hired help until the haying. Auntie was out in the fields too, but not Mother. Mother had to nurse the baby and look after Botolv and cook—but Auntie was in the fields, and Per was there too. The earth steamed, and Father's Brownie steamed sometimes too when the work period lasted a long time. Brownie often stood in the furrow, resting, when he was drawing the plow, and then Father would stretch himself out full-length on the field beside him. Per felt lighthearted then, for Father's eyes were gentle and happy. But he was no more talkative than usual.

"Look at your father again," said Auntie.

Per looked. Father was lying, tall and streaked with soil, alongside the plow in Brownie's shadow.

Auntie said, "Your father loves earth more than anything else in the world."

"No, he doesn't!" said Per.

16

"Oh, yes, he does; he's crazy about earth. He's impossible to be with."

Per's eyes widened, and Auntie hastened to improve on what she had said.

"Oh, you know he is, but—" she said, and then she snatched up the hoe and began working again. She was digging up couch grass. Couch grass was a weed and the most difficult to get rid of, so they said. Per was helping pick up the couch grass that the plow and the harrow tore up. Auntie was sweating; the sun was warm. Her arms were tanned already. By autumn they would be dark brown, Per remembered. Per watched her and kept close to her; it was safe and right to be there. There was a kind of fragrance about her warm body. Aunt Anne was terribly strict about washing herself—and about ordering Per to wash too.

Was Father impossible to be with?

He watched Father for weeks after that, throughout the spring plowing and while Father was at work on the cleared land after the plowing was over. Of course he was possible to be with. Mother showed that he was; she could sit so curiously still beside Father. Sometimes when Per woke up at night he could hear Father's voice in the bedroom like a low, comforting growl. He would call, "Ingjerd." That was all, but the sound had been comforting.

It *was* possible to be with Father, it was just that Auntie didn't understand him.

But Father sat silent, it was true, silent and still more silent. He came in, bringing the earth smell with him to the table, ate, and kept silent. He left earth on the chairs he sat in, so that someone had to go over them with a cloth when he had gone.

Per went over to the cleared land and burst out with this thing that was torturing him all day long: "Father, are you crazy?"

Father was digging around a stone that he was going to raise. He made four strokes with the mattock before he straightened his back and looked at Per. It had a calming effect, but Per cut in yet again: "Are you going to dig till you're crazy?"

"What are you talking about?" Father's voice seemed mixed with earth.

"Does the earth make you crazy?" insisted Per. Now that the question was finally off the hook, he seemed unable to stop.

Father shot out an arm. An incredibly long arm. Per was seized in a tremendous grip. Everything smelled of soil, but not only soil. Father was wearing a thin shirt, and Per felt how alive his muscles were inside the cloth, how hard and warm they were. And then Father turned his face towards him as he was caught in this iron-hard grip—and the eyes in this face met his own eyes and penetrated them. Per started to tremble, on the brink of tears, for something was going to happen now, he felt certain. And he didn't want anything to happen!

He screamed in terror, "Let me go!"

But no, he had it coming to him; he knew it would come. Father's grip, and his face, told him that something important was coming. Father said slowly, without letting him go:

"You too will love earth, Per. It's all that matters."

Per was trembling. He did not understand what Father was saying, but the words sank in. He would always remember them and the voice that spoke them: a voice full of dregs and rust because it was used so seldom.

"You will love earth too, Per. When you're grown-up."

"Let me go!"

But those eyes were on his; he could not avoid them. Father said:

"You will stay at Bufast to the end of your days."

"Let me go!"

"All right, now you can go. You can go to those who say I'm crazy."

The grip had loosened, but he stood paralyzed for a moment, unable to run as he had intended. Suddenly he had to defend Mother.

18

"Mother never said so!"

Then his feet came alive again, and his body, and he was able to run. But he did not run home; he ran downhill through the copse. It was summer, and tinder dry. The birch trees were thick with leaves. He came down to the river. It was small now and moved sluggishly. He went uphill again. Father's words and face pursued him. He would belong to Bufast to the end of his days.

At home Mother was sitting with the baby on her lap. The baby was called Åsmund, but his name was never used. Botolv was sitting on a stool beside Mother.

Per was trembling again. Mother was quick to notice that something was wrong.

"Well, what is it?"

"Father isn't crazy, the way you said."

"What are you talking about?"

Per stood there, overwrought and blinking his eyes.

"Did *I* say—?"

"Yes, you did! You said so to Auntie. And Auntie says so too. But it's not true."

"No, it's not true," said Mother.

"Why did you say so, then?"

"Oh—your tongue runs away with you sometimes. Be a good boy and don't think about it any more."

How odd they were. Don't think about it any more, they said.

"I shall stay at Bufast to the end of my days," he told her, in fear.

"Yes, what of it?"

He did not know what to reply. Mother looked as if she thought it was right.

"Now you and Botolv can go and run outdoors for a while," she said. "You're too small to know what you want to be yet."

He dragged Botolv outdoors. Father's face and voice and words pursued him.

Be a good boy and don't think about it any more. How could they bring themselves to say it?

3

It was haying time. And that meant it was time for Ivar to come. Father hired Ivar for the season every year. Ivar had a whiff of pungent blue pipe smoke about him and a fierce expression. Per looked forward to Ivar's coming and dreaded it too.

He was a year older than Father. He was bad-tempered but a good worker, and he was likely to be at Bufast for the season as long as mowing and reaping and potato digging continued. And there was always the worry of finding his wages.

The scythes were bought and polished. The grass hung heavy with dew, for it was tall.

"Ivar's coming tomorrow," said Aunt Anne.

At once Per began to look forward to it, forgetting how sulky Ivar had been last year.

Ivar came and was just as usual: tall and skinny, sharp-eyed, pipe in mouth. Per looked at his shirt and trousers and shoes to see if he recognized them from last year. But some of it was new.

How he longed for friends, for friendship! He studied Ivar again with new hope. Perhaps he would turn out to be a friend this year.

Ivar greeted them curtly and sat down for a while. Then he asked if they were not going to begin. He was a hard worker; that was why Father had searched him out. Father was a hard worker himself.

They started raking and mowing. In the grass round about them the grasshoppers fiddled and scraped in furious time: shirrr. . . . The sound came from the standing grass and from the grass that fell to the scythe and lay in rows. Shirrr. . . .

Auntie came and began spreading the hay. She did not speak to Ivar much; they had a permanent quarrel that neither of them took seriously. The sun shone more warmly. The cat came slinking from under the storehouse and began lazily stalking the green grasshoppers in the hay. Shirrr, they said. But he soon gave up and stretched out on his side.

Botolv was toddling about in the piles of green hay, and Per watched him to see that he did not wander up behind the mowers and into their scythes. The swishing scythe was not to be played with; it whispered slowly down into the grass roots, hissing like a snake. Per had seen snakes and heard the icy hiss before Father's stick put an end to them.

Per was waiting for the midmorning break. Then Ivar would eat his porridge, and afterwards he would go out into the yard and lie in the shade and smoke. Then Per could lie down beside him and look for friendship.

Everything went according to pattern. Ivar came out and lay down on the grass with his pipe between his teeth.

A fragrance came up from the new-mown hay; the sun was beginning to dry it. There was no fragrance like it in the whole world.

Per lay down three paces away from Ivar.

Ivar made no move. He simply went on smoking.

Per could not start the conversation; after all, Ivar had only just come. He would wait to see if Ivar would talk to *him* first. There was a buzzing of horseflies and shiny bluebottles. They swarmed close to Per, plaguing him. There were none around Ivar.

Ivar said nothing, merely smoked. Ivar had a sister somewhere; he lived with her when he was not at Bufast. They lived alone in a little cottage, he and his sister. Ivar supported her. Per knew all about it. Say something to me, Ivar, he thought.

No. Ivar was staring straight up at the cloudless sky. If he altered his position so much as to take his pipe out of his mouth and spit, that was as far as it went. He did not turn towards Per to show that he had noticed him. Per would have been grateful even for that, but Ivar did not do it.

And what should Ivar say anyway? No, Per did not know
—just *anything*. He had so much longing inside him.

Ivar had been a disappointment as long as he could remember. As long as he could remember that there had been
summer he remembered Ivar. It wasn't summer without him.

He remembered other summers vaguely. He himself walked
and stood and ran in those summers. He did not remember
it as fun. In those summers the sun shone most of the time.
It was hot. Up on the road rumbled the carts. Sometimes the
rumbling shook the house, and you could not see the cart.

"What sort of a terrible cart was that, do you think?"

"That was thunder," they said, raking the hay out in the
meadow. They were raking furiously. Ivar was helping, everyone was helping except himself. He just sat.

All of a sudden it poured rain, and then they did no more
raking. They went indoors and sat down. It was dark in the
kitchen. Then there were some terrible flashes, and terrible
carts rumbled. But it was not carts; it was thunder. Aunt
Anne hid her face; Ivar sat with his pipe in his mouth; the
others simply sat. Per had a clear picture of that. Other events
of those summers floated in a mist. Father sometimes appeared
in his memory along with some word or action: he remembered the shock these words and actions had given him.
Mother appeared, always linked with the picture of Botolv:
Botolv at her breast, Botolv asleep, Botolv sitting naked in
his bath, crying softly, Mother smiling at him. Whatever
happened, Mother was there. Her face was wider than the
sky; it was everywhere. She was the source of all food, of
socks and shirts, and of all punishment. At the edges he
could glimpse Aunt Anne and Ivar. Sometimes Auntie
emerged as the shining central figure. Ivar had never shone;
he had only been a stony face with a pipe.

But now Ivar must say something to him. He moved a little
nearer. His heavy heart was beating. But Ivar lay as before.
Per cringed in disappointment.

He could remember three summers. . . .

When the summers were over, Ivar would disappear. Then

winter came, and with it snow and cold. He floundered about in the snow; it was all part of it. But he was alone. Sometimes he managed to have fun in the snow anyway, but there was always something missing, and he did not know what it was.

Father would drive off with Brownie and spend his time in the woods. Carts never rumbled, but there were long, black evenings, and the windowpanes were black. Then calves were born. Calves were more important than people and kinder than people; they came to you and wanted to play and lick your fingers.

Now people were more important than calves. It was more important for Ivar to turn around now and say, I can see you! than for someone to call, A calf has arrived, Per!

Ivar did not turn around.

Mother came out with the baby on her arm and Botolv toddling after.

"*Here* I am!" called Per to her.

"Yes," she said, and walked on.

It was no use. Ivar lay on his back, smoking. And the midmorning break would soon be over.

"I'm here," he entreated.

"Yes, I know," said Ivar. "I'll be the one too many at Bufast when *you* grow up."

Per stared. Ivar had not said it in friendship, and it was friendship he was thirsting for.

"You'll get rid of me, you know," said Ivar again. There was a hard, dry sound to his voice, making it seem so very far away from Sunday, the comparison occurred to Per.

"I'll get rid of you?"

"Yes. When you grow up, I'll have to leave Bufast, my boy."

"Why?"

"To save them paying me my wages."

"Yes, they do seem to worry about it," said Per.

Ivar told the cloudless sky he knew that very well.

Per could not make head or tail of it. But he went away. Ivar was no different this year. There he was, getting to his feet and going over to the grindstone.

"Grindstone!" he called toward the open door of the house, swinging the scythe in his hand.

Aunt Anne came out and turned the grindstone for him. Per came and stood by them.

These faces had always been about him, through all these three summers that he could remember, as the house had been about him, and the tree in the farmyard, and the well. Mother, Father, Auntie, Ivar, Brownie—you could not slip past them. The calves changed, and the cows, and the pig —the others could neither change nor be changed.

"I've decided to get married this year," remarked Ivar as he sharpened his scythe.

There! With Auntie, Ivar could open his mouth and talk nonsense and bicker in friendship. Per groaned to himself. It hurt to be small.

"Oh, indeed?" said Auntie. "*I* won't have you."

Ivar leaned forward and touched the grindstone with his tongue.

"Just wanted to know if the stone was moving," he said.

Per could have hit him. The stone didn't move as slowly as all *that* when Auntie turned it. Ivar was only being spiteful.

Per left them. This summer would be no different from the others.

Shortly afterwards the scythes were slicing through the grass once more, flashing and swooping.

Father went first.

"Augh-gh!" cried Ivar harshly, as if scared, and shook himself. He had cut into a frog that lay hidden in the grass, cut it in two. Ivar killed it as quickly as he could and put it under a stone. Then he swept farther along the swath.

Augh-gh! The scared, harsh cry still hung in the air.

Augh-gh!

A shriek so wild that your heart stood still—Ivar's cry brought out the memory of *that* cry: Auntie had cried out like that once.

"What in the world—?" they had called.

"I almost sat on a horrible snake."

Auntie could do nothing but jump up and down from shock. It was at the edge of the woods; they were there cutting branches.

Father snatched a stick. The snake lay writhing in the heather, writhing and hissing. It sounded like a tiny little wind in the heather. Per stood spellbound, listening to the weak hissing—then Father's stick came down, and the snake began to make rings and figures of eight—Augh-gh! all of it.

"It might have run up inside my dress!" said Auntie, shuddering over and over again.

That too had happened during one of the three summers. . . .

"Are you crazy? Look after Botolv, Per!"

He ran across and dragged Botolv away. Botolv could not resist looking at the flashing scythes in the grass and had toddled up behind the mowers, was dangerously near Ivar's sweep, and Ivar had not seen him.

He could have run the scythe into him just like the frog! Augh-gh!

His heart would stand still.

"Sit there!" he screamed at Botolv, and Botolv sat down so suddenly in the windrow that the grasshoppers jumped into the air.

Botolv was too small; *he* wasn't the person he was looking for.

4

Brothers. He had never seen anything but brothers.

One day during the haying season Mother was down at the river bank washing clothes. It was so dry by this time that the brook at Bufast was too small. The Tvinna broadened out at this point, making a wide, shallow pool with a slight current. Mother had set up the wash kettle here.

She had Per and Botolv and the baby with her. Aunt Anne and Father and Ivar were busy with the mowing.

The air was warm and blue. Thick smoke rose up from the kettle; the driftwood and rubbish from the banks were damp. The baby lay on a big shawl in the shade. Botolv stood watching Mother stuff the clothes down into the kettle.

What was wrong with Botolv? Nothing. He looked like anyone else. He was terribly bowlegged, as if he had been straddling a log for an immense length of time. But there were other people who looked like that too. He had brown stockings which were darned with gray thread at the knees. Both Mother and Aunt Anne had tied his shoes today, but he was trailing the laces behind him again.

But there *was* something that Botolv did not have, or that he had too much of. Per had lain behind a willow thicket one evening when it was almost dark and had thought about Botolv until it hurt. He was half afraid of him. Now he was standing there looking like an old man, watching the clothes boil.

The baby suddenly let out a howl. He had been grasping at objects lying outside the shawl, got hold of a stone, and then dropped it on his face.

"Help the poor little thing, Per."

Per hurried over. But when the baby saw it was only Per, he screamed twice as hard and kicked in anger.

Mother had to come just the same.

"Someone who screams like that must grow into something horrible," said Per.

"You were exactly the same."

Botolv watched, his eyes wise beyond his years. It's a good thing I'm not like Botolv, at least, thought Per with a shudder.

The baby fell silent and looked straight up at the sky. Why couldn't you remember anything about the time when you were as small as the baby? Was it because you were allowed to be as angry and horrible as you liked then, without needing to feel bad about it afterwards? For you were never told that you had done wrong at *that* time. Perhaps that was what it meant: "Gentle Jesus, meek and mild"—he was supposed to say it as soon as he woke up, but nearly always forgot—did it mean that God loved the little ones so much that they could behave as badly as they liked? "Look upon a little child," continued the verse inside him. He remembered it at last. Still, God couldn't love him as much as he used to, for now he had such a bad conscience when he had been up to mischief.

Mother asked him to find something safe for the baby to hold. Then she went back to the kettle.

The baby was given a big bunch of grass. He liked it too; he put out his tongue and sang a lengthy song about the grass in his hands. The next moment he was asleep. Per pulled his bonnet well down over his face to protect him from the horseflies and gnats.

Per looked at the water in the river. Shallow, lukewarm water. In the spring he would have been punished for coming here and leaning over the green banks, but now it was shallow, and for the most part still. He would bathe.

"Mother, may I bathe?"

"Yes," said Mother.

Just then he noticed the sweat dripping from her forehead. She was standing close to the fire and in the sun. Per felt his own face. It was dry. You sweated more when you were grown-up.

He took off his clothes quickly. A horsefly came at once and settled on his back. It must have known; it found the exact spot between his shoulder blades where it could not be reached. Then it stung him. Per shot up.

"It's a horsefly!"

And Mother was there. She slapped at the horsefly so that it fell into the grass.

"Jump into the water and they won't bother you," she said.

He waded out into it. Mother didn't say take care, not once, for it was so shallow that it reached no further than his knees.

The bottom was yellow sand.

Per lay down in it, and it was cold, but immediately afterwards it was not cold but almost warm. And how strangely the slow-moving water trickled about his body. That was how it flowed night and day along the sides of the fish. There were fish in the river, they said. But they were difficult to catch.

Something nudged him.

What was that?

Yes, there it was again. It was the water. The slow current was holding him as if it wanted to take him with it downstream. Far away, mysteriously downstream.

The water nudged at his shoulders and frothed around them. It lifted him as he lay shining on the surface like a piece of freshly cut, pale pink wood.

Come. . . .

The current willed it.

If only you knew what it was, this thing nobody could see. The water was so clear you could drink it. You could see your shadow down on the sand. But there was power in it. When you shut your eyes, it felt as if everything *was* floating away. On a journey to something far, far away.

Come. . . .

What are you?

Come. . . .

He opened his eyes; he was still in the same place. Up on the bank Mother was doing the washing, flushed and hot. The flame beneath the kettle was pale in the sunshine. There was Botolv in his brown stockings. Why wasn't Botolv running about barefoot today as all the other children must be doing?

Come, said the current, or *thought*, for it was so still that it said nothing, only pulled and *willed*.

The horseflies buzzed around Per.

Just you try, he thought. He could easily dive under.

After a while he stood up and let the sun shine on him and warm him.

"Mother, look at me!"

"Yes, just look at you."

The current rippled round his knees.

Come. . . .

But he didn't want to go *that* way, for he could see where the river went for quite a distance. Up the other way were headlands, and the river came from behind them. He waded upstream towards the first headland. Mother must have noticed but let him alone; the water was shallow everywhere here, and she knew there were no dangerous pools in the river bed.

He disappeared behind the headland. There was a cove and then another spit of land jutted out.

Per halted. There were people in the cove.

A woman was sitting in the shade of a fir tree sewing something yellow, and in the water just below her and close to Per a little naked figure was wading, even smaller than he was, he thought. They both paused, then moved slowly towards each other. Per was astonished: this child was shaped differently from himself. And *he* was being stared at just as much. Now they were standing facing each other and looking at each other with expectancy and astonishment. It suddenly occurred to Per that this was a little girl. She had long hair cut straight at shoulder length.

"Are you a girl?" he asked.

"Yes, of course I am!"

"Is that why you're different from me?"

"You're different too," she said, her eyes round.

"Yes. I'm a boy, you see. I'm Per."

"Oh. I'm Åsne Bakken."

Åsne. He almost jumped with surprise. Was this Åsne? Of course it must be since she was a girl. He was tremendously happy. And fond of her. And the minute *he* felt happy, she too seemed to be happy—for her whole face lit up.

29

"Is it you?" he said.

"Yes!" she replied.

So it must be.

"It must be odd to be a girl?" he said, very cautiously.

"No!" she said.

"No," he replied, shying away from it. "I've heard about you," he told her, his face radiant. "I've been waiting for you so long. Have you been waiting for me at all, do you think?"

"Are you from Bufast?"

"Yes."

"Oh, then I have been waiting for you, because there's a little boy at Bufast who I can play with when I go to school in the autumn, Mother said."

"I'm going to school in the autumn too. I know where you come from if your name's Åsne."

"Yes, but there aren't any little boys there. The only person who comes is my cousin. She's called Signe Moen. Mother came down here with me today. It's a long way from home."

"Is that your mother sewing over there?"

"Yes."

"But what about your father?"

"I haven't got one."

"Why not? I've had one as long as—"

"He was killed driving the horses when I was small," she said proudly.

"Hm— Do you want to see *my* mother?"

"Yes."

"Come on then."

He grasped her hand. It was ready to take his.

He was very happy now. Åsne was here. They slipped behind the headland so quickly that her mother did not even notice and waded downstream to Per's mother so fast that the spray stood upright. Åsne stumbled in the water, for it felt like a band around your feet when you wanted to run in it, but Per pulled her up again quickly. He could not remember having been so happy before.

"She's come!" he cried.

Mother stopped doing the washing.

"Who?" she asked.

"She came because she wanted to!" said Per.

Mother stood waiting as they waded towards her and climbed up on land.

"So it's Åsne," she said calmly. "I've seen you before."

But now that she was with a grown-up, Åsne was shy. Not a sound came from her.

"What are you doing, Åsne?" asked Mother.

Åsne did not answer.

"Her mother's up here too," said Per. "Mother?" he added.

"Yes?"

"Were you an ordinary little girl when you were as small as Åsne?"

"Yes, I suppose so. What—?"

"Auntie too?"

"Yes. What of it?"

He fell silent and simply hid away the knowledge he had acquired. Mother began washing again. Åsne stood waiting for something. She was pink and beautiful. Never before had he seen anything so beautiful.

"That's Botolv," he said, pointing. "He's a little different from other people, but he's all right."

Åsne, surprised, looked at Botolv curiously. "How, different?"

"Nobody knows, but he is."

"Then he must be," said Åsne.

"Would you like to see the baby?" Per hastened to change the subject.

"Yes, please."

He took her hand and led her over to the shade of the aspen where the baby was sleeping.

"Well, that wasn't much," said Åsne rather contemptuously.

Per was offended.

"We'll wake him so you can hear him howl," he said proudly.

"All right," said Åsne without hesitation.

Per knew it was a mean thing to do, but he wanted to surprise Åsne. The baby was given a few hard punches, woke up suddenly enough, and began to howl.

"How's that for howling?" said Per, watching Åsne.

"Ye-e-s, but I've heard worse, that's for sure."

"Oh, I guess you have," he said, liking her a shade less. But only for a moment.

Then Mother came running and asked what in the world they were doing to the child. The baby was screaming in anger.

Per drew Åsne away.

"Would you like to see Father and Ivar and Auntie? There's plenty to see."

"Yes. I want to see everything!"

Then someone called from along the shore: "Åsne!" Her mother was standing waving.

Åsne gave a big sigh. "I have to go back."

"Yes, I suppose you have to," he said with a heavy heart. "Is your mother kind?"

"Yes."

"Does *she* fry pancakes when the calves come?"

"Calves don't come. We live in a house."

"What do you mean?"

"We don't have a cow as far as I know. If we did we wouldn't live in a house. We don't have a farm; we only have a house."

Per's eyes widened.

"Åsne!" called her mother.

"Yes."

Now she was running. She was white, and pink.

Her mother came no nearer but stood and waited. Åsne was running, and she was the most beautiful creature Per had ever seen.

He could have cried. He sat down in the grass and considered. Then he did cry. It made no sound, but began far down inside his breast, moved up to the surface, and broke free. Until the horseflies came and reminded him that he was naked.

5

His mind was full of Åsne; she belonged among his possessions now. Father and Aunt Anne and Ivar were busy with the haying. Father and Ivar scythed so that the grass leaped. They mowed at a great pace. Aunt Anne spread the hay to dry. They cut only the home meadow; there were so many fields that they had no time for more.

Auntie's arms tanned quickly.

Mother prepared the meals and bent over the baby. When he slept and the weather was fine, she came out on to the meadow and helped with the raking. The cows were in the home pasture all day long. The big bull was back in the barn; now and then he would bellow. In the evening the cows lowed at the fence. Then Auntie would go and fetch them home. Brownie was grazing there too and had to be fetched to bring in the hay. In the evenings tramps would sometimes come and ask if they might sleep in the barn. They were allowed to, after they had given up their pipes and matches.

Along the road rumbled carriages full of tourists. It looked as if the whole world was travelling from place to place. But at Bufast nobody travelled, and Father sweated so that his shirt stuck to his back and he drank milk and water like a calf. Mother and Auntie were very quiet and reticent some evenings after a long stint of haying. This was the mowing season: it was hard, demanding work and had to be done in a rush when time and weather permitted. It was like that on the other farms too, the ones behind the hill that you couldn't see.

Now and then hallooing and shouting would come up from the river. Someone was bathing there, rinsing away the sweat.

"Do people who just have houses do mowing?" asked Per. Ivar answered grumpily, "No, what should they mow?"

Per went away, almost angry. Why did Ivar say things like that? And in that tone of voice? People shouldn't *say* anything about people who live in houses.

Later he remembered that Ivar and his sister had only a house themselves.

A stranger came down to the farmyard and met Per and Aunt Anne.

"Good day. Is this where the farmer lives?"

"Yes," replied Auntie without thinking twice about it. "He's down there on the meadow."

"I'd like to talk to him a little," said the man.

"All right, just go down to him."

The man went down to Father. He was a well-dressed man with a collar around his neck. Per stood thinking.

The farmer, the stranger had said, seriously and with approval. He had not smiled. The man had asked as if it were something important.

Per left Auntie and went down to Father and Ivar and the stranger. The *farmer*, the stranger had called Father. Per looked about him and saw that the meadows were large. And at the edge of the meadows there was always the cleared land, and it was never in the same place. It was here Father dug, saying nothing, simply digging so that Mother and Auntie said he was crazy—

He seemed to hear Father's rusty voice: Stay at Bufast to the end of your days.

All Per felt was anxiety and a weight on his breast. He looked at the meadows and growing crops. The meadow was almost mown. The fields were green, the shimmering heads of grain not yet bent over. Beyond lay the cleared land, black and red, with upturned stones and tree-stumps, looking as if something tremendously powerful had struck down there, tearing and goring.

Love earth, said Father.

Per stood still and tried to find out whether he had come to love earth.

34

No. He felt nothing as he looked at it; he simply saw it. He came down to Father. The stranger was standing with a book in his hand, writing in the book as hard as he could. He was writing down what Father was saying!

Father was asked about number of years, so-and-so many acres of cleared land, and many other questions that Per did not understand in the least. Father replied abruptly and almost unwillingly. He stood with his scythe ready, prepared to carry on mowing again, but let it go and answered. The questions came rapidly.

Up from the earth came Father's voice, as usual. You seemed to feel it under your feet.

Ivar went on mowing. Now and then he looked at the stranger crossly, ready to grumble. Ivar was like that: any delay in the work irritated him. When *he* was toiling and straining, everyone around him was expected to do the same.

But Father stood still. The stranger asked questions, and Father replied. His words were written down as if they were curiosities.

All of a sudden the stranger turned to Per. "And what about you?" he said.

Per gave a start of surprise and turned pale. He had a few things to feel guilty about: various small bits of mischief. But surely this man couldn't know about them?

The stranger asked, "Are you going to grow up like your father? You must try to, my boy."

Per did not reply. Stay at Bufast to the end of your days, he heard inside him. He looked anxiously at the two grown-ups. Grow up like Father? He did not know what kind of a man Father was. The stranger could shut up.

Then came the earthy voice: "Yes, I expect Per will stay at Bufast to the end of his days."

Per stepped back involuntarily.

The stranger said: "Yes, I expect you'll stay at Bufast to the end of your days."

Per stared at them in fear. They seemed to flow together into one giant force.

He felt as if a wall were being lowered around him. No, it was as if an enormous mouth had opened and said crushing words and then snapped shut, and would never open again. No, it wasn't like that either, but there were those big grown-ups standing there: Father in just his shirt and trousers and shoes, with his shirt hanging loose, and the stranger well-dressed and ironed like those other townsfolk who passed by, and with a collar around his neck as if he were going to a Christmas party in the middle of the haying. They stood there saying something that Per did not understand but which made him terribly anxious. Why couldn't they shut up? They floored him with mysterious threats that burned into him so that he seemed forced to become what they said.

He ran away from them.

Indoors, Mother was sitting with the baby. The baby was sucking so hard that the milk was running out of the corners of his mouth again. Mother was full of milk. Botolv was sitting on his stool. Mother smiled at the baby and told him he was a greedy little creature. Then she smiled at Botolv. Nobody smiled the way Mother did when she made up her mind to it.

Per came in to them.

"Help Anne bring the cows home, will you, Per? You ought to make yourself useful now, big as you are."

"Yes," he said.

Stay at Bufast to the end of his days. Make himself useful. He perched on the end of the stool beside Botolv. Botolv looked at him inquiringly. Botolv was going barefoot today. Per laid his left hand on Botolv's bare, grimy knee, not knowing why he did so or why it was so good, but it was good.

"Per! Did you hear me? You're not usually so unwilling to be with Anne."

Per ran off. Mother's voice had sounded a bit cold. Was it because he liked being with Auntie best? But Mother saw only Botolv and the baby; they needed help and not he. So she thought.

He ran in anger, and understood nothing.

6

Per went regularly up to the gravel pits by the main road, where Jens was. He had spent time there with Jens as long as he could remember.

"Is that you?" said Jens.

Per was always welcome. For a while.

Gravel was taken from the pits for the long, long road. The gravel on the road had to be replaced all the time; it blew away in dry weather and ran away in the rain, and all the cart wheels and horses' hooves wore it out. Then the drivers came and loaded their carts with gravel from the heaps and drove it away and spread it over the long track. There was gray gravel and brown gravel. When the sun shone on the heaps you could smell a dry, peaceful odor, not good and not bad. Jens wore a red undershirt with a black vest over it. He chewed tobacco; Per would do that too when he was big.

"You must go back to your father now," said Jens.

"Why?"

"Oh, he wants you."

So Per understood that Jens wanted to be rid of him. He went down to the farm again. There was a clanging from the smithy. That meant Father was there whetting drills for dynamiting a huge stone on the cleared land. Father was a smith too. And a carpenter. His carpenter's shed lay alongside the house and was full of tools that were not to be touched. The smithy was a long way from the house, on a patch of scree. That was because of the fire. The risk of fire. The risk of fire, people said, and their faces turned stiff and dry, as hard and severe as if made of wood. The risk of fire had always lived with the matches, and it was the worst sin of all to play with matches.

Sometimes Father stood in the smithy working with the fire so that the sparks flew. Per had often thought what a dreadful sin he was committing. Later on he learned that the same things are not sinful for everyone.

Now Father was whetting drills, so there would soon be bangs and explosions. Then the other farms would hear that new land was being cleared.

Father did not dig gravel up in the pits by the road; he only dug in his own soil. He began in the early spring as soon as the snow slackened off, digging a deep, dark furrow with melting snow around it. Fresh April snow might fall, soft and wet, so that everything was white in the morning, but the black furrow thawed at once and moved slowly upwards.

Father's clothes were always streaked with earth, except on Sundays. There was a smell of gravel and earth when he passed. His face was often wet with sweat or rain, and he would touch it with his earthy hands. The earth stuck, and fresh sweat made furrows in his face. When it was so dry that the soil smoked, Father would get a narrow rim of it on his lips. It was not work for a sissy.

"You're all horrible and black," Per had said once.

It had been an unfortunate day for making such a remark. Father had been angry about something, and when Per commented on his black face, he had lost patience.

"Are you turning up your nose?" he had asked scathingly. "This isn't work for a sissy, and you'll learn it soon enough, my boy.

"Oh, well, never mind," he said in another tone of voice, hurriedly trying to shrug it off. But it was too late; the words had sunk in. Per felt a strong aversion for it all. But what was the use when two big grown-up fellows had sentenced him to stay at Bufast to the end of his days? His aversion only grew greater.

He went up to Jens. He would *not* stay at Bufast; he would dig gravel like Jens. Jens took shelter when the weather was bad; Father went on working in howling rain and wind.

"Jens can do as he likes," Mother had said once. "He has no land." She almost looked as if she wished she were Jens.

So Per went up to him again.

"Is that you, Per?"

"You can do as you like, can't you, Jens?"

"Who in the world says that?" Jens straightened up behind the cone-shaped pile of gravel he had raised.

"*You* have no land, that's why," said Per enviously.

A shadow came over Jens' face. "No, I have no land," he said wearily; "I just dig gravel where nothing grows."

Per was astonished. Jens said, "You can look forward to taking over a farm. Don't come here with that sort of talk. You should thank God for it, my boy."

Then he began hacking at the gravel again. It was all a riddle to Per. He went down to the farmyard and tried to tease Botolv to get him into a real fury. But Botolv did not get angry, merely looked at Per strangely wide-eyed.

So Per went away with a heavy heart, out into his loneliness.

"You go on digging out there till you neither hear nor see," said Mother to Father one day.

"Yes," he replied, and went on doing so.

Father was a silent man. It must have had something to do with his work; he dug till he neither heard nor saw.

There was a song he sang on Sundays when he sat with the baby. The song had a merry tune, and it was about everything the baby would be when he grew up. Per noticed that the song was different nearly every Sunday; Father found new things for the baby to be, and Per listened with excitement and delight, secret delight. *He* could never play with

Father; it was unthinkable. When Father turned his huge body and his huge face towards him, it never entered his head to play. He only watched him with respect. Aunt Anne was the same. Botolv was different; he ran just as willingly to Father as to the rest of them. Mother behaved towards Father in the same way as Per and Auntie.

"Why is Father like that?"

"Like what?"

"Like *that*." As if she didn't know what he meant!

"He digs too much in the cleared land. You don't understand."

No, he didn't. He asked his mother: "Do you have to stay at Bufast to the end of your days?"

"Yes," she said.

"Do you thank God for it?"

"I don't know," she said in confusion, and left him.

How odd it was: it was she who taught him all about God, and then she disliked him asking her about such things.

Now he began to think about Åsne a great deal. She and Aunt Anne had equal rank; maybe Åsne even took first place. But she never *came*. He suggested that they should visit the farms to the north of them, but nobody wanted to, not even Auntie. They didn't want to be anywhere but at Bufast, it seemed.

Auntie said, "You'll find Åsne Bakken again when you go to school. That'll be time enough."

How did Auntie know what was time enough? They were odd.

He longed for school and dreaded it. Aunt Anne taught him his alphabet and numbers. He must be able to read when he went to school, she said. And add and subtract as well.

Per stood watching, as if from a high mound.

About him revolved the year. Harvesttime came; potato digging; autumn plowing; autumn leaves on the trees. The autumn slaughtering season one gray day with crackling puddles. He was shut indoors and had to imagine what was happening: they're killing them out there. Brownie would snort in his stall at the smell of slaughter on the hands and clothes of those who came in to handle him.

Per watched from a high, rounded hill as the year revolved and the work changed with the seasons. He was not included. He had a clear picture of himself: he was standing on his hill watching. The others were in a world apart.

The first cow had calved: a heifer for breeding. The snow came.

Father could no longer dig in the earth; now he drove Brownie to the forest and brought home wood. Brownie was shaggy and warm in his winter coat.

Per played a little in the snow. Something was the matter, but he did not know what it was.

He was lonely.

Botolv preferred to sit or stand with Mother. Per preferred Botolv to be with her too. He was afraid of Botolv.

Christmas came after much fuss and bother. They passed the time quietly. On Christmas Day Mother and Father drove to church, and Aunt Anne stayed home with Per and Botolv and the baby. After that came two more quiet days. Per thought a great deal about God. Few strangers looked in, for they themselves seldom visited the other farms. It was quiet. And there was better food than usual.

On the evening of the fourth day Per and Botolv went with Mother all the way to the schoolhouse to a Christmas party. So he would see Åsne again.

The Christmas party *was* wonderful; it was wonderful every time. He saw a lot of children he did not know. Åsne was not there. He managed to find out that she had gone away with her mother to the neighboring village to see relatives.

He neither spoke nor fought with the other children. It didn't seem worth it.

My father was killed driving the horses when I was small, Åsne had said proudly. How many of these could say the same?

But she was not there.

He sat twisting and turning the orange he had been given along with all the others.

"Shall I peel it for you?" Mother tried to take the gleaming, golden apple.

"No," he said despondently.

Botolv sat on Mother's lap as if all the festivities were for him. The high-pitched singing of the children and all the candles and all the colored glass balls and swinging peacocks and the big silver star at the top of the tree—it all seemed to be for Botolv. He sat wide-eyed, drinking it all in. Per could see the whole Christmas tree in his eyes!

Botolv lost his orange. It rolled away between the feet of a boy who looked about him quickly and stuffed it into his pocket. Then he looked about him again.

Per wished he were twice as strong so that he could get the orange back. No one had noticed. Botolv himself was watching the party, but then he came to and missed something. "Here it is," said Per and gave him his own orange, not out of kindness, but in vexation because Åsne was not there.

Voices spoke and read to them, and he heard nothing. God could not love *him*, or Åsne would have been there.

But on the fifth day, when he thought it over, there *had* been a Christmas party just the same. He still had the echo in his ears and the flickering of the candles in his eyes and the scent of the Christmas tree in his nostrils.

He was taken to church twice that winter, but Åsne was never there. The service was long, and people dozed. Mother dozed too.

Mother had stopped nursing the baby long ago, so Aunt Anne could look after him now as often as necessary.

"Did you see Åsne?" asked Auntie teasingly when they got home.

He reddened, wondering why Auntie wanted to hurt him.

"Perhaps you'll be *my* boy again now, won't you?" she asked.

42

He did not reply.

She put her arm around his neck. There was nobody to see, and so the arm was good.

7

Father owned timber, but this year he had cut down nothing. Yet he *took* jobs driving throughout the winter. He drove supplies for the storekeeper and took his pay in food and clothing. Per was too small; he was not allowed to go the long way to fetch the stores. Brownie was tired when he arrived home after these journeys. Later Father drove timber for the neighboring farm. Per was not taken to the woods either. It was dangerous, said his father; logs and snow might fall on him from the piles of timber, so Per had to stay at home. There were snowdrifts at home too, and Per dug tunnels in the drifts and built houses where he sat inside alone, staring out in front of him. Father came home with wet clothes when the weather was bad, the seat of his trousers soaked from sitting on the logs and on icy tree-stumps.

"It's bad for your health," said Mother, wiping the chairs where he had sat. "Couldn't you at least take a sack to sit on, on top of the load?"

"Yes, I suppose so," he answered indifferently.

After a while he said, "Have you ever seen me ill?"

Father was never ill.

"No," said Mother, "but I expect I will one of these days."

Per's heart turned over. Such prophecies were so dreadful— They could just shut up. They stood there saying things like: You are to stay at Bufast to the end of your days; I expect I shall see you ill one of these days. He felt as if it would have to happen once it was said.

Father's clothes smelled of resin now. It was a good smell.

He was afraid of Father. He felt it more and more. He had been afraid of Father since he had taken hold of him on the cleared land and seemed to pronounce his sentence. Father had laid a burden on him. And he had renewed it the day the stranger had come from town.

The stranger had written about Father in a newspaper and praised him to the skies. Father had been sent the paper. Mother had kept it in a safe place, even though it was full of boasting.

In the barn the calves were arriving. They kept one of them a long time, even though he *was* a bull-calf; he drank milk fit to burst. Then Father slaughtered him one day and bartered him for goods from the storekeeper. Whatever Father got for driving the logs went to the storekeeper. They fattened two pigs: one day they were slaughtered, and one of them was driven to the storekeeper. Mother and Aunt Anne churned butter, and Father took that to the storekeeper. The hens laid eggs, and the storekeeper got most of them. The sheep were sheared, and the wool was sent to the storekeeper to pay off credit.

"Is he going to get everything, that storekeeper?"

"Yes. We're still in debt to him. We had to ask for credit."

Per harbored a grudge against this storekeeper who had given them credit so that they were in his debt.

Each time they slaughtered an animal on the farm, Brownie went wild. Father always did the job himself. Per did not see the animal until it lay dead on the bench. He did not find it horrible; it was certain and settled beforehand that they had to be slaughtered, just as certain and natural as that one would eat and sleep oneself. But when Father went into Brownie's stall afterwards to give him his feed, Brownie snorted wildly, shivered, and cringed against the wall. The stink of the slaughter was in Father's clothes and on his hands. Brownie smelled it no matter how well Father had washed.

It was a strange sight: big, strong Brownie cringing because of a smell on someone's hands.

Per heard talk of slaughterers who went the rounds of the farms. Why didn't Father use them?

"He's too good to animals to do that," replied Auntie. "Don't you think the animals know when they're going to be killed? He'd rather do it himself, not have strangers to do it. Don't you understand?"

"No."

But—he's good to animals, Auntie had said. It was reassuring that she had said so. It *sounded* safe and reassuring. Perhaps he too would be good to animals one day?

People came leading their cows to Bufast. The cows plodded along in the snow, looking out of place. Cows belonged to green meadows and leaves and horseflies. Now they were being led through the snowdrifts to the great bull that belonged to Eilev Bufast. There they were given calves. Then they plodded home again through the cold, white drifts. They ought not to have been out of doors at this time of year; they were out of place.

The bull was dangerous and was never let loose.

Towards spring fewer cows came, and then the bull was slaughtered. He was too old; Father wanted a new one.

Per got a glimpse of the slaughtering of the bull through a hidden peephole. He saw the savage bull standing tied behind the barn one morning. All four feet were tied, and he was tied by the ring in his nose. There was one man holding each rope. The bull raised one of his forelegs and pawed the ground slowly.

Then Father went straight towards him to make an end of it, his rifle in his hand. The bull straddled his legs, terrifyingly strong. Per was too far away to see the whites of his eyes. There was an explosion, and the bull toppled. Per was glued to his peephole. Now all the men were on the ground holding down the bull. It was a black lump. Per tore himself away, trembling. He ran to the stable and stroked Brownie over the nostrils again and again. Brownie stood quietly, enjoying it, bending his head without shivering.

When Father came today, Brownie would shiver and fuss.

One day Father would go up to Brownie with the rifle, he thought. Somebody had said so.

What did it mean, to be good to animals?

Father was out of sorts the whole time the snow lay. Everyone knew what the matter was, and everyone waited for the snow to go so that Father could begin working on the cleared land, digging in the earth. After all, his affairs were theirs as well.

And then the snow went. The river began murmuring again. Father began digging. At this time too, the last cow calved. Per heard a question inside himself on the morning of pancake day: Do you love earth, Per?

The earth lay there around him; he looked at it, but it said nothing to him.

He was asked to *do* more that summer: now this, now that. "You do it for me, Per." "Perhaps you could do it, Per." "You must try, Per."

He was seven years old. In the autumn he would start school. He had learned to read a little, stammering through it. More and more often he was told: "You must try, Per."

To the end of my days, he thought, and ran to do as he was told. Father, over there on the cleared land, had sentenced him.

8

Mother taught him more reading and arithmetic. Then the autumn was there, and school started.

He was both glad and sorry. Mainly glad, so that he told

himself he would not have missed it for anything. Åsne Bakken had been pushed into the background that summer, but as he was trudging to school with his mother the first day, the image of Åsne reappeared. He would see her again today.

It was a long way to school. Bufast lay on the very edge of the district.

There were lots of children. But Åsne Bakken was not there to begin with. He looked at them all, and many of them looked shyly at him. Some knew each other already and kept each other company noisily. This gave them a kind of advantage at once. Those standing there singly were inferiors, searching the faces of their leaders for a smile. If they were given one, they smiled happily back.

Mother left, having dumped Per into the crowd.

There was Åsne, and another little girl with her. The other was sure to be Signe Moen. Per remembered clearly that Åsne had a cousin called that. They came hand in hand and halted, without a grown-up since there were two of them. They were from the opposite direction; they would never keep Per company along the way.

Per looked away. Åsne also looked away. They never would have believed that seeing each other for the second time would feel like this. Down by the river everything had happened by itself. Signe looked sideways at Per, since Åsne was doing so.

He had no idea what to do. Then he noticed a stick lying at his feet. He was saved. He picked up the stick and threw it in front of Åsne. She bent down quickly and threw it back again, and then they could smile at each other and go up to each other.

Signe Moen stood beside them, half smiling with them. She was about the same height as Åsne. They were very much alike.

"Why didn't you ever come down again?" asked Per.

"Couldn't go by myself."

"Is this Signe Moen?"

"Yes."

Signe was suddenly standing with her back to them. She was shy.

Per said to Åsne, "You know, I've been waiting for you so, and you never came to Bufast."

"Yes, I've been waiting for you too," she said. "You can turn around now, Signe. Walk around her, Per; then you can look at her."

Per went around Signe so that he could look her in the face. She did not mind letting him look at her, so then they could smile at each other and make a threesome.

Now they were three. They looked about them at once.

There turned out to be a crowd of inquisitive people: around them stood four or five young boys, staring.

Per was angry for some reason. Wasn't it right to stand with the girls? Was it something to be ashamed of? He was suddenly angry with these gaping fellows. And he was *at least* as big as they were. He'd show them.

"They stand staring like new-born calves," he said, to their faces.

Åsne and Signe laughed proudly. The gapers were left flat. Per was so proud of himself that he flushed and felt quite dizzy.

"Chase them away," said Åsne.

There was a fight in the air, but then the teacher arrived and took the whole crowd indoors.

Per managed very well that day. He wanted to sit next to Åsne and Signe but was not allowed; he had to sit with the boys. But he had already made enemies of the boys, and he did not look at the one sitting beside him. During recesses he and Åsne stood together. Signe drifted away to some of the others.

He went home pleased with himself. It had been a good day. He had no company, but he was used to being alone, and for most of the way there was nobody to be with anyway.

The autumn grass was faded, and the leaves had fallen.

48

There was a scent of moisture and of earth. The scent jolted him, and he stopped to find out whether he loved earth.

No. But he loved Åsne Bakken; he had found that out easily enough.

One school day followed the next. School was fine. There were wet autumn days. The earth smelled black and wet. Per smelled it in the morning on the way to school and in the afternoon on the way home. He tried to find out again and again whether Father's prophecy had come true. But it had not.

He still preferred to be with Åsne Bakken. Åsne said to him when the first week was over: "My, you're bright at school."

He did not reply but felt happy. She had said it enviously.

"Are you going to be a pastor?" she said again.

He did not understand.

"A pastor?"

"Yes. Signe has a brother who was so bright at school that he has to be a pastor. He goes to school even though he's grown-up! Because he's going to be made into a pastor."

Per was on the point of bursting out that he was going to stay at Bufast to the end of his days, but then it struck him that this was a way out! He would be brighter than all the rest of them at school; then they would have to make him into a pastor.

"Are you?" she asked, demanding a straight answer at once.

Immediately he was terrified that this escape route might be closed if Father and the others got to know about it. He must keep it secret! Simply be so bright that they would *have* to make him into a pastor.

"No, *I'm* not!" he said cuttingly. "You do talk nonsense."

The term continued. He noticed how light-hearted many of them were about their lessons. He *had* to learn his and had to know them better than the others. He *did* know them better.

He kept Åsne company, but less and less. She was a girl,

and it was difficult to be with a girl in the middle of a crowd of boys, even though nobody dared tease him to his face. They had felt his fists by now.

Signe drifted away from him entirely. When he saw her, she was always with another girl, and it didn't matter to him what she was called.

Then he found Olav Bringa.

They were about the same height and were a little afraid of each other—afraid of being the loser—so they did not test their strength except in friendship. The others hated them at once because they did not draw in a third. It was sweet to be hated a little when you felt strong.

9

He had found Olav Bringa.

Per had found something that he had no name for, any more than for all the other things he wondered about. It was *in* Olav, and he had always longed for it. Before school began he had not even known about Olav. Then, during one recess, each had stood facing the other, noticed the quiet, questioning, bewildered face in front of him, and recognized in it a friendship that would last forever.

It was unlike anything Per had experienced before. It was not in Botolv or the others at home, but it was in Olav—in the searching expression in his eyes, about his temples, and around his mouth.

I will never let him down, he thought, and something shot through his breast. It felt good. What was it?

They had to share the same desk in the schoolroom, and when they stole a glance at each other during the lesson, it felt as if this was the right way to sit if life were to be as it should.

"Do you have any birthmarks?" Olav had asked in great confidence as soon as they were alone.

"No."

"I have. Do you want to see it?"

Olav clearly asked as if giving him a present.

"Yes, please!" answered Per, wondering what he could do in return. He felt proud as well; this was for him alone.

They went into a little shed, and Per was shown the birthmark. It was in the small of the back, jagged and uneven, and quite long.

"Can you see what it looks like?" asked Olav.

"No."

"They say it looks like a country called England in geography."

Per looked again. He did not have much idea of what England looked like yet. He had not started geography, nor had Olav. It was a fine birthmark; he envied Olav greatly.

"I'll never really see it myself," explained Olav sorrowfully. "But they say it's made like England on the map. It's a big country, England."

"Yes, I'm sure it is," said Per, impressed. He had nothing that could compare with this, he realized. All the same there grew in him at that very moment an extraordinary affection for Olav. This was between Olav and himself. On the other side of the wall the rest of the children were playing; *they* had not been allowed to see it or know about it. Per and Olav went out to join them. Per was grateful; Olav too was grateful. Now they would be together.

He dreamed about Olav Bringa at night. But when he woke there was only Botolv beside him, Botolv's thin, warm body.

Events at Bufast became more and more remote. Father was driving timber and longing for the spring. Now and then he went to the woodshed and chopped wood, or he was in the carpenter's shed repairing something. Botolv sat around as good as gold. Mother and Aunt Anne looked after the cows, milked and churned, and brought in eggs from the henhouse. The storekeeper got more than enough eggs and butter. They were perpetually in debt to the storekeeper. Per hated the sight of him.

He longed for something. He was always longing for something: for invisible things and things he *knew* he was longing for.

There was Auntie, and Per longed to be close to her as in the old days.

Mother looked at him only fleetingly. "You're a big boy and must look after yourself," she said bluntly, busy with the baby or Botolv.

He did not feel big. Inside him he was tugged and pulled, and there were whisperings and orders and threats. It all slid away when he tried to catch hold of it. Then he remembered that Olav Bringa was still there and could not disappear.

Auntie was washing butter, standing with rolled-up sleeves washing yellow butter. She took it out of the churn, kneaded and slapped it, and changed the water. Per watched those arms which were so busy doing all kinds of work.

"Come and drink some buttermilk, Per," she said. "It's good for you."

She filled a cup with buttermilk. He watched her do so, and came and drank it. In the buttermilk floated small lumps of butter. While he was drinking, Auntie was very close. He thought he could catch the fragrance of her. He drank a great deal of buttermilk; it ran easily down his throat.

He knew she was watching him calmly. She must not be lost either.

"You're not my boy any more," she said.

"What?" He started and flushed.

She said, "Is Olav Bringa the one you like being with best? That's what I've heard."

"Yes," he said mercilessly.

She stood looking at him as if accusing him of something. His heart was heavy.

Only at school with Olav did he come alive. Home was just a place to do homework in. He *had* to know his homework; he must never arrive late. He had to be the best.

Olav had to be next best, and he was. The other boys hated them and called nicknames after them when they stood in a group thick enough for them to dare. They never shouted singly.

The spring was coming. The snow disappeared, and Father was able to start digging on the cleared land. School came to an end. The river churned. Per and Olav sat for a long time behind a thicket of willows the last day they were together. When they parted they had not said a word. "Good-bye," they said, with their backs to each other.

Åsne Bakken and Per only looked at each other fleetingly in farewell. Signe Moen did not even do that. She simply left with some girl or other. It was all the same to Per.

The earth lay bare and black once more. The whole of Bufast smelled of soil. Father chuckled. The sheep came out onto the new spring pasture and had lambs to look after: newborn, long-legged lambs who skipped in flocks across the green grass.

Brownie sweated in the fields. Per was in the fields too, weeding and planting potatoes. Perhaps he *would* stay at Bufast to the end of his days? The escape he had thought of seemed so far away now that he could scarcely believe in it. When Father said do this and that, he did it on the spot. He was bored and sweated. Father sweated. Aunt Anne sweated.

Auntie was lightly dressed to let the sun shine on her body. *She* must never leave Bufast.

Botolv had stopped growing. Now and then Per noticed that Father let his eyes rest on Botolv longer than necessary. The baby toddled and then walked, but he was a sleepyhead and was often in bed.

You will stay at Bufast to the end of your days, heard Per from the corners of the kitchen, from the woods around the meadow, and from the evenings.

I will not. . . .

Summer days. He met Olav. There was no school, and each came barefooted down his own short cut to the river. When they found each other and sat down on the turf side by side, Per was at peace.

Their hands and wrists lay side by side on the slope: narrow, bony wrists, not quite white.

They bathed in the backwater. Olav ran about with England etched finely and sharply on the small of his back.

They sat on a rock and let the sun dry them. The moisture ran off them and down onto the flat, warm stone, making runnels which dried up before they got any farther. Per's body gave off a fragrance as he dried; Olav's body was also fragrant as it dried close beside him.

It seemed as if there could be no barrier between them when they sat like this. But there most likely was. They did not discuss everything with each other.

Per asked suddenly, "What is it you don't want to tell me?"

"What?" said Olav, standing up. He had been lying stretched out on the comfortable rock.

"There's something you know that you don't want to tell me."

Olav reddened. "No," he said.

It shot through Per that Olav was lying. "Yes, there is!" he said.

"No!" said Olav, scared, and got up and went over to where his clothes were lying on the grass. His birthmark stretched and changed shape when he bent down for his shirt. Then he put the shirt over his head, slipped into his trousers, and was dressed. He set off through the copse toward Bringa farm.

Per remained sitting on the rock. The Tvinna slapped gently against the edge of the stone, shallow and harmless.

No, they didn't talk about everything hidden inside them. He didn't do so himself. They didn't do so at home at Bufast either. He had noticed it: from time to time they fell silent and hid something away. Olav had something hidden too. He himself had a great deal that was painful and confused and nameless, that simply was there and must not come out. If you talked about it, the heavens would fall, or something equally terrible would happen.

He shouted so that it echoed: "Olav!"

He shouted a second time. Then he got dressed and took the same path as Olav had. There he sat, breaking a twig into small pieces. He got up.

"I know where there's a new thrush's nest," he said.

They went to see it.

It was in the cleft of a birch tree. The young birds were half grown. The thrushes screamed.

Olav fumbled, trying to say something.

"I spoiled a thrush's nest once," he said quickly, looking straight in front of him. "There were four eggs and I smashed them to bits. It was a long time ago, but still—"

He did not look at Per but moved slowly away. Per moved after him, ill at ease. Olav had told him a little of what he kept hidden; now he would have to do the same. No, he would not! He *could* not; they were only shapeless tangles. He had to attack Olav in order to defend himself.

"You're a liar as well," he said.

"Am I?" said Olav.

"Yes. You said there wasn't anything you didn't want to say. But you knew about this."

"Yes, but I've told you now," said Olav.

"Not everything. There's so much you haven't told me, that—"

Olav let fly at him and knocked him down. Per had such a guilty conscience that he felt sick. He ought to have hit back. But. . .

"I have to go home," said Olav.

He really did this time. Per watched him go. Olav looked

back. Per turned away quickly, but then he watched him again. There was Olav, barefoot, dressed in shirt and trousers, the white shirt hiding a birthmark that looked like England. Per thought: We must always be together.

10

The summer passed with toil and busyness. The autumn was welcome. The autumn seemed to arrive along with Skrim, the cattle dealer, who came and bought all the cows in the district which could not be used for breeding that winter. Skrim came and bought; he was welcome but held in affection by nobody. He left with many loved animals. He was unavoidable, like the seasons. He sold the animals he bought at once, some to live and some to be slaughtered. When you heard that Skrim was in the district, a pang went through you, and you thought: It's autumn. Skrim is in the barn and in the pasture and will take the cows away.

School started again.

At school there were only Olav Bringa and lessons. He could not be with Åsne; he was a boy. Signe Moen meant nothing to him. He and Olav walked and stood about together and were happy. "Couple of dopes!" shouted the rest at them, but the label did not stick. They were the two best. At home there was homework. He *had* to be best. What was going on outdoors and in at Bufast was not important. A whole year passed. The baby was strong and filled the yard with echoes, eager to play. But Per was too big to play with a baby. Aunt Anne did so. Per was waiting for the baby to be big enough for Mother to remember him, Per, a bit more as well. No. You're a big boy, you can manage, she said. She had gone on saying it until it had become a habit.

Father stood in the earth. He growled now and then, and that was all.

A voice would be raised: Mother, Auntie, Father. "Hurry up, Per. What are you dreaming about?"

He would hurry to do as he was told. They always had to find something for him to do. *He* wanted to be enormously clever and read and read.

"Didn't you *hear* what I said, Per?"

Yes, he had heard.

"Run then."

He ran.

It was summer. Botolv's summer.

A rainy evening.

In the morning there was thick mist. You saw nothing. When Father went to the cleared land, he vanished into the soft whiteness.

That's how it should be for Father, thought Per suddenly, soft around his cheeks and shoulders.

But if you followed him in a little while, you would hear his spade grating in the stone-filled earth, striking against the stones. Nothing was soft there.

A mound of mist came rolling in to crush the whole of Bufast. But Per ran into the mound, and it made room for him inside. He saw not a house nor a tree but ran with wide-open mouth towards the grayness to find out what mist tasted like.

There was no taste. And not even enough of it to spit out.

Then the mist swirled away. Nobody had done anything, but it was gone. You could see where the sun was. There was Father standing wiping the sweat from his forehead. It wasn't work for a sissy.

In the evening it thickened again.

"There'll be rain before bedtime," said Mother, sniffing at the weather.

But it did not come until they were in bed. Botolv was already asleep when Per undressed and crept down beside him. Out in the little bedroom lay Father and Mother and the baby. The baby's name was Åsmund, when you stopped to think about it. The door between the bedroom and the kitchen was open as usual.

Then the rain began whispering. It sounded like the things Per didn't know about, snug and peaceful. Lots of strange things must be happening now out in the meadow and out in the woods—at least, that's what it sounded like. Per dozed and listened to it. Botolv's breathing was shallow; his body was feverish, as usual. Per lay and thought and thought. The rain whispered. There was great peace in the rain, but it did not put him to sleep; he only dozed.

In the bedroom he heard Father say Mother's name. Only once. Mother's name was left hanging in the air for a good while. Then Mother finally seemed to answer what Father had said, even though he had only used her Christian name. She said quietly, half asleep: "Yes, it's the hardest stint now, until Per can help you."

The earthy voice mumbled something in reply. Per could not catch it.

He wished he had not heard any of it. It worried him. A chill gust from something merciless that was facing him. And then an unexpected glimpse into Father's affairs. Was it a struggle for Father? Per had never heard him complain.

But there was more. It was Father's voice, full of gravel and incautiously loud: "This business of Botolv is the worst."

Per started so that he gave Botolv a nudge. He looked quickly to see if he was awake; it was light enough to see. No, he was lying just as before. Per trembled, certain that there was more to come, that what he had dreaded hearing for a long time was coming. Now the grown-ups in there would say that Botolv could not live.

And it came. Mother was the one who had to say it.

There was Mother's quiet voice. But she spoke clearly, and the calm whispering of the rain drowned nothing.

"Yes, it doesn't look as if Botolv will ever grow up healthy," she said. "He might die any day now."

At that moment Botolv looked at Per, wide-eyed with terror. He had been lying awake listening. Botolv was six years old. Their eyes met in the summer evening light, but so warily that it was no more than a blink; Per looked into shock and fear, then Botolv shut his eyes again. Per only felt Botolv's body trembling and shivering as if from cold, only it was feverish.

His own body felt strangely numb.

Silence and yet more silence. Now it had been said. The rain increased to a great sizzling downpour. Peace. But here Botolv lay trembling.

In the bedroom Mother said, "Goodness, what rain!"

Father mumbled indistinctly, "Yes, the ground will be sodden."

Afterwards there was no sound. They had fallen asleep.

Per lay without moving, filled with a great love for Botolv. They had been small together and played; Botolv had clung to Mother, and Per had been a little sulky and felt a little neglected. Now it was not important. He had often been irritated by Botolv's grown-up eyes: those eyes that *knew*— as grown-up eyes do—and he had been afraid of them and felt inferior. Now it was not important.

And Botolv's eyes just now, when he heard! Deep down there had been nothing but blind terror. Botolv understood more of this than Per did. Per put out his hand and touched Botolv. He had to nerve himself to do it, burrowing his hand under Botolv's nightshirt. Botolv was alive and trembling.

"Botolv," he said.

No answer.

He took his hand back, feeling poor. *He* could not comfort anyone. And Botolv was six years old, but much older.

Per was nine.

He tunnelled down into the bedclothes, moving away from Botolv so as not to feel him. But then Botolv moved after him. He was still trembling. Per lay and endured it. The rain sizzled; even if you lay deep down in the bedclothes, you could hear it. The sound forced its way in and was good.

Tomorrow the ground will be sodden.

Per felt sleep coming in spite of what had happened. It's annoying that you can never see it, see it and feel it just as you're falling asleep, he thought. It creeps up on you. Ugh, all the things the teacher talked about and the pastor in church preached about. Death comes like a thief in the night. They stood there saying things like that, frightening you.

Dear God, you must let Botolv live, he thought, but he barely thought it, for he was heavy with sleep. So that won't be much use, he thought. God was supposed to be very particular about such things.

But how soft it was here now. Soft. Like diving into new-mown hay. . . .

11

It *was* wet in the morning. Otherwise everything was just as usual to begin with. Botolv was asleep; he too had finally managed to sleep. Per looked at him the minute he woke, and felt a stab of distress.

He hurried out of bed, looking timidly at Mother and Father. They showed nothing. Father ate and got ready, then went out to his digging. The ground was indeed sodden. His feet squished as he walked, and a thin haze of moisture rose up about his shoulders.

Mother gave Åsmund his breakfast. Today as yesterday. Åsmund woke up early. She showed nothing. Aunt Anne, who slept upstairs, had heard nothing in the night, so of course she was normal.

But nobody besides himself had seen and felt Botolv last night.

Botolv slept later than usual. At last Mother went over and shook him. Per sat with his heart in his mouth. Botolv woke up and yawned a couple of times. Saw his mother above him. Per watched closely. Then Botolv remembered what had happened last night: he gave a start and remembered, looked about him, and got dressed.

Mother noticed it too.

"Are you sick, Botolv?" she asked.

"No."

"I think you are."

"No!"

Botolv had raised his voice in fear. Shortly afterwards he sat picking at his food. Per was paralyzed, incapable of helping him in any way.

It was terrible to watch Botolv all that long day. He sat on his stool as usual, picking at something, looking over at Per with eyes that knew. He blinked his eyes wildly, desperate for help. Then he got up from the stool and began following Mother wherever she went, trudging after her with his shoelaces undone and his socks falling down.

At last Mother, in despair and fear, said, "Whatever is the matter, Botolv?"

He did not reply, merely went on following her, not close to her, but if she went outside so did he; if she came indoors so did he. It was such torture for Per to watch that he did not know what to do with himself. Botolv's face was pale and taut and seemed even smaller than before—and his eyes much larger.

Mother looked around for relief from this situation, this tenacious following after her.

"Can't you *tell* me what you want?" she said. It was an agonized cry.

He looked up at her. No more. His face was still, his eyes tense.

"You must tell me, Botolv. What is it you want of me?"

He only looked.

Per sat paralyzed.

Auntie tried. But Botolv had never bothered about her. Now he did not even see her. Father came home with muddied clothes, picked up Botolv in his clumsy way, and tried to get him to play as usual. But Botolv hit out at him—Botolv, who never hit anyone. Father became angry, muttered something, let him go, and went out again. Botolv began following Mother as before. Åsmund came toddling in and pulled at him, but he shook himself free with a whine.

Per did nothing, noticing only that the evening would come soon.

"For goodness' sake, Botolv!" said a harassed voice in the kitchen. Mother behaved as if pursued in her own kitchen, and he seemed to have no mercy, but kept following her.

It was bedtime. Father had come indoors. They were all afraid that Botolv would refuse to lie down and keep on walking all night. Per suddenly leaped at Botolv and dragged him across to the bed.

"Go to bed!" he said wildly.

"Yes," said Botolv and began to undress.

Mother came over to him. "Will you tell me before you go to sleep?" she begged.

"No," said Botolv from inside the bedclothes.

Per stood beside him, and Mother turned to him. "You keep him company then, Per." And she left, powerless to do anything.

Per lay down close to Botolv, frightened to death. Botolv lay with a slight quivering in him, and this quivering transferred itself to Per as soon as he felt it in his brother's body. He had to say his name; he could think of nothing else to say.

"Botolv."

Botolv lay still. The night was light. Botolv *saw* nothing with those eyes; they were merely open.

Mother came in after a while, without having undressed. She leaned over. Per smelled the odor of her body. She said, "Go to sleep now, Botolv, and I'll sit by you all night."

"No!" screamed Per. "You mustn't!"

"What is this, Per?"

"You'd better go in again!" said Per dizzily. "I'll look after Botolv."

Mother was so uneasy and irresolute by this time that she obeyed him without question and went.

After a while Father came in and stooped over them. It had darkened a little. Now there was a smell of earth.

"How's Botolv?" he asked.

"There's nothing the matter with him," said Per with difficulty. "He'll fall asleep soon; you'll see. I'll manage."

Father padded away again.

Per and Botolv lay quivering, both of them. What in the world was this that could scare one so horribly? It wasn't true that Botolv was going to die soon. Dear God, you must let—

Botolv quivered. No sound came from his lips. He and Per were struggling with something together. Struggling. They were so weak and exhausted that it seemed hopeless; they would have to give in. After a while Botolv clutched Per's thigh.

"Shall I fetch someone?" asked Per, his tongue paralyzed.

Botolv did not answer. His hands did not let go. He and Per only terrified each other the more by being together. Then Åsmund screamed from the bedroom, a scream from out of a bad dream. Perhaps it was not such a dreadful scream, but it *sounded* wild and terrible. Botolv and Per both gave a start, almost out of their minds with fright. God, dear God. Botolv groaned. Per screamed, "Botolv!" Botolv did not answer, but his grip on Per's thigh loosened. He must have fallen asleep. In the bedroom Mother could be heard hushing Åsmund after his bad dream. The baby had awakened her hundreds of times.

Everything fell silent. Botolv was no longer quivering. Exhausted as Per was, he became calm. Half slept. Nice and quiet. Thank you, God. Botolv had fallen asleep. Per would sleep too, but he lay dozing, still too tense.

He noticed that Botolv was no longer feverish. He was getting colder and colder. He felt him, and understood, and called out.

The next day the doctor came and decided that Botolv must have died of heart failure, and said it was rare for children to die of it but that it might happen if they had been badly frightened.

Mother said, "But Botolv wasn't frightened."

Mother and Father seemed *almost* glad that Botolv had died. Even though Mother cried.

There was a funeral. People were invited from the neighboring farms. To Per they were just people. It was remarked scores of times that children like Botolv never grow up healthy. It was repeated until Per felt ready to throw up. Neither Åsne nor Olav had been invited; they lived too far away.

Per went to church, saw the grave, heard the bell. They said that Botolv was an angel now. The church was full of staring people. Per seemed to see Botolv's eyes in every single one of them.

Then he drove home with Father and Mother. He would never dare tell them what he knew about Botolv's death. He believed that if he were to tell them, something monstrous would happen. The earth would open up, the house plunge to destruction.

12

Little by little Per's shock subsided. At first there was yawning emptiness where Botolv had been; then it lessened. Only later did it return.

Olav Bringa had heard what had happened and came to Bufast. He came over time after time. Per was less often allowed to visit Olav at Bringa. But he went there now and then. Bringa was like all other farms. You recognized it all from what went on at home.

When school began everything was back to normal, in appearance at any rate. Per had to work and be the best. There was little pleasure in it, but it gave him no peace until he did.

He came no closer to Mother and Father because Botolv was dead. Now Mother concentrated on the baby, Åsmund. Per was big and could look after himself, they said.

Around the people there was a ring of animals. Per was with them a great deal. He was in Brownie's stall and in the barn with the cows and the calves, the sheep and the pig. Nearly all of them except the pig would greet him with outstretched muzzles.

Could *he* become good to animals? He wondered about it, not knowing exactly what it meant.

Father didn't seem to do anything to be good to animals. The horse got a solitary pat, a cow too on occasion. All the same, Father was what Aunt Anne had said. You knew it and saw it. Father was something mysterious and valuable: he was good to animals.

Brownie was too old and had to be put away. Per knew nothing about it until Father went over to the stall one morning with two men. Father's voice was normal—deep and calm just as when he remarked that the ground was sodden or something of the kind. He said, "We're taking Brownie away, Per."

Per knew at once that this meant Brownie was going to be killed. He had a strange feeling in his feet the minute he heard it. Father's large, set face showed no grief.

Per tried to slip out through the door, but Mother stopped him. "Stay indoors."

From the window Per watched Father lead Brownie out of his stall. Brownie was hanging his head. Suddenly he seemed oddly naked as he was led out without his harness. He had been led like this so many times, but not until today had he looked naked because of it. His back was hollow; Per had heard the word *swaybacked* used to describe it. His belly was enormous, and he had broad, heavy hooves.

Father went first, leading naked Brownie. Two men followed them, looking as if they had done something wrong. The whole procession had a silence about it; you had the feeling that they were making no noise as they walked.

Per felt an ugly expression forming inside himself: old plug.

Old plug, old plug. He could not get rid of it. *Brownie himself* was walking across Bufast yard, where he had plodded his whole life, naked and an old plug. Father was looking straight in front of him, as if unable to turn his head. The two men followed him stiffly and noiselessly. Then they all disappeared behind the barn.

This was death.

Brownie, who had shivered with fear when people approached him with the smell of slaughter on their hands— now he had to face it himself.

It was dreadful. Per felt giddy, gripped with shuddering anxiety much the same as he had felt that night with Botolv. *Death!* Botolv had died as he was holding him. He could not help thinking of nameless dangers. Quiet, noiseless people with heads that could not turn. Plug. Old plugs. Savage bulls were tied down to meet death. The silly, gentle calves were slaughtered when they were two weeks old. Naked old plugs with pot bellies. . . .

This was death.

On this side of the barn Aunt Anne was standing waiting with a bucket in each hand. Two empty buckets.

Boom! came from behind the barn.

At once Auntie ran around the corner and disappeared. Now the buckets would be filled.

Mother was indoors. She was holding on to Åsmund to stop him from running out. The shot exploded, and the air indoors was choked by the event they had not seen.

Per asked, "Is it true that Father is good to animals?"

"Is what?" said Mother.

"Good to animals."

Mother smiled, and Per had thirsted for that smile. She said reassuringly, as if reassuring Brownie, "Yes, Father's good to animals. He has been all his life."

Auntie came in with the buckets.

Father came in with red hands. His face was just as calm. In one red hand he had a long knife. And yet he was good to animals.

"Get me some water," he said.

Mother asked how it had gone.

"It went well," said Father.

Per was certain that Father was good to animals, but if he tried to explain to himself *why*, he got nowhere. It was just that it made what he had done less dreadful.

It was late autumn, and the ground was encrusted with ice. The slaughtering season. The slaughterers were going the round of the farms. Father wanted to do it himself because he was good to animals. The world was full of riddles.

13

Spring again, after a long, uneventful school winter. He had been the best all the time. Olav Bringa had been next best. The winter had been a gray one. He had nothing in common with Åsne Bakken and Signe Moen any more; they were girls. He went home to Bufast only in order to do his homework.

Homework, homework! To have the cold joy of praise from the teacher's desk, of seeing himself envied—and of seeing himself laughed at by the helpless, stupid creatures who *couldn't* learn and who fell back on sneering instead.

"Why should *we* work harder than the others?" asked Olav.

"Don't you think it's fun, then?"

"No," said Olav.

But Olav did not give up working. Per's cold joy was infectious; Olav felt it too. They kept their place a notch ahead of the others. It was a gray winter. Per scarcely noticed what they were doing at Bufast. He was swallowed up by school.

Then it came to an end. Here was the spring. And Per was ten years old.

"Now you can do *that,* Per."

He ran. Shortly afterwards they were saying: "You ought to be able to manage *that* now that you're so old."

He made the effort. It felt like going up an endless hill in hot weather. Endless.

This spring he was to mind the sheep.

So he minded the sheep. He did everything that was expected of him. He took a bitter delight in the knowledge that they could find nothing to complain about. Then something happened.

Auntie stood in his path and said, "Now you're going to tell me what's wrong. You're so strange."

He looked at her and suddenly felt stiff with sorrow. He could not answer.

"Aren't we kind to you?" she asked.

He looked at her in fury. People could bring themselves to say things like that! Making it impossible. The tears welled over. How utterly impossible people could be!

He was caught up in the arms he had longed for when he was smaller. Auntie did it suddenly and roughly: he was lifted up from the ground and squeezed against a bosom which gave gently under the weight of his body, and then he was kissed all over his face. He hit and kicked, but she was strong. He struck her full in the face, but she laughed strangely and happily and kissed him. He tasted her lips and smelled the faint fragrance of her hair and her bosom. She had a misty film over her eyes.

He was cold with anxiety and hot with shame, for this must

be shameful. One blow struck her on the nose so that it started to bleed. How beautiful her face was, how frank and warm. How good she was, and her eyes, so misty and kind. He struck her once more, and the blood ran faster.

"Put me down!"

She put him down and went out and wept bitterly. That was how he thought it: she went out and wept bitterly. He remembered that sentence from the Bible story amazingly clearly.

He ran into the woods. It was midsummer. The sheep were fenced in; he had to go out with them again after dinner. It was warm and dry. He ran down to the river. He would go home to Mother and tell her. No, he wouldn't tell anyone; it was so shameful.

When he came home, he was afraid of meeting her again. But she was nowhere to be seen, and he did not ask after her.

But then he did ask. His mother replied, "She went up into the woods with the cows. What did you want?"

"Nothing."

Mother was sitting alone with Åsmund. The door stood open. In the ditches lay withered birch leaves.

"Looking for her again?" asked Mother. Her voice was teasing and a little envious.

"No!" he said and went out. In the doorway he met a bumblebee buzzing its way in. The bee would soon die, buzzing against the windowpane for a while and then lying on the sill with its legs in the air. That's what happened to bumblebees who came in. No, Mother would open the window and let it out at once.

Father was on his cleared land. It was a bright reddish-brown. Father was hunched there like a tireless ant. Never, never any rest—he was an ant father. There he was, hunched up. No, of course not! He wasn't an ant; he was a mountain, crushing and oppressive.

Shortly afterwards Per was on the path that wound in among the fir trees. All the puddles were churned up by cow hooves, and cow droppings had been left. It even smelled a bit of cows, they had trampled here so regularly. The grass was good.

He came down to the grassy hollows where he guessed Aunt Anne would be. Yes, there were the bells. Cautiously he crept closer; now he could see her. She was sitting on a stone. A calf was standing close to her, licking her hand. Now she put her arm around the calf's neck. The calf stood stock still; Auntie had given it food and petted it since it saw the light of day. Auntie's fingers had been the first things it had had to suck.

Per stood behind a juniper watching. Then he went home and sobbed harshly and miserably.

14

For several days he avoided Aunt Anne, and she was more distant than ever. He would never tell anybody.

He and Olav Bringa were sitting beside the river. They met sometimes on the bank at a place halfway between the two farms. It was Sunday, but it was not all it should have been.

"Are you herding the sheep today as well?" asked Olav.

"Yes."

Their guilty feelings were numbed a little since each of them had run away from the sheep to come to the agreed meeting-place on the river bank. The sheep would wander home, into the fields and meadows, and everywhere they shouldn't, but— Per and Olav sat down defiantly. They seemed to be sitting on their consciences, holding them down, just as when you fought and sat on the loser. They could imagine with unpleasant clarity how the irritated sheep would run home through the luxuriant barley fields and the lush meadow and perhaps even through someone else's property, but—

"Don't you ever get out of it on Sunday?" asked Olav.

"No."

"Neither do I."

But the grown-ups did nothing all Sunday. They smoked and went the round of the farms and talked about each other behind their backs. Why should we herd the sheep when nobody else does?

Some people had children who never did a darn thing, while *they* were ordered here, there, and everywhere. That was what Per felt, and that was what Olav felt; they had found out that they were alike. But Per had not told Olav about the judgment which hung over him about staying at Bufast to the end of his days.

There was a marvellous rushing sound from the big, cool river; it had been swollen recently by torrents of rain. The earth and the glistening leaves were fragrant—but what was the use when you had to herd sheep on Sundays? Bumblebees hummed and butterflies flickered. It was all so *strange:* you wanted to mourn over yourself for having to herd sheep on Sundays in the middle of all these marvels that you didn't understand. Herding, herding—may all the sheep drop dead! thought Per and turned cold in the pit of his stomach because he had thought of something so wicked. He looked quickly at Olav and asked, "Do you believe everything in the catechism is true?"

"Don't know," replied Olav uncertainly. Olav was uncomfortable; that was obvious. Per was pleased. Olav must have thought of something wicked too.

Now God was close by; they both felt it. He was close by, looking into their hearts. God was watching the sheep too, the sheep who were going home through the fields and everywhere they shouldn't. Per felt uneasy; he had to bring Olav into it and make him uneasy too.

"Something will happen to the sheep," he said.

"Yes," said Olav.

"Would you like to find them all lying dead in the copse?"

"No!" said Olav with a start of surprise.

"Yes, you would!"

"No."

"Don't you believe that God sees you and the sheep and everything?"

"I haven't even thought about the sheep lying dead in the copse, I told you."

"Now God sees you're lying," said Per, cold in the pit of his stomach, he was so shocked at himself. The river rushed past; the fragrance of the earth reached him; but it was horrible here, and he himself was dreadful and committing dreadful sins.

Olav winced when Per said this and became a different Olav, who wanted to hurt and who knew quite well how to do it.

"Did you *watch* Botolv dying?" he asked abruptly.

Per, in a cold sweat, stammered no.

"Oh, yes, you did. They say you lay there watching—"

The way Olav said it made it feel like a dreadful accusation, as if it had been Per's fault that Botolv had died. For the moment Per thought it *was* his fault.

"Shut up!" he shouted, tormented.

"I expect God knows all about it," said this fellow Olav who was a new Olav, an evil, dangerous Olav.

"What does he know about it?"

Per was terrified. He *saw* that it was his fault Botolv had died.

"About Botolv, he knows it all."

This fellow Olav had not existed before. Now Olav was lost to him; he too was lost. Auntie was lost. Botolv was lost. Åsne was lost. Per groaned in dread. Botolv weighed down on him like a stone. All that misery had come back as vividly as ever. And this fellow Olav was an evil Olav. He must hit this stranger in self-defense.

He hit him.

Olav hit back.

"Do you think I'm afraid of you?"

"Bum!"

"Bum yourself!"

"Bum of a father!"

They exchanged blows with each insult. Neither of them won.

What? Bum of a father? thought Per, and hit out with both fists at once. "How dare you say anything about *Father!* If I were to tell you what I've heard about *yours*—"

"You're lying," said Olav, gritting his teeth. And hit him.

Yes, I was, thought Per. And hit him.

Neither of them won. They only smarted from the blows, both of them furious—furious because of the blows and because God was watching, because they felt guilty about the sheep, and because it was Sunday. They stopped fighting and went away, each in his own direction. And wept bitterly. Again it came into Per's mind: He went out and wept bitterly.

Per walked alongside the Tvinna, downriver towards Bufast.

Sinning . . . he thought.

At school, in the long, long, solemn lesson, they talked about sin. Committing sin. Today he had committed a sin, he knew very well. But Olav had committed a sin too, hadn't he?

What was sin? How was it made?

He did not know. Its complexion was dark; that was all he knew. For the teacher talked about black sin. The worst sins were black. No, he could not picture it; it was just something huge and dark.

He wanted to swear. He knew very well how to do it. He hardened himself in defiance. Whatever happened, it would serve them right. When you had to herd sheep on Sunday, it served them right that he should be walking along committing dreadful sins. He thought two oaths, one after the other, but did not say them out loud.

He knew all sorts of swear words. When you heard words like that, you didn't forget them; you carried them around with you. And when you heard other wicked things being said, you didn't forget them either. They stuck as if hammered in. You went about full of swearing and wicked words when you came to think of it. But you weren't allowed to say them yourself. You didn't let them escape.

Now Olav was lost.

Per stopped short beside the river and stared at it with empty eyes as he realized that Olav was lost.

He was losing everything.

He saw the whole sequence again. Åsne was lost, for she was a girl; Signe went around with a girl and was a girl herself; it was shameful to be with them. Botolv was dead. Olav had gone away from him today. He was shy of Auntie.

He stared down into the river. Life was miserable. Mother was always with the baby, Åsmund. Åsmund was no company. Father had set up a flaming text over his head: You are to love earth; you are to stay at Bufast. He couldn't help being afraid of Father because of that. It seemed as if Father wanted him to be miserable. Father dug in the earth until he was different from other people, and then he rose up out of the earth and said things as if he were God.

Per tried to see whether he loved earth and laughed scathingly and with satisfaction. No.

How lonely he was. He pitied himself, and that made it seem worse and worse. There couldn't be a living creature as friendless as he was.

When he got to the place where the sheep ought to have been, there they still were. Auntie was herding them. He knew she had found them among the crops. How would she take it when he went up to her? What would she say? He was excited. No, he wasn't excited; it would be just as bad whatever she did. He would make himself angry with her whether she scolded him or pretended that there was nothing the matter and was friendly.

She was sulky, and left without a word when he came and took over. He wondered whether that was the worst she could have done. Yes, it was the worst. In a fury he watched her go.

A sheep came up to him, greedy for salt. Instead of salt it got a painful blow on its black muzzle.

Father was good to animals, said Auntie, so Per struck the

sheep on the muzzle. Here was someone who was going to be different.

Sin.

Today he would commit sin. Sin upon sin. It was Sunday today, and everything was at cross-purposes and impossible. He threw himself down. Immediately he saw his sin. Once he had seen a polluted well in the yard of a derelict farm; the well had been half dry and full of mud, and smelled rotten. He was like that inside now, he was certain of it. It was so bad that the mud was spurting out.

15

After that Per spent many days with the sheep. The sheep came and nuzzled him and were given salt, not blows. There was plenty of time to sit and think, especially in the evenings when it was nearly time to go home, when the sun sank low so that there was shade and it was quiet and cool, and when the sheep had eaten their fill—then it was good to sit and think.

I wonder what Olav Bringa is doing now?

And he thought too: I wonder what Åsne Bakken is doing now?

At home everything continued as it should. Things were set in motion and not allowed to get out of rhythm.

One day the sheep were to graze in the home woods no longer; they were to be driven up to the moorland and the mountain. This was the day all the shepherds looked forward to: the sheep were leaving. Little brown herdsmen scurried about, not knowing what to do with their arms and legs. They were free.

Per and Aunt Anne were standing by the roadside minding

the Bufast sheep when the whole flock arrived with shouting and noise and dust. Somewhere farther along the same road Olav was standing waiting.

Auntie laughed and looked at Per. "So now you're free."

She went in front of him down to the farmyard. Auntie herself was spending a good deal of time in the woods these days with the cows. She swung her arms delightedly. Per watched her.

Auntie must never become old and wrinkled and stooping like some old women he had seen. Auntie must *walk* as she was walking now, swinging her arms and humming—and he himself would be a short distance away.

Free. Free of the sheep. Free of school. He tried to forget what he was *not* free of, and did feel free as the air.

Smoke rose up from the chimney, slowly and freely. And it felt like Saturday. The river murmured placidly. Father was over on the cleared land, Mother was down in the hen-house and Åsmund was running after her, shouting. Everything was almost right. Per stood watching them, and was free. Auntie let the cows out and took them with her into the woods. Mother began washing clothes at the well. Father came home sweating, was given food, and left again. Everything was right and in full swing; he was standing still and was free; the sheep had gone; he was a bit giddy, and his body felt light. It was like Saturday even though it was a Tuesday.

In the afternoon he walked slowly down to the meeting-place by the river. And Olav was there.

Per asked, joy flooding through him, "Have you been here long?"

"Yes."

"They left today, I suppose?"

"Yes, that's right."

"Ours did too."

It was good to be there.

Nothing lay between them. No sin. No word. No stubborn

look that read into your heart. Just Olav and himself. As they lay there side by side kicking the grass with the toes of their shoes, it seemed unthinkable that it could ever be any different either.

They said nothing about it.

Per picked up stones and threw them into the river. Olav picked up the same kinds of stones and threw them too. Olav wandered about in a copse for a while; then Per wandered about in the copse for a while too. There was a smooth wall of rock there and soft stones that you could write on the rock with. Per wrote on the wall in big, clear letters: OLAV BRINGA.

Olav wrote, in the same kind of primary school writing: PER BUFAST.

The river sang a friendlier melody. There was no sin here. They looked into each other's eyes. Each of them winced. All the rest of it seemed to be lying behind a thin wall: misery, fighting, sulks, boring work, wicked words—they hurriedly looked aside and chased it back to where it had come from. It was nothing. It did not exist! And when they looked at each other again, it really did not exist.

They had fought and become enemies forever, and had been eating their hearts out for each other; they knew it at this moment—and yet they were *not* enemies, but friends!

Per was ready to tell Olav everything he knew now. If only Olav had asked, Per would have told him. He knew it and was thinking about it.

Don't ask me, he wished.

Olav did not ask.

Yes, he would have told him all the hidden things. About Botolv. About Auntie who had kissed him, about the meeting with Åsne Bakken in the river long ago. Perhaps many other things—oh, it was unsafe to be so ready to tell someone if only you were asked.

Don't ask me, he thought.

Olav did not ask about anything.

That was strange too, and almost suspicious, that nobody should ask you when you knew about such things. Per began to wonder whether he ought to tell him without being asked.

No, no!

Yes, I will.

He cleared his throat, his cheeks hot. But before he got started it was too late.

"We must go home," said Olav, and got up. He had not noticed anything.

"Home?" Per breathed more easily. He felt freed from a sudden temptation. The things he knew had been lying like open hatches; now they closed again with a bang. He would not tell him.

"Yes, I suppose we must go home."

"Yes, we must."

"See you."

" 'Bye."

This happened the day the sheep left. Olav had been found again. Per remembered Åsne as he was walking home. During the whole of their meeting, she had not so much as entered his mind.

16

The summer passed like the previous one, except that there was more work suitable for Per.

You do it, Per. Per can do that; he has plenty of time.

Do you love earth, Per? asked God, rising up enormous from behind hills and out of valleys. You only had to shut your eyes to see him.

No! replied Per in fear.

Then God did not ask for a while.

Sometimes it was God who asked, sometimes Father. Sometimes *both* of them as *one* man appeared out of the hollows and asked.

Father dug on his cleared land again in the autumn after he had finished the harvest. In the field beyond was the new horse. He was yellow and was called Goldie. Father and Goldie had got to know each other that summer. Now, after the harvest, Goldie was browsing on the second crop in the meadow, wandering about in an atmosphere of great peace and repose, feeling at home on this farm. In the evening when it began to grow dark, he stood in the home meadow, tall and solitary and comforting, and grew dark too. But Father never forgot to go down and fetch him in the twilight and put him in. They would appear in the yard, emerging from the soft darkness, large and indistinct. Then they were gone.

The yellow horse had known for a long time who Father was. Per did not know, however much he wondered about it.

Per and Olav were in the fourth grade that winter. So were Åsne and Signe—but that wasn't important; they were never with them. They seemed to be quite clever, the two girls, but it wasn't important. And yet, not entirely unimportant either, perhaps.

To be the first! That was the first commandment, now as before. And then you *were* the first.

There was much more homework to do now. The world widened around you. Some of the big boys were preparing for confirmation. Some girls too. It was not so easy to show off in front of *them,* but Per and Olav slaved away and surprised the big ones on one occasion after another: there was Per on their heels, sometimes even in front, and Olav close behind. They were praised and looked about them boastfully. It was no fun.

In the morning darkness on the way to school God would tower unbelievably huge behind a hill and say: Per—

Per stood still. He could see nothing, but there was a presence round about him.

Per, it said from behind the hill.

He hurried on, his conscience pricking him. You're only doing it to get away from Bufast, said the hill.

It was no use denying it, but he did so just the same.

Per—

Yes, that's why! he made haste to say, and ran past the threatening hill.

Late that winter he noticed something that surprised him: Åsne Bakken was the center of attraction at school.

How had that come about? Had it happened now, all of a sudden? He had noticed it all of a sudden. He had noticed that she was often the most daring and had heard that she was unafraid and frank in her speech. But he had thought no more about it. Olav and he had been self-sufficient. Now they noticed Åsne. She was number one. She gave orders, and they were carried out. Boys who were older than she allowed her to boss them about. She had no control over the oldest of them, but they let her do as she liked. After Christmas many of the biggest ones had left school, the ones who were preparing for confirmation. Then Åsne's power increased.

Per and Olav were displeased when they caught on to the situation.

One day towards spring Åsne laughed at the two of them to their faces.

"And what about you?" she said teasingly.

"What about us?" they replied, but without much resolve or certainty, for Åsne had her whole crowd of friends behind her.

"What are *you* up to?" she said, laughing fit to put you in a fury.

"Mind your own business," said Per.

"Couple of dopes," she said.

She even stooped to *that*. That insult which had only been thought up in envy, which had never meant anything and had not even been heard for years.

This was aggression. They were in the woods near the schoolhouse. School was over for the day, but here in the woods the snow was lying in the trees, and there were fine glades, a suspicion of spring light over it all, and mild air. The afternoon sun fell in broad patches of gold. At night there would be crackling frost. It was like a fairy-tale in the woods —but what was it now? Per and Olav saw that they were surrounded by the whole bunch of schoolchildren and were going to be made fools of.

And it was Åsne's work.

Here she stood, alone in front of them, rosy-cheeked, round, and laughing. Her eyes flashed at Per and Olav, alight with mockery, and her mouth pouted.

Was this Åsne?

Per stared at her in disbelief: Åsne whom he had met in the river one day that summer before they started school; Åsne whom he had longed to be with. Since then she had been at a distance. Now she had suddenly come forward again in order to make him look foolish in front of everybody.

He stood rooted to the spot with astonishment, trembling before the unknown. Olav seemed to be taking it more calmly; he simply laughed scornfully back. Per was incapable of it; he could only remember that he had led Åsne through the water, and looked at her, and cried when she had to go. This was terrible: here she stood, about to say something scornful so that the laughter would rain down on him. They were standing around waiting, in such a tight circle that they had the courage to laugh, every filthy little brat among them.

Why would the laughter rain down if Åsne let it loose? He had not done anything laughable. But it would rain down if Åsne opened her mouth once more.

He wished wild, silent wishes: Don't do it! Be quiet, Åsne! Åsne, have I done you any harm? Don't—

But the crowd wanted blood, and Åsne let them have it. She stood there laughing happily.

"Did you know your homework today?" was all she said. But she said it in such a way that the laughter rained down. Per and Olav were laughingstocks. Each one who was envious of their being the best laughed heartily. Each one they had fought and crushed because of their superior strength laughed. Some of them laughed coldly and nastily.

The afternoon sun sent broad patches of gold into the glade where Per and Olav were being sacrificed.

Then Åsne had finished. It was all over in a moment. Per could not see anything clearly any more. A flaming tongue of sunshine fell on Åsne's face and seemed to set it alight. In the circle he made out other faces. He heard Olav hurl a couple of nasty cracks around him and saw him hit somebody. Yes! That was the only thing to do now. Hit them.

Olav had already started, and Per rushed in blindly beside him, hitting out. He got into a ray of sunshine and had to blink his dazzled eyes for a moment; then he planted his fists into the dark heap once more.

There was uproar. The girls shrieked and cried. Per and Olav were dizzy with shame and anger and cleared a space around them. And then a voice that they did not seem to recognize, perhaps someone who had never spoken up in any commotion before, said, "Onto them quick and get hold of them."

The voice had authority, and in a flash Per and Olav were powerless, crushed, knocked down, beaten up, and held under. Beaten up yet again. Then this voice that had never spoken before said, "You don't need to keep so much to yourselves. Why can't you be with us?"

They left them lying there in the snow. Their heads throbbed; everything throbbed. They looked up sideways at the person who had spoken. It was one of the big boys, one who never said very much. He left, and Åsne went with him.

All of them left. Not one of them bothered to see whether they could get up or not. They lay thinking it over. When the last one was out of sight, they got up. The world was hateful. Life was hateful. They might as well have killed them; it would have served them right. Then they would never have dared go home afterwards!

The evening sun was shining into the glades like flaming swords. The spring snow sent up a slight fragrance. There was a trace of frost in the air wherever there was shadow. It would be chilly tonight. Tonight Åsne will cry, thought Per suddenly.

"What's the matter?" asked Olav.

Per was about to tell him that Åsne would cry that night. But he stopped himself.

"Nothing," he said roughly.

Olav drew back, hurt.

They parted to go home, each with his swollen face. Things would be different at school after this.

As Per walked home he considered what Åsne's face had looked like. A ray of sunshine had set it alight; that was the last he had seen of it.

Åsne had reappeared suddenly and powerfully and let loose revenge and envy on him. Tonight she would regret it bitterly. He worshipped her.

Later that spring things *were* different at school. Per and Olav spent more time with the others. But they kept ahead. Per had to.

Åsne *was* a leader. All she had to say was, "Let's!" and you wanted to at once. Per came no closer to her, only watched from afar and wished many vague wishes.

Soon school was over, and the wishes lost their urgency. He began reading the paper. The whole world was in the paper, and at school he had been given a clear picture of the world.

17

The earth smelled raw and warm. Sometimes it smelled bitter, sometimes heavy, sometimes mild and lukewarm like milk fresh from the cow. Father's earthy voice could be heard when he came in from the cleared land, muttering or saying a word or two. Then he would leave again. Summer had come.

Per had herded the sheep and been freed of it again. But he was most taken up with Aunt Anne.

There was something the matter with Auntie. Something had happened.

He could not get rid of Åsmund these days. He had to play with him, even though he was so big himself. And Åsmund was grateful. But Per's thoughts were with Auntie while he was thinking up games to play with his brother. Åsmund was six years old now. Per would soon be twelve.

Auntie . . .

Of course he had noticed, he who was so strangely close to her—noticed that she was different. And he was so big now that he soon guessed the reason. He was tortured by it and strongly attracted as well.

She walked differently and lay down on the ground in a different way when she rested. Her eyes were different. She carried around in herself all the rawness and strength that the earth was smelling of. Per saw it with observant eyes.

Aunt Anne was in love with someone; he could see that. He looked at her arms and at her mouth: he ached bitterly at the memory of those arms and that mouth. He had been burdened by it for a long time.

He could not rest until he had made certain—and one evening he lay in the copse down by the river and witnessed how Aunt Anne was in love, was full of love. He heard the words she spoke, and they were full of love.

He dug with his fingers into the earth. This was torture. But he listened, excited and fascinated—listened and hid it away. It was full summer, a warm, still night with clouds in the sky, but light.

Auntie's voice was that of a stranger. Per dragged himself away from the copse and thought that it was hateful to be alive. As he crawled, the earth around him smelled raw and fertile. He got far enough away so that he did not need to be

84

so careful any more, and then he ran as far as he could. It was dangerous and hateful to be there.

He had recognized the man Aunt Anne was in love with, but it did not seem to matter who it was. It was all the same, just a man from the district.

At home in the farmyard everything was silent. The earth will be your business all your life, said God to him as he crossed the yard. He stood paralyzed with fright, so clearly did he seem to hear that voice.

Leave me alone; I haven't done you any harm, he said to this presence around him.

The haying was strenuous, as usual. Ivar was there, blunt and cross. Per helped a little with the mowing, not just raking what the others had cut. It was such tough work it made him forget about Auntie off and on. He ate and worked and slept. In the evening he read the paper and any books he could get hold of.

Auntie's state continued. Per did not tell Olav Bringa this either when they sat by the river on Sundays. After a while there were many things he did not tell him. Then one day *Olav* told Per about Aunt Anne and her friend. Was that the way with secrets, Per could not help wondering?

Auntie would laugh for joy sometimes in the Bufast yard and out in the meadow, laugh at the top of her voice. She stood on the earth and lay on the earth. The whole of Bufast was glad and seemed to rejoice because of her that summer. She went about as if blessing the whole farm and bestowing on it her riches. Per saw that she was beautiful. He knew that already, but now he saw it and found her incredibly beautiful.

He himself felt ugly and small.

Father's voice interrupted him sharply: "What's this? Aren't you ever going to get that finished?"

Per brought his attention back to what he was supposed to be doing and bent over the earth once more. He was beginning to know Father now, and Father proved to be strict in his demands. Do *that* today, said Father curtly, and you had to do it. Father clearly took note of the fact that he was bigger and stronger—and Per never tried grousing to that large, set, earthy face when it opened its mouth and gave an order.

It would never be given casually. As he obeyed, sick of it all, he tried to prove that Father's orders were wrong. But he had to give up and admit to himself that Father was right.

Father never lost. He had never been wrong as long as Per could remember. Mother had sometimes even blamed him for it, but Father had simply left the room, taking the earth smell with him, and gone to his tools on the cleared land. It was Mother, who stayed behind, who was the loser.

But you had to keep your distance with Father. Per tried many times to imagine that he was friends with Father in the same way as with Olav Bringa, but he never managed to believe it. Father and God had scared him too much, saddling him with burdens and judgments, writing the ten commandments for him. Mostly he tried to stop thinking about it now and just slogged along, working. Thinking about it would only make things more complicated.

Åsmund came and tugged at him to come and play.

"Go to Mother," said Per. "I have to work."

He pitied himself profoundly. Åsmund trudged off. Per bent down again. He was always having to bend down, picking up weeds, picking up the heads of grain after the mowing, picking up stones from the cleared land. Picking up. He thought about those mornings long ago, mornings with newborn calves in the barn and with spluttering pancakes the first sound in his ears when he awoke. It happened now as well, but not as it did *then*. Then there had been something different about the long jets of the first milk spurting into the bucket. And Mother had sat close to the cooking-stove with the baby in one hand and the frying pan in the other—and she had been so full of milk herself that it overflowed when the baby sucked.

Mother was no longer as she had been then: not slow in her movements, and gentle, and full of milk. Now she was brisk and firm and never had time for anything.

But there was Auntie . . .

The whole summer was Auntie's summer. Her eyes looked drunk sometimes when they met yours. Per could bear it better now than he had to begin with. The first smart had dulled.

The smart does get dulled, he learned. What was exceedingly painful to begin with hurt less and less.

Harvesttime came. Auntie helped in the fields and was happiness itself. Everyone had known about it for a long time.

It was time to dig the potatoes. One day as they were lying and sitting in the field, resting among strong-smelling, blackened potato plants, Per watched Father enjoying Auntie's happiness.

There was nothing around them but earth. The fragrance of black potato plants was the fragrance of earth, as raw and genuine as it could be. Per's back was aching, and he lay stretched out at ease on the soil, and there was Aunt Anne, sprung up out of the earth too. Father sat leaning against a sack of potatoes, watching Auntie.

She was lying contentedly on the ground, resting her head on a heap of potato plants. She lay there as if she owned the riches of all the districts round about. She moved slightly; her dress rearranged itself; all was riches.

Per was in the middle of all this. It was good to be here. Suddenly he felt it was good to be here. He did not go into what was good or how it was good. It was good to be here at Bufast. Per lay still. There was a fragrance of potato plants and raw earth—and Aunt Anne was lying here with something you couldn't put a name to, and Father was leaning against the potato sack making everything seem right.

It did not last long. When Per bent down to dig the potatoes again, the feeling had gone.

18

Now he saw *Mother* better. She was always where she was needed, when clothes were torn and when any of them wanted food and drink. But she was not close to Per. He did not *want* to come closer to her. Sometimes Mother looked as if she were about to say something that he was sure would prove embarrassing. On these occasions he either went away or scotched it by talking nonsense. Mother must not read his heart; nobody must do that.

Everything glided forward, interlocked as it was supposed to be, so that nobody paid any attention to it. What was to be used appeared; what had been used was hidden away and only brought out again when it had to be used once more—and then it was mended and clean. It occurred to Per that Mother did all this. The *days themselves* passed through Mother's hands and were ordered by her before they reached other people.

Then another idea occurred to him, an uncomfortable one: without Mother everything would come to a standstill, grind to a halt, go to pieces. All would be changed into dark night.

But she never came to a standstill. There was no darkness. So there was no need to think about it again for a long time. Mother had always been there.

Was he fond of her? Yes, he was; he knew that. Sometimes he thought about her with great joy and affection. But he did not want to be involved in her thoughts; it would embarrass him. And he did not want to talk about his own thoughts.

Occasionally Mother's voice was impatient, usually in the evenings. Then she was tired, and they listened to the impatient things she said with a guilty conscience, without replying. Mother was tired because of them.

Sometimes it startled Per to see how dreadfully tired Mother was. He got a very guilty conscience and wondered what could be done so that Mother need not work so hard. Then he would do some chore or other in the house without being asked, throwing out water, fetching in wood. Mother would sit half asleep, staring into her lap.

Father would sit the whole evening with the smell of the earth about him, powerful and calm like a statue.

They went to bed, and in the morning Mother was once more the one who set things in motion so that Bufast went on running.

Mother was not disheartened. She was contented. It was only when she was over-tired that she could startle and disturb you. Sometimes she sat with a book in her hands in the evening; then the book would fall to the floor, and Mother start up out of sleep.

Mother's tired, they thought. Sometimes it seemed good, because it was late and the whole farm was looking forward to sleep and night.

In any case Mother was behind everything here. Nothing must ever happen to her, so that she was no longer there.

They were settled here for good.

There were great differences between people.

Up on the road people travelled incessantly. Townspeople came to the farms, stayed for a while, and were gone again. A pastor had come to the district a few years ago. Now he had left, and another had moved in. A doctor came. Then he left too, and a new one moved in.

But Per and his family here on the farm did not travel. They were settled for good.

There was a great deal to read in the newspaper which the postman left in the mailbox at the roadside, but nearly always it had to do with movement and journeys and restlessness. You got the impression that the whole world was moving about restlessly like pastors and townspeople.

Per stayed at Bufast summer and winter and all seasons. Sometimes he longed to be able to travel and see things. He read the papers until his mind was full of pictures. He read every word in them.

Much was written in the books too. In the schoolroom there was a cupboard reaching from floor to ceiling full of books that they were allowed to borrow. Per devoured books. So much was in them, and they changed you inside. There were a few books at Bufast too, which he read and reread. Some of them were very old and yellow. Father preferred reading the yellowest ones. Father read the paper as well and sometimes threw it away impatiently, as if what he read was all nonsense. Mother and Aunt Anne read in a different way and quarrelled about some of the things they read about. Father never quarrelled with anyone. He gave his opinion once only.

The paper brought news about great events too. Towns were burned to the ground. The earth opened or spurted out flame. Somewhere people were at war with each other, shooting each other down in heaps. Kings died. Ships sank into the ocean. It was strange: as you read about it, all the pictures inside you seemed to begin to spin and drift, just as if someone were stirring a pot with a stick. Then after a while the world stayed still where it ought to be, just as before, far away, tempting, and frightening.

Per was settled for good, planted on the same patch of earth like a tree.

The hidden wish to get away was still there. When the work he had to do was heavy or boring, the wish emerged; or when the struggle to be rid of the debt to the storekeeper haunted him.

He would have given much not to have to listen to the conversations between Father and Mother about money matters and what they owed the storekeeper the nights when they talked about debts and struggle.

Mother's voice would reach him from the bedroom: "I don't know what we can do to pay off that debt."

Per was lying awake in the kitchen and could not help listening. He lay writhing.

Mother said again: "No matter how much we save it makes no difference."

Father said nothing. Mother continued: "You get nothing for what you sell these days either."

Still Father said nothing. But Mother had more. "Where shall we find the wages for Ivar this year?"

The darkness was thick; autumn was far advanced. Everything outdoors was whispering slightly. No, not everything; it was only the river. Indoors, Mother's voice was making it torture to be awake.

Why couldn't Mother shut up about it! He turned poor and cold inside as he listened. Everything else he might have been thinking about and enjoying was chased out of sight.

Father said nothing.

"Are you asleep?" she asked.

"No," said his earthy voice at last.

Then Mother said nothing more. Per lay awake for a long time. Oh, to get away from all this, he wished. Why did Mother say things that made him so unhappy?

In the morning he expected something dreadful to have happened. Just *something*. But nothing was dreadful. Aunt Anne came down, energetic and pleasant. Mother came, and things wove themselves out of her hands and turned into things for others. One of her best smiles could come on such a morning after such a gloomy night.

She had regained her courage, and it made you glad. Last night's remarks lost their force. Bufast lay ready for the day. Bufast was eternal and immovable.

Per expected Father to repeat what he had said about staying at Bufast, but he waited in vain. Now that Per was a tall schoolboy, Father seemed to have forgotten about it.

But he knew better. It was not forgotten. He knew Father counted on it, counted on the fact that it had been said. It was as if written in stone.

Per wished: Say something about it, Father!

It was a mystery why he should wish it. It would have been comforting and helpful, however strange it seemed. But Father never said it again during the whole of his life.

19

Frost, school, homework came round once more.

The earth echoed beneath his feet as he tramped off in the morning with his homework simmering in his head, like soup still on the boil. To be the first. That was what mattered at school.

Many things were painful, but when you knew your homework the best and wrote the best essay, then it was all a little less painful.

There was Åsne. She led the group because she was reckless and fun when they played pranks. She was the first to jump down from a wall of rock or climb up a boulder or slide down the frozen rivulets swollen with ice. He looked at Åsne with different eyes now. She wore a dress with three-quarter length sleeves, and when she wrote dictation, she pushed her sleeves even farther up her arms. He never tired of looking at her arms this year. He was full of strange wishes. Things were different this year.

There was Olav Bringa beside him. Didn't Olav notice Åsne's arms? Did Olav think as he did: Åsne's arms, Auntie's arms, girls' arms? He didn't say anything about it. But Per didn't say anything about it either. It was good to sit so close to Olav at the desk that he was nudged by the shiny elbow of his jacket. Olav was next best, and he could just try to be more.

Arms were curious. Something heavy sank to the bottom inside you when you looked at them. You *had* to look and look. *Could* they be the same arms he had held when he led

Åsne through the warm, shallow river? They were rounded and quietly busy on the desk, while the dictation sprinkled down from the teacher's desk, dry and gray, like ant dust from an old tree-stump.

Something had happened to Aunt Anne. An icy horror late in the pre-Christmas winter, poor in snow.

Auntie had laughed happily that summer and autumn. Then Per overheard a conversation one evening out in the passage of the Bufast farmhouse. He was shut in so that he could not help hearing; it was impossible to leave. Father and Mother and Åsmund had driven out that day with Goldie and not yet come home. Auntie and her friend had met up on the road, and the strange man had come down with her. Now they were standing in the dark passage.

"You're not in love with me," said Auntie's dear, familiar voice.

Per felt as if slashed with a knife.

"Really?" said the stranger indifferently.

This was icy horror. Dreadful to listen to, unable to move a finger.

"I didn't know you were like that," said Auntie. "Are you a good-for-nothing?"

Per felt furious hatred for this strange man in the dark. The blood pumped hot into his ears.

"No, I'm not in love with you," said the stranger callously. "I can't help it."

"No—" said Auntie.

A long, painful silence.

"But you *were* in love with me?" said Auntie anxiously.

Silence.

"Weren't you?"

"Oh—I—"

"And you *still* did it!"

"Oh—"

"Oh, yes, I understand," said Auntie laboriously, her voice hoarse.

Then the way was free; they had gone. Per could go where he wished, but he stayed on the same spot, trembling. The world was a dreadful place. People killed each other. Auntie's voice had sounded as if she were torn apart.

That he did not fall at her feet, that man, and lie there, stone dead! There was no justice in the world.

Per pulled himself together: the icy yard was rumbling and echoing. Goldie had come home with his load. Aunt Anne went to meet them. He could hear her talking calmly to Mother.

Per dreaded meeting her in the lamplight. Then he saw her. She was a little paler than usual, and Mother asked her whether she felt all right?

"Oh, yes."

Then she began to play with Åsmund, lifting him up, holding him on her lap, teasing him noisily. Åsmund laughed happily.

Per sat frozen through and through. What did Auntie look like inside now?

You were powerless. Defenseless against everything that came and crushed you.

It was almost Christmas. Between Christmas and New Year it began snowing heavily.

Later that winter Per helped Father to clear tracks in the snow and dig out the piles of logs on the days when he was not at school. The woods were snowed under and broken down with snow. In the twilight you could be half afraid, there were so many distorted shapes. In sunshine it was like a fairy story, and even more so in the moonlight.

The timber tracks were deep gullies. It was heavy work to clear them. The piles of logs lay like sleepers deep in the drifts. You had to bring a shovel and bore your way in. Hi, wake up!—and when you had made a hole, the logs breathed strongly and warmly through the opening. The logs were dark, living animals down there; they had been lying breathing all the time. Mice had been running along them.

You're big now, Per; you must be *good* at clearing timber tracks and log piles.

Nobody *said* this, but it was demanded just the same, and he shovelled snow until his shirt was wet. When he took off his mittens, steam rose from his hands.

Father and Goldie slid along the deep channels Per cleared in the drifts. Father piled on heavy loads and Goldie pulled them.

20

There was an emptiness around him.

Per stood clearing snow. Father slid away with a fresh load. Per had to dig out a new pile.

He had a hollow feeling. What was this? Was it God calling? God was no longer so frightening; he was not afraid of him now. As long as you were not a scoundrel, God would do you no harm. He thought about God more shyly now. It was impossible to talk about him. What were those people made of who thought it amusing to talk about him? Ugh, the teacher in school who moralized and chattered about Jesus as if it were an ordinary name passing his lips—this name that Per found impossible to say unless ordered to do so, that he would rather not even think about, he felt such awe and diffidence towards it. But some adults chattered and moralized about Jesus, pronouncing this wondrous name without a downward glance. Such people made you despise them.

Mother and Father kept silent about it, and he was glad. If they had started on *that* he would have been deeply disturbed.

What was the Holy Spirit?

He felt a fine vibration pass through him as he stood shovelling the snow: the Holy Spirit! There he was. No sooner had you thought about him than he shot through you, announced himself, and was gone again.

He stood empty-eyed in the snowy twilight. *All kinds of things* shot through you; this time it was the Holy Spirit.

He went on shovelling.

Åsne might have come along now, skiing between the bending trees. She would glide lightly on skis. The drifts had settled, so that her tracks would remain here all day.

She was reckless on skis. Yesterday she had jumped from a wall of rock where nobody had ever jumped before. But if she were to come here today, she would glide past lightly and quietly, and he would say something to her as she shot past him. Then he would go on shovelling until suppertime.

A thought struck him and cut through it all: Is Aunt Anne going to have a child by that good-for-nothing?

No, no!

But it was not impossible.

He shovelled and pondered. He was well enough informed about all *that*. It was no secret; he knew very well what happened. From the time he was small he had seen animals come together in order to have young. People came together too. He had understood this long before anyone had stated it, and it was nothing to laugh and whisper about as some of them did at school. All the same he often thought of all the ugly stories he had heard. They burned themselves into your brain the first time you heard them.

Was Aunt Anne going to have a child?

She would be kind to it! was his next thought. And she would be full of milk. The baby would drink until it burst from all that milk. No, no, she must not have a child!

He could have ground his teeth.

Åsne kept on getting mixed up in this. But Åsne and this did not belong together. Around Åsne hovered the Holy Spirit.

At that point he came back to earth, in the middle of his shovelling. The logs were fragrant. Pale straws and bits of heather were frozen fast to the chunks of snow loosened from the ground. The mice had been running up and down, gnawing pieces of bark.

There was the black earth, the faded grass. Did he love it? He could say neither yes nor no. He no longer tried to see if he was, as he had done for years. He was big now. Next year he would be confirmed. Yes, but what then? What was this hollow longing? Something was calling come, come, and yet there was nothing.

The thing to do is to slip away and let nobody see me.

No, I ought to go up onto a high hill where everybody could see me and see how difficult and unjust everything is for me.

I ought to go up on a hill and pray to the Holy Spirit.

The snow was falling more thickly; he was shivering from the sweat inside his clothes and the melting snow outside. A wild wish came into his head: I wish something good would happen!

He went on shovelling. The snow too had a fragrance when you stood cutting it into slices with a shovel. It gave off a faint scent, like that of spring water and rain. The logs gradually appeared, lying rough and tall on the faded grass. Father and Goldie came gliding along. They were large and wet, both of them. Goldie stamped his hooves. His black eyes were like wells. He tore off birch twigs with his teeth and did everything that was expected of him. He worked for a man who was good to animals.

Father looked about him despondently. This was what life was like in winter. It was an unpleasant time for him: snow lying at a depth of many feet above the earth he was thirsting to dig.

The fresh load moved slowly along the channel.

Per went on shovelling alone. Then Åsne Bakken came.

Per straightened up in astonishment.

Åsne came alone on skis and stopped beside the long, open grave that the log pile resembled. With her ski pole she struck at a little fir tree bent over by the snow. The fir shook itself, righted itself, awoke.

97

"What are you doing?" said Per without the slightest introduction, alarmed because there seemed to be no reason in *getting* what you wanted! He felt as if he had conjured her up. He was incapable of speaking pleasantly to her. Why had she come?

"I'm going to the farms," said Åsne, and it seemed quite natural after all.

"Is the snow good enough to ski anywhere now?" he asked skeptically.

"Yes," she said.

They just stood.

"Are you shovelling snow?"

"Yes," he said, at a loss what to say next.

She struck the skis with her pole to get rid of a lump of snow and then went on downhill. It was steep; she was soon gone.

Per stood looking at her tracks. It had not been a vision; the flesh-and-blood Åsne had sped past: there were her tracks. She had come when he most wished it. Why had she come like that and ruined his thoughts? Now he could not be fond of her again for a long while!

The Holy Spirit had nothing to do with *her*, he thought crossly. There had not been the slightest suspicion of it about her. A tall girl, that was all there was to it. To come like that—and make him disappointed.

He went on shovelling, so tired that his arms were trembling. But it didn't matter.

Then the evening came, and came early. The bending forest was full of strange animals. The log pile had been cleared and was a long, dark grave in the drifts. Per took his skis and followed Åsne's tracks as far as he could; then he turned aside and went home. All of a sudden he felt incredibly happy.

Throughout the spring he and Åsne spoke very little to each other. Sometimes he dreamed senseless things about her.

He could not look her straight in the eyes. When she turned

up her sleeves to write dictation, he felt hot and strange. Why did she do that? None of the others had turned up their sleeves until now, when they began aping her. Nor did any of them besides himself seem to notice that *she* did so.

All the others looked at her openly and talked to her and quarrelled with her—as if she were an ordinary girl. The biggest and strongest girl. Not even Olav noticed that she was quite different from before. It was incredible.

Then he realized that he did not think the way the others did when they were with girls. He brooded, ashamed, and hid it away.

One day just before school broke up, a girl stood looking him straight in the eyes. It was Signe Moen. She simply studied him with her clear eyes. He knew that Åsne and Signe were together most of the time. Girls always kept together. Signe was looking at him as if trying to find out something. She must have been doing it for Åsne. She had noticed something and wanted to know more about it.

He could not shake off those cold, searching eyes for several days. What did she want to find out? It had to do with Åsne. Everything had to do with Åsne Bakken now. But the fact that it was so must be hidden, or dreadful things might happen.

It was the spring thaw, and there were light evenings and a tall, tall sky. Per went about staring. He had a stone in his breast. On the day of the examination it rained: strange, spring rain; tender, impossible spring rain and the smell of all that was *to be* throughout the length and breadth of the country. In the afternoon when everything was over, Åsne Bakken and Signe Moen went home along with the others. Past Per they walked, in the middle of the crowd, and he stood waiting for a voice to call out his innermost secrets all over the school yard—and for the heavens to fall afterwards.

The voice did not speak. He was saved. Åsne and Signe went on. They disappeared behind some dripping black birches. It went on raining, cool and fresh. Gray snowdrifts sighed and received the rain.

Far, far away there *was* something. Hopelessly far away. It was in today's rain, and in the black earth beside the wet snow, and in the concluding Our Father that had been read slowly and solemnly today, and in Åsne Bakken's eyes, and in the yawning emptiness after Botolv; it swirled around confusedly and was nameless.

Olav Bringa was standing in front of him, looking sideways past him.

" 'Bye. See you."

" 'Bye."

"Are you herding the sheep this spring?"

"Yes. Are you?"

"Yes."

Olav went home. He too disappeared behind the wet birches; he came to school the same way as Åsne and Signe. Nobody else came to him to say good-bye, nor did Per go over to anyone and say it. He went home to Bufast, with his worn books and his pencil-box hidden under his jacket because of the rain.

21

Aunt Anne was not going to have a child.

For a long time Per had been expecting somebody to talk about it. Such things were always talked about by someone. But nobody said anything. Auntie was just as before. So he was relieved of that worry.

All this idle gossip you heard: She's landed herself with a child now, I suppose, said people about this person and that.

They said it without feeling the slightest sympathy for whoever they were talking about. Rather, they said it in such a way that it turned your stomach. People were full of idle gossip.

Auntie would escape their wicked tongues.

But she would have been wonderfully kind to the baby; he would have had more milk than he knew what to do with.

Now she looked just as before: good to look at. And yet, as they toiled in the steaming field during the spring plowing, there was a difference from last year all the same. Per thought about the happy days in the potato field last autumn.

Father was sitting resting in front of Goldie. The horse was dozing with fatigue, his head hanging almost as low as Father's shoulders. Per's back was aching from weeding. Aunt Anne was sitting close by, resting her back too.

So she was not going to have a child by that good-for-nothing. Per could not help thinking of him with horror.

He was still alive. Per saw him on the road sometimes and a flash of horror shot through his body. That man must be on the brink of death and destruction—and yet he went like others to the storekeeper and bought coffee and sugar and shoe leather as if nothing had happened. He talked about the weather, and gossiped about people, and laughed. He was still alive, and it had happened six months ago.

"Look at Goldie," said Auntie, close to his ear.

He started out of his thoughts.

"What?"

The yellow horse was resting his muzzle on Father's shoulder. Father was sitting stock still.

"Look at your father and Goldie," said the soft, pleasant voice behind Per.

Per ran about in the woods after the sheep. He was so bored he could have screamed, but in the evening when the sheep took the permitted, direct route home again, his heart was soothed.

At home life continued unwaveringly as usual. Mother prepared their days and their clothes and their food.

Per learned to swim in a creek of the river while he was herding the sheep that year. He read the newspaper that was wrapped around his food to the last letter of the alphabet.

The driest matters, which would never have been noticed otherwise, were read with enthusiasm when you were a herdsman sitting on a stone.

Next year he would be confirmed. And Olav would be confirmed, and Åsne.

Father came and said he must help him weed out stones while the sheep were fenced in during the middle of the day. He was choked with anger, for it was unfair. The herdsman was supposed to be free then. He gave Father some dirty looks and threw the stones onto the heap so that they bounced.

Unfair!

He would tell Father to his face that this was none of his business. This was his free time.

Father was digging stones out too, turning over and piling up the biggest. He straightened up and looked at Per with a sneer.

"Quite right, Per," he said, when Per sent a stone into the heap with a clatter. "It's good for the stone to feel it; that's only right and proper."

And he laughed coldly. His laughter felt like a ducking in cold water. This was not work for a sissy, and nobody asked what the herdsman's rights were.

Father merely attacked another heavy stone with the crowbar. The words that Per had thought of hurling at him were never spoken. Per saw that they would roll like bilberries off that homespun back and those square shoulders and that tanned neck.

Father had scorned him. He felt as if he had been beaten. There was another feeling too: it was like having your mouth full of earth. He wished Father would turn around and look in his direction.

No. Father kept his back turned to him, clearly on purpose. It stung.

The midday sun was baking hot, and the ground had a different smell, sending gusts of warmth back again. Per was standing in the middle of the patch of red, barren, newly-cleared land. A short way off lay the pieces which Father had cleared in previous years. Some of it was thick meadow now. On last year's patches wheat or oats were growing sparsely. Father had sweated over every foot of it.

Turn around, Father, and look at me just once.

No. Only that back and those square shoulders and those elbows showing through the holes worn in his shirt.

"Home!" called Mother from the doorstep.

It sounded reassuring. Of course, everything was all right. Mother and her call home were part of it and were always there when it was time. Mother never forgot the routine.

They straightened up, answered yes! to the call, washed their hands in the stream, and went in to dinner.

Per looked down at the table that day as he ate. Åsmund refused his food, was spoken to sharply, and sat pouting.

"Eat," said Father. "It's good food."

"No," said Åsmund.

"Then leave the table and go to bed," said Father curtly.

Åsmund left, red with the sulks. He went and lay down on his bed, with a sidelong glance at Father.

A thundercloud lay over the table. Per sat and chewed, knowing whose fault it was; it was his fault that Father was irritable and that Åsmund had been sent to bed.

No, it was Father, who was hard as rock. Father will destroy me. . . .

A strong gust of earth came from Father's soil-spattered clothes. Father takes the earth with him all over the place; he's impossible; he'll kill me soon; he's. . . .

Per chewed.

Father chewed slowly.

Mother and Aunt Anne chewed.

Åsmund lay staring through the wall.

Aunt Anne was letting the cows out. They were making a good deal of noise and commotion; it was their first day out, and they were frisky and boisterous. The calves stood as if blind, unable to walk. The grown cows fought each other

savagely, clashing horns getting entangled, and horns prod-
ding necks and shoulders and flanks. It looked highly dangerous but was unavoidable. Mother and Auntie, hot and short
of breath, went among them flailing their arms to part them.
Father came and parted them if there was any real danger
of a cow's being gored. Their hooves gripped the earth so
that they sank in deep and clods spattered up. The bell cow
ran amok, and none of them dared touch her; she was an
experienced fighter and threw a couple of the young ones
aside as soon as she came out, to let it be known that she was
keeping her position.

Åsmund sat in the shelter of the doorstep, but Per ran
around the yard with a switch. *This* was fun! Dangerously
strong horns glistened and thick strong necks writhed. Their
white backs gleamed above their red flanks, reminding him
of milk; milk reminded him of Mother and Auntie. Hooves
clashed. The two heifers stood still, young and slender. The
two calves looked stupid, standing with eyes like marbles,
not knowing what to do with their feet. Then they found out
and ran like mad things, and then stood still again, staring.

The big bull was still in the barn, butting the wall and
bellowing. He was the father of almost all these heifers and
calves running about outside. But he could not be with them
today; he must never get loose. He would chase the herd,
knock them about, destroy them. He stood bellowing and
turning up the whites of his eyes.

Olav Bringa and Per met that year too at the river the day
the sheep were sent away. They took stock of each other:
they were tall and brown and thin. They had herded the
sheep for the last time. Next year they would be working on
the farm, and some little kid or other would have to run
about herding.

"Are you so very glad?" asked Olav uncertainly.

At once Per felt it too: he had been happier in previous
years when the herding had ended. Why was that?

They lay on the bank skimming stones across the river. Thinking. There was something missing; they had no desire to yell at the tops of their voices and take wild leaps. The bank was thick with windflowers, the tall, coarse windflowers that last far into the summer. The young aspens were pale green. They were not glad.

Ought they to be?

Yes, they ought. It was said over and over again, and repeated in print, that these were the best days of their lives. And every time it was said, it was a lie.

The truth was, their hearts were heavy. If only they had known *why* it would have been a help.

Per asked, "Have you seen many of the others from school this spring?"

"No," said Olav.

"D'you think they've been herding sheep?"

"Don't know. Yes, I suppose so," said Olav crossly. "Åsne's been herding for her aunt. Did you know Åsne had learned to swim?"

Per stared at him. "No. Yes, I did. No, I don't know—"

"She told me so one day when I met her at the post office, a long time ago."

There was a long silence.

"I learned to swim this spring too," said Olav finally, and threw a stone into the water.

Per looked away. "I learned this spring too," he said, his mouth dry.

Long silence. Strange, shy thoughts.

"Shall we?" said Per, not knowing what to do next.

"Yes."

They threw off their clothes and swam in the river. They were not very good at it yet. The water was cool but not cold. The bottom was yellow sand.

Something nudged them.

Come! willed the current, wishing to go far and see many things. The water was clear. You could see the outline of England on Olav's back when he floundered.

They climbed up onto a big flat stone and lay there lonely in the sunshine with their shy thoughts.

Their bodies dried. They were both equally tall and equally slim.

22

"What's on your mind, Per?" asked Jens up at the gravel pits.

"What do you mean?"

"Never mind. I was only asking."

Per wondered whether people noticed any outward sign of all he thought about. Why did people ask things like that? They pecked with their questions dryly and tiringly like a woodpecker drumming into a hollow aspen.

What do you want, Per?

He had not told anyone that he did not want to stay at Bufast when he grew up. All the same they asked as if they knew something. They could just shut up.

The haying season arrived, bringing hard work and warm weather. Per mowed, raked, trod down the loads. If he and Ivar were alone in the field, he would try to keep up with him in the swath. Ivar would laugh and leave Per far behind in an instant.

"No, you're not going to chase me away yet," said Ivar.

In the evenings Per was often dead tired. He would sit in a corner, too tired to read. There sat Father, there Ivar. Mother and Aunt Anne could not rest until the last dishes were washed and the cows milked; then they fell quiet on their chairs in the corners. Tired: it was the haying season. The door stood open and great gusts of summer came in: the smell of drying hay, the buzzing of dung beetles, the tiny whine of gnats. They sat limp and blind, for the haying was no joke. Only Åsmund was noisy; he was not tired enough.

Did Father over there know he was sitting wishing for something else? Just something else. Yes, he must know.

Over in the corner where Mother was sitting, a book fell to the floor. Mother's tired, he thought vaguely.

"—Per!" said a voice, and a kind hand gripped his shoulder. He tore his eyes open and looked into Auntie's. Auntie smelled of hay when she came so close, and of cows and milk, but mostly of hay.

He had fallen asleep.

"There are only the two of us left," said Auntie. "You've been sitting asleep."

There was no one in the kitchen besides themselves. He suddenly felt he wanted to tell Auntie something.

"You must go to bed," she said, and went up to her room. There was a slight creaking up above, then silence. Auntie was asleep.

He went outside. His body was full of memories from the haying that day, from treading down the loads as fast as he could, from treading and pressing it down in the barn while Father tipped in the load of hay. The barn had been hot from the sun-warmed hay and filled with dust from the dried grass and flowers. You sneezed and sweated in there. Now the barn lay dim, sending a fragrance of hay out through the vents. Farther off the barley field glimmered; it was not yet ready for cutting but was yellowing fast. From the barn came the childish bleating of a calf.

Per stood there watching and listening. It was as if he were left alone at Bufast. All the others were asleep.

This is my farm, he thought.

He went indoors to bed. It was not dark, but dusky and peaceful. Åsmund was hot to lie next to, as Botolv had been before him. There was a gnat in the kitchen, singing its tiny song.

Per lay reliving the haying. Many things were mixed up in it; he was sleepy, and the haying was confused with his sleep and with Aunt Anne. There are only the two of us left, said Auntie. Milk in warm jets. Hay. New-mown hay breathing its fragrance through all the vents on all the farms at this moment. Fragrance of cows, of big warm animals—and again the fertile spurt of milk into buckets with a frosting of foam. . . .

Per confused it all with his image of Auntie.

Auntie has not been killed. It must not be possible to kill her.

What? A thought chilled him, cutting across all that was good and reassuring: Father's lying awake, staring out at nothing, knowing I want to leave.

One Sunday in the late summer Mother and Aunt Anne went visiting the other farms and took Åsmund with them. Ivar had gone over to the farms too.

Per was walking in the yard, thinking how long and boring Sunday was. You looked forward to it all week, and when it came it was boring.

The yellow horse was tethered in the hayfield. The barley field was cut. Father was nowhere to be seen. Usually he was in the habit of lying out in the yard on Sunday.

When Per came indoors, Father was not there either. Only the cat lying in a chair, and a low buzzing from a couple of flies up in the ceiling. Per was surprised and went out into the bedroom. There sat Father reading an old newspaper. Per came in so quietly that he had no time to hide it. For he started in surprise and tried to hide it!

He was reading that piece about himself written many years ago. A PIONEER, it said in big letters. Beneath it was his picture. Father was standing in uniform; he had been on army exercises. It was faded too.

"What do you want?" he said to Per sharply, putting the newspaper with the picture face downwards.

Per did not know what to reply.

"You can go out again, then," said Father, still sharp and hostile. "Can't a man be left in peace?"

Per left. He felt as if he had committed a sin. He regretted having gone in. Father had been helpless, sitting there with the old newspaper, reading those bragging words about himself.

No, he did not regret it. He was glad he had seen him.

23

School started, and at the same time the candidates enrolled for confirmation classes. There were quite a number of them. Åsne Bakken and Signe Moen and Olav Bringa among others, and Per Bufast. Per was nervous about being with them again.

It turned out to be nothing to worry about; there was no more of what he had felt that past spring. Åsne looked at him calmly, and he was able to look calmly back. They were friends and busy with lessons.

They often felt solemn about being prepared for confirmation, yet it was impossible to find out *why*. There *was* something solemn about it; none of them tried to make fun of it.

At school Åsne was the center of attraction, now as before. She did not dislike it; you could see that. She was even wilder and noisier than the boys, so they idolized her. The girls were jealous of her, and taunts were often exchanged.

Sometimes Per would be startled to feel that it had not gone. With the passing of time it certainly had not gone. It made him strangely glad and strangely depressed.

Olav sat at Per's side daydreaming.

"Olav," whispered Per.

Olav gave a start. "What is it?" he said, blushing.

"Nothing."

The teacher unrolled the big map of Europe. "Olav, will you come here and show us on the map what you know about England."

At once Åsne turned to Olav with a smile. Olav groped his way to the front.

Per felt as if he had swallowed something strange, and saw a dim shadow pass in front of his eyes. Olav had let Åsne know about his mark. Anger and sorrow rose inside him.

Olav stood stammering and knew practically nothing about England that day. Per felt it served Olav right to stand there being stupid. He tried to catch Åsne's eye across the desks. He managed it; she was as open and frank towards him as to the others. Then she turned back to the map.

Per couldn't make her out.

"What's the matter?" asked Olav when he came back to the desk.

Per did not answer. His friendship with Olav was hanging by a hair.

There was no showdown afterwards. It did not occur to Per; it was too painful to talk about.

It receded, the matter of Olav, as so much receded. At any rate it went to rest somewhere like a deposit at the bottom. One thing after another sank down to rest there. You tried to be careful and not stir it up again.

So he did not lose Olav. He and Olav would stick together always. Many times it was his salvation to remember that when he was torn by puzzling sensations. He was torn by futile thirst and longing.

At home the routine continued as before. The only difference was that Åsmund had started school that year. Per helped him with his simple little pieces of homework. Åsmund made friends who came to Bufast on Sundays. Per was not invited to join them; they played together and seemed to manage very well on their own. Sometimes Per joined them just the same and was astonished at how grateful they were. They became twice as enthusiastic; the game was given new interest and turned into a new game. Per felt touched and grateful himself. He could not understand it; he had always been the eldest.

The Holy Spirit was often in his thoughts.

He had so many Bible stories and explanations to read that winter, and it sank in whether he wanted it to or not. Strict Jehovah, and Christ before whom he felt so shy—he hurried over them in order to stop and rest with the Holy Spirit.

Not that he understood a word of what was preached and presented to him, but sometimes he had felt something within himself that was as delicate and as quickly gone as a Holy Spirit *ought* to be.

They sat for long hours in the pastor's office. It was warm there, and the air seemed terribly dry, while outside it was snowing. They sat stiffly, repeating their homework to the creaking accompaniment of the pastor's chair.

Dull homework. Per felt empty, yet solemn. The girls sat on the bench nearest the stove. Laughing, adored Åsne sat strange and solemn. Some of them sat listening in amazement, with astonished expressions. The heavy spring snow had stopped falling and simply hung in the cherry branches outside the window.

The chair creaked.

Per tried to push out everything that haunted his mind and cling to the thought of the Holy Spirit reverently and long, while his head throbbed and ached. Beside him, Olav looked at him with empty eyes.

With all his heart he wished for what it seemed he could not have: something for this thirst and hollowness in his breast.

This Spirit! Only a touch of flame. Help me! he thought.

24

Finally he found himself in church, standing in a row of dark-clad boys, a row of new clothes and shoes and stiff faces. Across the aisle was another tense, solemn row: the girls they had known through hundreds of schooldays. Now they were standing tensely. You dared not start looking at them one by one, only saw them as a row.

Around them on the chairs sat people staring at them. Small children hung over the backs of the chairs watching them importantly and searchingly. Per did not know what to do with his arms and his feet. You were not supposed to do anything with them.

He stood trying with the best will in the world to feel what he should. He knew he did not feel as he should according to the precepts, and this was bitter, but not unexpected. But he knew, in spite of everything, that something about the day had *some* meaning for him. He was freed a little from the daily struggle. What passed through him now like a soft wind was holy, and yet. . . .

Outside it was spring. A brook was foaming. If they had been outdoors, they would have smelled the fragrance of the willows along the brook.

Per was the one who came off best in answering the pastor's questions. That was only how it had always been and had to be; it gave him no pleasure. Learned by rote. He rattled off the dry rigmarole with his mouth, trying at the same time to save the splendid day this was supposed to be.

Beside him was Olav Bringa. That was right and proper. Olav's clothes smelled of the pressing iron. How much care and trouble had gone into all these new clothes? wondered Per suddenly. Many a bitter struggle must have taken place before enough money had been saved for so many brand new clothes and shoes. Each one kept the memory of it to himself, hidden behind his stiff confirmation face.

He looked at the worn people sitting in their chairs with folded, worn hands. They had a son or a daughter standing there today. Some sat more quietly than others, as if it had cost them more.

The pastor had said something one day as he sat creaking in the office chair: Your parents have brought you thus far; it has cost them fifteen years of worry and struggle.

It made you feel guilty. Per looked at these quiet, worn people in their chairs. Fifteen years of worry and struggle. It gave you a guilty conscience. It was not a holy occasion any more, only a bad conscience about something you could not help.

He looked across at Father and Mother. They were sitting with their hands in their laps, like all the rest, looking this way at him and the others. What were they thinking about? Probably about fifteen years of worry and struggle. But it was *not* his fault. All the same, he had a guilty conscience; it was strange. . . .

Now came the worst part: the pastor's voice calling him out to something unknown, calling loudly and clearly, "Per Eilevson Bufast." *

The holiness was now. The strangeness was now. Yet he got to his feet again with a bitter knowledge: he was no different from before. Not one person present could have *borne* what was being enjoined on them that day. Every living soul among the adults sitting there knew it. He understood it all right. All these silent mouths in here could have said so had they wished: that it was no use trying to bear it.

He looked across at Father and Mother when he returned from the altar. He saw at once what they were thinking. It was not about fifteen years of struggle. They were simply thinking: Now we have a son who is confirmed.

It obviously meant more to them than it did to himself.

Per Eilevson Bufast. The name had had a curious ring to it when it was called out. Bufast. He repeated it to himself. It had rung out beneath the church roof and was still here. It drew the whole of Bufast into the crowded church. He saw it in his mind's eye—the color of the house, the tree in the

* Formerly Norwegian children would use the father's Christian name with "son" or "daughter" added as a suffix. Thus the patronymic might change with each generation. The addition of the farm name shows that the system had already been officially abandoned by this time in favor of one surname common to all descendants, but that this valley evidently clung to the old tradition.

farmyard, the glitter from the river below. And the meadow and the field and the animals. It smelled of sunshine mingled with scores of other things. It was warm and heavy and alive, and was a farm. Cows were milked there. Calves were born there. Animals were slaughtered there when the time came, and the man who slaughtered them was good to animals.

He glanced at him quickly. He was tall and capable, with square shoulders.

Per Eilevson Bufast. Per Ingjerdson Bufast. He tried it out to see what it sounded like.

He met a pair of eyes in the row of girls across the aisle. Randi Bratterud. The eyes slid away again. Randi Knutsdotter Bratterud had sounded above her bent head a few minutes ago. She was holding her hymnbook and her handkerchief in her hands.

She had always given brief, straightforward answers, he remembered. And she had never tried to be the best.

There were others here whom he knew better, but he could see only the backs of their necks. Beside him were Aunt Anne and Åsmund.

It was over. They all rose from their chairs at once and lost each other in the crowd. Outside, a brook was roaring in flood; the rushing noise met them at the door. The willows met them with the fragrance of their strong, sweet sap. Outside the door he found Olav again, was pushed right into his face. Olav Aslakson Bringa. Now he was confirmed.

Somebody came up and took his hand. "So now you're grown-up, Per. Good luck to you."

Per looked up, surprised. Grown-up? He didn't feel grown-up.

A couple of others came over and congratulated him. But it was really because Olav was standing beside him. Olav knew a good many of the people in the district. Per knew practically nobody. They came and told him he was grown-up.

Platitudes. *Boring*, that was what people were! Full of empty platitudes.

As they were standing there together, Åsne came over to them. She pushed her way across and stood in front of them, familiar and good to see. She stretched out her hands to them with a big smile. They took a hand each. Åsne Torleivsdotter Bakken. They must have returned her smile; they could not tell.

For a second he looked into her eyes, remembering scores of things about her.

"What's to become of us now?" she said, and then released them and went over to the other girls. She would stay at home, and at home circumstances were narrow. Her father had been killed driving the horses soon after she was born.

Olav and Per could not very well stand together any longer. They turned towards each other at the same moment, flushed and generous.

"Well—" said Per.

"Well—" said Olav.

So they parted. They had meant to say a great deal to each other. So they said nothing.

Father and Mother were waiting. We have a son who has been confirmed, was written in their faces. Aunt Anne busied herself looking after Åsmund. A man hurried past her. It was *that* man. Nothing happened.

Mother nodded and smiled at Per. It was a relief that he did not have to dread admonitions and speeches and solemn talk from his family, bless them. They did not say a word about what had happened as they walked home.

What's to become of us now? Åsne had asked, perplexed.

It occurred to him that she had been holding her hymnbook in the hand she had given Olav. That meant that Olav had had to squeeze the hymnbook as well as her hand. It couldn't have been as good as the handshake Per got. He tried it out as he walked along, squeezing the hand that was holding his own book. No, it was nowhere near the same.

What's to become of us now? Åsne had asked. As he walked along he gradually realized how boundlessly perplexed her eyes had been. Even hers. In spite of the smile in them.

Åsne's words began swelling, like a piece of food too dry to swallow.

He would be staying at Bufast, wouldn't he? There went the man who had the power to make assertions that were as much in force now as the day they were spoken, assertions that he had struggled against in every way since. He did not know.

The wish to get away was still there, but he doubted more and more whether there was anything in it. He had fooled himself with all that struggle to be the best. He did not put so much faith in it any more. How could he know! Wait and see! he thought hastily, and pushed it all aside.

Olav would stay at Bringa to the end of his days. And he talked about it as if it were right and self-evident and good. Why didn't Per have the same feeling?

"Åsne Bakken will have to find a job with her aunt now," said Aunt Anne, finding herself beside Per on the way home.

Per was startled. He could tell that this was no chance remark, but that Auntie *wanted* to talk to him about Åsne. It was as if she wanted to do him a kindness. He was grateful for the way in which she said it.

"Will she?"

"Yes, I suppose so. There's nothing for her to do at home *there*, you see. She won't be able to stay there when she's grown-up; it's more than enough for her mother, looking after herself. Åsne's a nice girl."

Her voice was kind and comforting, and quiet so that Father and Mother would not hear her. What did Auntie know? If he had been as strong as a bear, he would have crushed her with gratitude.

They came to Bufast. There was lowing in the barn. *That* always meant something. Cows didn't stand lowing for nothing.

"What do you bet—?" said Aunt Anne, hurrying down.

She came out again quickly, throwing on her smock. "The calf's lying on the floor!" she announced.

Then she turned to Per. "That's what happens when you have to confirm young boys."

She and Mother got busy. They had been expecting a calf, but not so soon as today. Now it was all over while they were at church. Per stood remembering the wonderful, well-known feeling: beestings and pancakes. It was not the same as before.

Mother put water on the stove. "You'll have to wait for your dinner," she said, and hurried out again.

Åsmund went with her and stood in the stall beside the calf. If Åsmund put a finger in the calf's mouth, he would smack his lips and suck it.

Per left Åsmund standing there and went to sit in the kitchen beside Father. Dinner was half ready; it had been prepared before they went to church.

It was difficult sitting beside Father like that. Per would have preferred to go out again to Åsmund and the calf. Father was sitting with something unsaid.

Don't ask me about anything, wished Per. Don't ask me.

Father turned to him. "Well, well—" he said decisively. Not a word more.

Now *that's* over and done with, was in his tone of voice. Now we have brought up a son.

Per returned his gaze as frankly as he could. Father would not ask him about anything dangerous.

Mother came in with a frothing bucket full of the first milk.

---

*Bufast will give you
all you need.*

1

Now you're grown-up, they had begun saying.

Per was told this from time to time during the course of the summer. He did not feel grown-up. He felt nowhere near as grown-up as they all seemed to expect.

It never sounded as if it were a good thing when they said, Now you're grown-up. When Mother and Aunt Anne said it, it was a complaint. It meant that he had acted childishly again. Or they said it as a reason for finding more and heavier work for him to do.

Father did not say it.

But if any of the neighbors dropped in, they would say, "Yes, Per's grown-up now, oh, yes—" And then they would smile in a friendly, well-disposed way, even though they knew they didn't mean a word of it. He felt like grinding his teeth over all these empty habits people had.

What was the next step? The future was vague. He had not decided to stay, yet he went on with the daily round just the same, doing what he was asked, doing it like a sleepwalker, taking no part in it.

Bufast held him in an iron grip. He was to be here to the end of his days; it had been inscribed on tablets of stone. That was how it would be.

He felt so small and impotent that he had a desire to throw himself down on the earth, kicking and screaming.

Yes, now you're grown-up too, Per, they said.

What did he *want*?

He did not know. Yes, he did. He wanted to be rid of all that weighed on him and of all memories—and then he wanted to *go elsewhere*. That was how he thought: go elsewhere. Everything was uncertain.

To go elsewhere sounded so easy and splendid that it made him think of light little clouds high up in the sky, or a pleasant

Saturday afternoon free from work and with the longing stilled.

That year was a drought year. The drought summer, they said for years afterwards.

Per minded the sheep no longer. A poor little wretch from the neighboring parish came and did it, a boy called Knut, who was so poorly clothed when he came that Mother immediately found more suitable rags for him to put on. Knut Prikken was his name. The farm he came from was not really called Prikken,* but was so small that it was known as such all the same. Knut was ten years old and was to mind the sheep with Åsmund. Åsmund was to be made use of too now. Bufast had seized him.

Not a single question was asked as to what Åsmund himself thought about it. He was just to be with Knut Prikken. The two boys were simply awakened in the morning and given food, and then off to the woods they went. They were as if dead and gone for many hours. But they returned the minute they were allowed home. They had a watch. They came shouting and leaping, swept the sheep behind the fences, ate, and were gone from sight, off to more important affairs of their own behind the house or down by the river or up in the gravel pits. Then it was noon, and the sheep bells jingled again on their way to the wood, to the long, long afternoon of herding.

Per saw and heard them from the cleared land or from some other work place out in the meadow or among the crops. He was the farm hand at Bufast now. He could not deny that he liked it better, even though the work was harder. He would not have changed places with the two shepherds.

This year as every year Father had a patch he was going to convert from wasteland to cultivated ground. Per dug there with him. It was exhausting. The new patch had been there as long as anyone could remember, so that you no longer *saw*

* A point or dot.

it. It simply moved a bit, and you dug and dug. Thin soil that had never seen the sunlight was turned up with great effort. The sun came pouring down. Then the earth was fragrant for the first time.

Drought summer.

The steepest slopes turned brown. There were withered patches where the rocks lay just below the surface. The grain grew sparsely and turned yellow when it should have been green.

The cows came home thirsty from the pasture and jostled around the well in the yard. Aunt Anne went among the big animal bodies, pushing them about, pouring water into tubs and pails, standing in a cloud of small black flies that had followed the irritated herd of cows home from the woods. Auntie was as brown as copper.

It was hot week after week. At Bufast day after day they turned up new earth, which was burned and baptized in a flood of sunshine. The sweat poured off them.

There was no more conversation this year than was usual when working with Father.

It occurred to Per that Father had a disease. It was a disease, this digging of his in the earth.

It was dreadful to watch how he dug. To see the gleam in his eye. He was sick and crazy about digging in the earth. It blinded him to other important things so that he did not see all that he should. Mother and Aunt Anne had said so many years ago when they said he dug till he was crazy.

It must be a disease.

Father did other things on the farm only because he had to—and then he turned back to his patch again with an altered face and dug and shovelled until he sighed. But there was no complaint in his sigh. He dug until you could see it was painful for him to straighten his back, but there was great peace in his expression. He was where he belonged; so he would sit and lean against the red edge of the unturned earth and let his back straighten out a little.

There should not have been anything dreadful about it. But it was easy to see that Father was overtaxing himself, wearing himself out over it, the way he kept on without being able to hold himself in check. Besides, he was breaking up too much ground at a time. Per did not know very much about it, but he had heard people say so; Ivar told Father to his face that if he couldn't manure all that newly-turned earth properly, it would be better to take on no more than could be tilled little by little. They knew very well he was too hard up to buy manure.

Father only smiled, presumably thinking they could just try to take away what he took pleasure in. He must have been wrong, but he smiled and went on as before.

He was not strict with Per in that he stood over him and drove him. He simply enjoyed himself in silence, digging tensely and urgently. It was difficult to avoid being drawn into his rhythm. Per was so drawn.

The sun shone, and there was no end to its warmth. But the water dried up in one well after the other on the neighboring farms. At Bufast water had to be carried up from the river in barrels. The cows came home and drank thirstily. Auntie pushed them about, flailing her arms, so that each one got a drop.

Olav and Per met occasionally, but Per saw nothing of Åsne and the others. That was both good and bad. He was uncertain how to behave if he met them now; it had been quite different during their school days.

Everyone they met complained about the sun and the drought. The crops were ruined, they said. The small amount of grass left was mown before that was scorched too.

"This year we'll have to reduce the herd," they said.

One Sunday there was something Olav wanted to say before they parted. He seemed to have to struggle to get the words out.

"Åsne's going to stay with us at Bringa this year. For the haying."

Per said, "Oh, is she?"

"Yes. She's coming tomorrow."

"Is she going to stay after the haying?"

"Yes, I expect so."

"Is she going to stay for the winter too?"

"Yes."

They each went their own way.

Olav had told Per as if confessing a crime, and Per almost felt it as a crime, a sin.

He watched Olav walking away between the bushes. A lump came into his throat. Olav would not come to meet him any more.

It was unbelievable, but that's how it was: Olav won't come any more.

He felt a sharp, stinging pain, as if he had breathed in smoke. Tomorrow they would start mowing the thin grass that was left on the scorched meadow at Bringa. They would be starting at Bufast too. Ivar would be coming to Bufast. Åsne Bakken would be coming to Bringa.

Olav was lost. There, he had gone!

We'll have to reduce the herd this autumn.

It hung over the herd of cows more threateningly than the black cloud of flies. It was said each time two men met on the road. It was said each time anyone dropped in at the kitchen at Bufast. At the counter in the store it was said more often than anywhere else.

"There'll be fine herds going to the town this autumn," said Ivar.

"Don't talk about it," said Auntie. She felt haunted. There was something about it from which you recoiled; you refused to think about it. Mother said, "Go get us more water, Per."

He went to get Goldie. He had learned how to harness him. He did so and rattled down the slope towards the river with the empty water barrel. Father and Ivar were lying in the yard resting after dinner.

It was fun holding the reins, but not while others were resting. Åsmund went with him. Knut Prikken had left, so Åsmund tagged after Per wherever he went.

Per carried the buckets across the dried-out beach of sand between the bank and the little trickle of water still flowing like an eel. Goldie stood stamping and flicking at the flies. Åsmund stood and held the reins, Goldie looking at him as if wanting to say something.

Per walked along the white mounds of dry sand. It wasn't right: this was the bottom and should have had clear water flowing over it. This was what it was like outside himself, and he was like this inside as well, plodding along through dry, hot sand and fields of thistles.

2

Per waited expectantly every Sunday: today Olav will come. He did not come. The precious Sundays were long and empty and worthless. Then he worked six more days and earned another Sunday.

It was impossible for him to go to Bringa. He could find no reason for this, except that he could not bring himself to do so.

"What's happened to Olav Bringa?" asked Mother. "We never see him nowadays."

It was just such a long Sunday, empty and with a heat haze in the air. He could feel the six days of hard work in his body.

Per did not answer his mother. How innocently she asked, "Have you quarrelled?"

"No."

He left her. Ivar was lying out in the yard. In the field stood the poles for drying the sheaves of grain. The stalks were only half their usual length. But the little grain there was, was firm and rounded. The flour would be good this year. Rain had fallen at last, turning the scorched meadows green, and there was water in the well.

Ivar took no more notice of him this year than last, and Per did not care; he had no need of him. There he lay yawning. He was a hard worker and seemed quite lost on Sundays.

Olav did not come that Sunday either.

Judgment hung over the herd. Towards autumn Skrim began going the rounds of the district buying up the cows that could not be kept through the winter. He hastened from barn to barn like a pestilence.

There were cows for the asking everywhere. He came to Bufast and took three. He did not take them away at once, but simply marked them with an invisible mark, writing them down in a worn notebook. It was a sad day. There stood Father, selling cows. It was done quickly. Father wanted to get it over with. "Oh, yes," he said, fed up and dejected, in answer to Skrim's talk.

Skrim in his haste noted Per too: "I shall need drovers when I go to town. Will you take the job? Come with the herd in about a week?"

Yes, yes! thought Per, looking at his father.

"As you please," said Father to Per, fed up with the whole thing.

So Per said he would, and Skrim promised to send for him later.

Skrim went on to other barns. Nobody could avoid him. He was like the plague. It was not *he*, Skrim; it was the pitiless drought summer that was behind him. He was only a part of it.

Father stood with the money in his hands. The price had been low. In a year's time, when rain had fallen and there was grass again, he would have to buy cows. Then he would probably have to give twice the price.

In a year's time there would be rain and grass once more. The conviction was there. In the middle of this burning

drought was the certainty that the meadows and fields would
be bountiful from the rain and bear fullfold. Their spirit would
not be broken.

3

Skrim did send for Per.

Per reported for duty some distance away, in the northern
part of the district. He was going to town. He was tingling
with excitement. He knew what the town looked like from
many books and pictures, but still he was excited.

Another boy was there to help with the droving. His name
was Hans, and he was the same age as Per. They had been
confirmed together, since they belonged to the same parish.

And there was a surprised cow waiting to be led away by
Skrim and his drovers. It was the beginning of Skrim's herd,
like the source of a river. A woman was standing there waiting with the cow. Skrim checked in his book to see if it was
the right one.

"Off you go, then," said Skrim to the cow. It was the
drought speaking out of his mouth.

Per and Hans were absorbed and solemn. They had food
in their knapsacks; they were going far. The single cow soon
had company: at each lane leading off to the farms, cattle
were waiting for them. It was a bright autumn morning, with
frost in the grass.

So it went. All the farms had been forced to make their
sacrifice to the pitiless drought summer. Per and Hans followed the herd; Skrim walked in front.

They came to Bringa. Per had been thinking about it all
along. Now they were there.

Bringa lay a short distance above the road. It had a good

position in the woods. Above it was steep mountainside. The lane down to the main road was gravelled and well kept. There at the gate waiting for Skrim stood the farmer, and Olav, and Åsne Bakken, each with a cow on a rope.

Olav did not know that Per was going as a drover, it was clear. He looked confused. Åsne stood calmly, watching Per. A whole summer had passed over her since he had seen her last. A brown summer. She had grown a good deal too.

"Good day!" she said.

"Good day."

There were the cows. Per noticed that they were standing beside Åsne and that they were accustomed to her. She untied the ropes and gave them up to Skrim. Per watched Åsne, noting how she had grown and changed.

Olav was standing stiffly. He and Per did not look at each other. But just as Per was about to leave, they did so. They gave each other a long look. There was no yearning in it; it was simply long and silent.

"Get going, will you?" said Skrim sharply from up in front.

"Have a good trip!" called Åsne, and raised her arm. Those arms that had raked hay and milked cows this summer; Per gazed at them.

"Why don't you come along too?" called Hans to Åsne teasingly, being free of Per's restraint. He knew Åsne from the confirmation class, and besides he had nothing to hide from her. He was free.

Åsne laughed. "Wish I could," she said. There was longing in her voice. She could say nothing to Per, and he could say nothing to her. Only Hans stood there free.

"Get moving," said Skrim roughly. "See you," he said to the farmer from Bringa.

And they left. Now the Bringa cows were on their way to the big slaughterhouse. Now Åsne, who had milked them, was on her way back to Bringa to stay there for the winter. She would work in the house and milk big, warm animals. Per saw it in a flash, saw her milking big, warm animals.

Now Olav was on his way home to Bringa.

Per pulled himself together and began to drive the herd. The slaughterhouse was the goal of this journey.

More farm gates. More cows. Skrim checked in his terrible book to see if they were the right ones.

They came to the farm called Bufast. Father and Aunt Anne were standing at the gate. It was strange to Per to be approaching it from the north, almost as a stranger—to be stopping at Bufast only briefly while this broad-shouldered farmer and this young woman gave up three cows to the herd.

"Have a good journey," said Auntie.

Father said nothing. He let the cows join the herd and then left. He went down to the farm called Bufast. Per was going out into the world.

Per tried to tell himself that he was going out into the world and would never come back again. At once he felt sad, for he could see it was good to live at Bufast. The buildings were old, weathered to a fine gray; there was a spreading rowan tree in the yard. It was his own farm, and now he was leaving it.

"Have you never seen that farm before?" teased Hans. Hans was drunk with joy because he was going to town that day. Per returned to reality with a start.

The gravel digger came out of his pits. Per had always seen him; he would never change or die, but would pile up round heaps of gravel forever.

"Hi!" he said to Per, like a handshake. Per was proud. Old fellows came out of their gravel pits and called hi! to him. They hurried on.

The Bufast cows kept to the back of the herd. They knew Per and walked just in front of him. That, too, affected him. He could not help remembering that he had seen them as new-born calves with the first milk dribbling out of the corners of their mouths. Now it was another story; now they were off to the big slaughterhouse.

They walked and walked, Skrim relentless and lean up in front. Relentless and lean as the drought summer itself.

The consignments of cows ceased when they left the areas where Skrim did business. In these districts the cattle went to other traders.

It must have been because Per knew they were going to be slaughtered that they seemed to him to be walking differently from other cows. Some of them set up a sudden staccato lowing. Then they dropped their heads again. Per thought about this until he forgot to be happy about the journey for long stretches at a time. Yet Hans remained plump and jolly, without a care in the world.

It was exhausting plodding behind a herd of cows all day. The cows were hungry and snatched at the grass along the wayside, the fresh, tender grass that the rain had at last tempted out. Rain and grass and cattle and flowing milk— you felt it all as something pleasant and attractive. But this herd was written down in Skrim's list and was frightening.

The scent of the potato fields was in the air. In some places people were digging the ripened potatoes. Those on the road could only breathe in the fragrance of the withered, drying potato plants.

Hans laughed aloud.

"What is it?" asked Per.

"Nothing—Skrim crabbing along at the head of his slaughter-herd, and everything!" said Hans.

For two more days they trudged along driving the cattle. The road to town was long when you had cows with you and were unable to drive or go by boat.

They passed through districts that had been spared by the drought. All the cows that were meant to live could do so there.

"We'll get there today," said Skrim.

They arrived late in the afternoon. It was a long way from Bufast.

Per and Hans entered the town. First they left the cows in a pen outside the town, and then they walked in. The air smelled strange.

"It's coal smoke," said Skrim.

Clatter and noise: the roar of traffic, the roar of factories and mills. Tall chimneys pouring out black smoke. Crowds of people and crowds of stores.

Per and Hans certainly did not throw themselves into it. It was like this and like that, just how it ought to be. It tallied with what they already knew. It was like this in all the pictures of towns and in all the stories. They almost had a feeling of being cheated, for they had expected it to be very different from the pictures and the books.

A little later they noticed that they were walking in a fever of excitement just the same. Hans said, "It's fun, but strange." He said it quietly and frankly. Per too thought it fun but strange.

Skrim and the boys went into a small café to eat. The man who was going to buy the cows from Skrim was there too. They sat there for a long time. When they came out again, lights were shining in all the windows.

It *was* splendid! In some places there were trees growing close to the lamps. That was almost the best thing: the leaves in the strong lamplight.

This was the town. Per and Hans walked about looking at it all. They had very little money to spend. They found themselves wishing they had pocketsful of money so they could go in and buy.

Skrim took them with him down a long, brightly lit street. But the street ended at the dark pen where the cattle were standing. A prolonged, astonished bellow came from the pen.

It was well-built. None of them could escape. Everything was quiet; then one of them bellowed. It was ugly. As they went back through the lighted street, the bellow rang in Per's ears, giving him thoughts which he pushed away from him.

Skrim had reserved rooms for them at a small hotel. They started to go to bed, but there was too much din in the street outside. They sat in their chairs for a long time. Skrim had gone away again.

Hans turned a somersault on the floor. "Hey!" he said.

Per wished he could accept the light and noise of the town as simply as Hans. Hey! said Hans, and let what would happen, happen. Nothing seemed to affect him.

Skrim did not return. They crawled into bed. After they had turned out the light, a muted glow shone through the window. It was not the moon; it was the town shining in. On the one side of them came the sound of laughter through the wall, on the other the sound of water—someone was washing himself. Then the washing finished; the laughter ended. Out in the street the noise abated, but the light shone in.

It was impossible to sleep.

"What's the matter with you?" asked Hans.

"Me?"

"Yes, you."

Per did not enlighten him, and Hans did not ask again.

Fear of death was in the room. It gripped Per. He could not rid himself of the image of the dark pen full of cattle ready for the slaughter. Fear seeped in through the walls and the window, the old feeling that dreadful things were going to happen, that he would hear the destruction toppling around him.

He thought about God and then about Hell. Something was hanging on a thread and would snap. . . . That lonely bellow from the pen. There was nothing but death all around.

Hans was asleep beside him. Per dozed.

Why had Botolv trembled all over when he realized he was going to die?

Now the street was quiet. But the light shone in. They were in the town. Here it was never dark. Yes, it was dark. Who was that speaking?

"Per!" it said.

"Yes," he replied.

"Can you see me?"

Per was numb. It was dark. And a voice was speaking out of the darkness.

"I'm coming, Per!" said the voice threateningly.

"What!"

Hell—thought Per, Hell—

A hand came out of the darkness, he could not see it, it grabbed at him, he was dying, and he began bellowing wildly, turning up his eyes like the big bull at Bufast. He was dead and was sitting in a bed, thrashing out around him. Someone was lurching and babbling close beside him. He heard a curse. That was how Skrim used to curse when Per was alive and was with him on earth—

Skrim.

"Will you come to your senses!" said Skrim thickly. "You'll knock me out."

It was Skrim! He was alive and drunk. Per was alive too. Thank God, he was alive, and here was Skrim, drunk and smelling of brandy.

The room was there too; the light streamed in. Beside him Hans was sleeping. Alive and asleep. Thank God.

Skrim stood unsteadily, nodding and babbling.

"Go to bed in your own room, Skrim," said Per, curtly and commandingly.

Skrim obeyed on the instant. He muttered something and left. He even remembered to shut the door behind him.

Outside it was silent. What was the time? Here it was peaceful.

The light streamed in through the window silently and uninterruptedly in order that no one should die.

In the morning they woke late. But that was as it should be in town. Townspeople slept late.

The town woke too. Carts rattled past, and people's feet in increasing numbers clattered past as well.

Per and Hans dressed and sat waiting for Skrim. Skrim woke very late in a bad temper, but he gave them breakfast. Then they were allowed to do as they liked: Skrim was going to sell the herd, and that was of no interest to boys, he said. "Here's five *kroner*, and we'll meet again here this evening. I'll have to send you home tomorrow morning by the boat."

They stood thunderstruck.

"Don't you have eyes in your heads? It's five *kroner*."

They rushed for the door. Five *kroner* was a lot of money, and their wishes were many and ambitious.

The town was in full swing again, noisy and crowded. Their joy increased. They looked around them, smiling. They smiled so happily and openly that a young girl stopped in front of them and smiled back without being aware of it. Then she started in surprise and hurried away. They were happy; everyone was happy today. Per hid away the anxieties of the night. They took care not to stand staring like country bumpkins, but looked critically at everything they came across.

They went into the shops and bought objects that were cheaper than five *kroner*, pleased with themselves, paying in cash. They went down to the quay and looked at the boats. They recognized it all from books and pictures.

They forgot to buy food; they were not hungry. They kept away from the slaughterhouse and the cattle. Then they started on a fresh round: boats, tall factory chimneys, a rushing mill, well-dressed people, carts, enormous loads, pretty young girls—more than they had imagined could exist—a huge clock face up on a church wall, people, shop windows, a funeral procession, children, more pretty girls.

At the end of the street they were brought up short: they had come back to the cattle again. It looked as if all the streets finished up at the cattle. The big slaughterhouse lay close by. Skrim and someone else were driving six or seven of the cows in through the gate of the slaughterhouse. Per and Hans turned without a word, dead tired. The clock on the church tower told them that it was five o'clock in the afternoon.

They were hungry, and their money had been exchanged for goods. They went to the hotel and waited for Skrim. A little dejected, a little regretful, they tried the stimulation of their newly-purchased cigarettes, but rather apathetically. To-morrow morning they were going home. Would it be good to be home again? They did not know. It was good not to have to choose.

4

Father was given a reminder that autumn. A warning.

After the potatoes had been dug and the barley field plowed, Per and his father worked on the cleared land. Father was compelled to do so; Per had to help him. Then the warn-ing came, one day in the middle of the work period. He was using the crowbar to lift out a large stone. Per was helping him. They put all their strength into it. Father groaned and dropped the crowbar. The stone, with all its weight, fell back towards Per, and he barely escaped being crushed. Father was bent double, his face white.

"It's my stomach," he said.

He scarcely managed to walk home with Per's support. What will Mother say? thought Per. Yes, haven't I told you so plenty of times? she would say. Don't let her say it! Let her take him in and put him to bed and not say a word about how right her prophecies have been. But she will say she was right. . . .

They got home. Mother met them in the yard, white in the face. Aunt Anne and Åsmund came.

"What is it?" said Mother.

"Oh—I've torn a muscle—"

"Yes, haven't I told you that's what would happen in the end?" said Mother.

Per groaned inwardly.

"Oh, yes, you've told me so," said Father wearily and with

annoyance. "How fortunate that you should be proved right."

Per wished he could run away. That they could talk like that to each other when they had been together so long, worked together, and slept together. And that they could say it in another person's hearing, and torture him.

Mother's color shifted from white to red.

"Come along," she said shamefacedly, and took hold of Father, took hold of him with infinite care. Suddenly she was infinitely gentle. Hands that had cared for newborn children. They were different from Auntie's hands. Auntie would never have been able to take hold of him so gently.

"Come along, Eilev," said Mother.

He went in and lay down.

Per was told to drive for the doctor. There was a low, tense ringing in his ears as he went. Was Father going to die?

The doctor said there was nothing to be done but sit still. It was a torn muscle and was dangerous.

"Will I mend?"

"Yes."

"No, I won't," said Father bitterly in his thick earth voice. He was caulked with earth. His tongue was bitter. He was impatient and offended.

The doctor left. Father lay in pain all that evening and through the night. They stayed up fully dressed. In the morning he fell asleep.

They sat feeling how important he was. All night they had felt it. They saw in each other's eyes that morning how important he was. There he lay sleeping. Mother began preparing the new day that was dawning. Aunt Anne went to the barn. Only Per and Åsmund could go to bed.

Later that day Father sat up quietly.

He sat like that all the autumn and during most of the winter. He had been warned. His eyes were impatient; he had never been able to sit still.

That winter it was Per who drove the firewood. As soon as the snow was right, Per and Goldie slid down a long, white lane through the trees and came home with wood. Then they left again, and again returned.

What was the matter now?

He felt poor inside. He felt thirsty. He felt everything that was uncomfortable, inside himself.

Some days differed from others: a low sky and mild air, a dead calm with mist on the surrounding mountains. Then the echo was there, in places where he never heard it normally. Per sometimes felt a desire to call out in the tremendous silence. He sat on the load and gave a long shout. It echoed back to him and made him feel better. Goldie turned his head in amazement.

One day Per left Goldie in the woods to search for a way through to new piles of timber. After a while he heard him give a single wild whinny. It sounded as if he were afraid of being left alone. Per was seized with guilt; instinctively he gave a bellow and came back again to Goldie to keep him company.

What should he do?

There were wide snow-covered marshes to cross, and the desolate landscape filled him with wonder and strange thoughts: that wild whinny of Goldie's, that bellow from the cattle in the darkness, that trembling body of Botolv's when he was about to die.

God wishes nobody harm; you don't need to worry about that.

No, and yet—

The snow-covered landscape marched past his eyes. Goldie, drawing the load, seemed a symbol of peace. But Goldie, too, had revealed something about himself in that wild whinny when the man left him: he was afraid of something.

The Christmas party came around, as did everything that was routine. Per was there. He had thought he would not bother, but he went just the same. An old habit from his schooldays. It was the best party there was, the only one really.

The tree had always been a blaze of light and had always tinkled with bells you could not hear but knew were there. It blazed and tinkled today too. The children sang carols around it with shining eyes. Per sat among the grown-ups around the walls feeling left out. Each time the door opened, a cloud of vapor poured into the room. It was frosty outside.

If only I could be given the tree! Be given it shining and sanctified. Be given just one thing once more—

Olav Bringa walked past. Olav had grown. Shortly afterwards Per felt somebody's eyes on him. It was Olav again. Then he disappeared into the next room.

Per sat and sat, or so it seemed. The time dragged. The children tramped up and down in front of him. Åsmund was among them. He and Knut Prikken, his shepherd comrade, were singing hand in hand.

Åsne Bakken appeared from somewhere out of the crowd and sat down beside Per on the bench.

"Good evening, Per."

She said it as if it were quite ordinary to be saying Good evening, Per. To Per it seemed as if the lights on the Christmas tree had begun to dance.

"Have you been here a long time this evening?" he asked indifferently. "I haven't seen you."

"Yes, I've been here all the time."

"*I* haven't seen you."

"No, but I'm sitting next to you now," she answered, with embarrassment.

"Yes, so I see," said Per.

He had only one thought: let it last, let it last.

She was so close to him on the crowded bench that he felt her weight. She had changed again since he saw her last, he thought. He looked at her. She was silent and not at all gay this evening. Her eyes shone when she looked at the tree.

"What are you doing now?" she asked.

"Hauling firewood," he said, and was glad he could; it sounded grown-up. "And you're at Bringa?"

"Yes, I'm at Bringa."

The light from the tree made her face radiant. Per thought that now Åsne was grown-up.

"Do you like it at Bringa?" he asked, and then was angry with himself for asking such a stupid and intimate question.

"Oh, yes. Why don't you ever come over on Sundays?" she asked.

"What?" he said, although he had heard very well.

"Why don't you ever come over on Sundays, I said."

He felt he wanted to doze off, to relax and fall asleep. He did not reply.

A girl stretched her hand out to Åsne: "Come on!"

It was Randi Bratterud. A circle of older boys and girls was forming outside the ring of children. Åsne stood up and took the hand. Then the circle began to move, taking Randi and Åsne with it.

When they reappeared on the other side of the tree, they were singing with wide-open, little-girl mouths. They went past incessantly; there were innumerable verses to the carol. The tall, shining tree hid them for the space of a wink each time they circled it. Once when they reappeared, Olav Bringa was between them, Åsne on his left and Randi on his right. Olav was holding their hands. He opened his mouth and sang. Per saw Olav singing and went straight out and walked home. It was bitterly cold, and the ice crackled underfoot. The stars in the sky were crackling with cold too.

5

The hauling of firewood came to an end. Per wished it could have lasted longer. He wished he could have tried to do Father's job of hauling the timber. But this Father who sat at home said no.

"You're too young to lift logs."

"Yes," said Mother. "You're too young."

So there was nothing else to do but to stand threshing in the barn.

They threshed in the old way, laying the sheaf of barley on the floor of the barn and beating it with a flail. The straw rustled as you walked. If it was cold, the heads were tender and easily crushed; the grain danced around you. If there was a thaw, everything was sticky and tough. For hundreds of years threshers had stood flailing like this, flailing empty-eyed and rustling in the straw. The dust was piled high up in the crevices in the walls.

Aunt Anne came past the barn door many times a day. She hurried by with hay and meal mixtures and milk. Auntie seemed to be connected with everything that was lush and fragrant. She paused at *his* door, too, occasionally. It lightened his long day of threshing.

The layer of grain on the barn floor thickened to a depth of six inches.

Then they sent for Ivar, and they winnowed the grain so that the dust and chaff smoked.

Ivar sat with the shovel and threw the grain the length of the barn. Ssshooog! said the grain as it hurtled from wall to wall. Dust and chaff fell close to Ivar, the lighter grain went far, but the hard, full-kernel grain swept in an arc all the way to the wall and lay there as if saved.

Father sat indoors. He was not going to die; he was improving. It was just that it went so slowly. He developed a habit of holding his head in a different way. It came from having to sit so unwillingly.

As soon as the barn was cleaned and the grain carried away into the bin in the granary, Per laid down more sheaves and flailed and rustled in the straw. The sound of the flail against the straw was a muted, satisfied sound. This was what it was like to thresh barley.

Per was waiting all day, and waiting all night, and in the morning. Something must happen. He was only provisionally living like this. The pronouncement about staying at Bufast had been pushed aside; he did not want to think about it. He thought only about the unknown future.

In the meantime he threshed and looked after the yellow horse. Father sat strangely washed as if for Sunday, all the earth smell washed away. Occasionally he went for a walk among the farm buildings, looking unfamiliar and pale. One would meet him now here, now there. They could see that he was consumed with impatience.

When the grain was threshed, Per chopped wood. He stood day after day in the woodshed, sawing and chopping.

Åsmund went to school, and the one day he was home he spent most of his time with his friends. He did not take his lessons very seriously; he just about knew them and was never the best. Per envied Åsmund, who never thought of working hard so he could run away, as he himself had when he was at school. Åsmund simply *was* at Bufast, and it looked as if that was what suited him.

But Per read all evening and all through the rest breaks. There was a library in the district, and he went there regularly to borrow books. He consumed books, now as before. Having something to think about helped him through many a long stint.

He was chopping wood. Mother came out to the shed and said unexpectedly, "Your father will mend!"

"Yes, of course he will," said Per, as if he had known it all along.

"Yes, he's improving," said Mother. "I know more about it than you do."

She went away again. Why had she made that last remark? It was a good thing she went as soon as she had said it. It was a good thing she was there.

As the spring advanced, Father improved quickly. When the time for the spring plowing approached, he took over as before. He was just a shade more careful. He had not mended completely.

All of Bufast improved when he was back at work. It was

easier for Mother to prepare the days for them to live in, and the rest of them lived more easily in the days she made for them.

People would call at the farm. They would usually say to Father, "You've mended again. You were lucky."

"No, I'll never mend," answered Father.

Per felt a stab of sorrow each time he heard it. Then he would forget it, since Father *seemed* to have mended.

The earth could not be destroyed. Last year there had been drought, but this year it was green. Rain fell on the countryside, and the earth was green and fertile.

Inquiries were made about cows. Everyone had too few and wanted to buy more. The cows that were for sale came in herds from districts that had escaped the drought and slaughter. And not a single heifer was slaughtered that winter, in the certainty that the earth did not let itself be destroyed.

Now Skrim *came* with cows and sold them into life. He was merely an instrument in the cycle of the earth and the seasons.

Knut Prikken came, small and pale after the winter. He had not grown much. Åsmund was glad to see him. They ran about the woods with the sheep.

Father and Per were out on the cleared land. But the old work rhythm had gone; Father had to be careful. Per, on the other hand, worked at full strength and was not held back. Father let him do it.

"You mustn't let your father destroy you," said Mother.

"How?"

"You're too eager, and he's far too happy to see you driving yourself. But you must look after yourself. He can't manage much on his own."

"No, he can't manage anything," confirmed Per.

He would have liked to say to his father: Go home! Don't you see you can't manage anything? But he did not say it. It would have been impossible for him to open his mouth to say anything like that. And so Father hung around.

It was haying time. Ivar ought not to have taken part in

it this year. But he was sent for. Father could not be counted on.

The earth was thick with grass.

6

Aunt Anne did not let herself be destroyed either; Aunt Anne was like the earth.

For the second time the summer was hers. It began some time during the spring. It must have been going on inside her for a while before it burst out with such radiance that everyone noticed it.

Auntie's in love again! he thought. One after the other, all of them at Bufast came to regard it as a gift to himself personally. It was like being given something in the palm of your hand.

She had not been killed, as Per had thought and feared. She was like the earth.

Auntie did not try to hide it. Her heartfelt laughter rang out openly through the farm. She did not tell them *who* it was, but that seemed to be less important; they would soon know. It was most likely someone who was worth it this time.

Åsmund went to Per looking important. He wanted to be asked about something. Per asked him.

"Auntie has a sweetheart," said Åsmund.

"Who says so?"

"Knut says so," said Åsmund haughtily.

"Tell Knut I knew about it long ago."

Knut was standing at the other side of the yard watching them. He had loaded Åsmund and wanted to see Per getting the shot. Åsmund ran back to him, and they disappeared somewhere again. Nobody really knew what the two of them

144

were up to. Knut was thin and small, but Åsmund followed him in everything. They appeared when there was food to be had, and then were gone again.

This was Auntie's summer. And soon it was no secret who the man was who had given the summer to her. It was Bjørn Moen, Signe Moen's half brother. Signe's father had been married before and had this son, Bjørn.

Per did not smart as he had done the last time Auntie was in love. His heart simply softened when he saw her. He watched Auntie walking away in the evenings, walking slow and fulfilled down the road. Per would lie down on the ground, and think and think. He gave Knut and Åsmund a sharp, angry thrashing one evening when he found them about to sneak after her.

"Go home and go to bed!" he snarled at them finally.

"And what about you?" asked Knut.

"He's grown-up," said Åsmund scornfully.

"Did we get in your way? I suppose you wanted to go after her yourself," said Knut again. They stood there beaten and angry, not daring to do anything but slink home and go to bed. Per lay down again and thought about many things. About girls, and about friendship with girls. It was painful and strangely weakening, and he could not stop thinking about them.

One evening the following week Auntie disappeared again. Knut and Åsmund vanished the same evening. Per kept a lookout for them, full of anger. He'd give them a thrashing. But when they came back, they got nothing. He saw them coming and got to his feet to confront them. Then he paused: they were walking oddly, shuffling their feet, and stood in front of him scared and guilty. Knut looked thinner than ever. They did not run away, but seemed to be waiting for a beating to relieve their consciences. Their faces reflected something they had heard and seen which had made a deep impression on them. They stood waiting silently. Waiting for their release.

Per simply turned away and left them. They need not find release in a beating and yells and bad temper. They stumbled indoors and went to bed.

Per lay on the ground thinking. This was difficult and dangerous territory. He thought about girls.

The river was making a rippling sound. He went down and bathed. Swam in the pool. Lay on the bank. It was warm; he could lie naked even though it was late in the evening. He dressed, went home, went to bed. It ought to have been cold, miserable, windy, not this weather that stole one's sleep and peace of mind.

Not until the haying season did Bjørn Moen appear at the farm openly and in full daylight. He made no secret of the fact that he had come to see Aunt Anne. Per watched him with admiration and a twinge of envy: this was a grown man.

There was grass in plenty in the pasture. The home meadow was lush with it. There was water in the brook. The cows came home to be milked. Aunt Anne milked them, and the sweet milk flowed. It was pleasant to see that nothing let itself be destroyed.

Aunt Anne is going to get married in the spring.

Long before she herself said so, someone else did and made it known. It was all very orderly and peaceful, and Auntie herself said it after a while, towards autumn, as if it were good news for them all: "I'm going to get married in the spring."

Per looked at her, too, with admiration and a twinge of envy. How openly they talked about such things! But he, who was seventeen—

Auntie struggled with the cattle. She came home in the middle of the herd of red cows and round-eyed calves. The bull in the barn bellowed in a fury of joy when the herd came home and the cows were back in their stalls again. He butted the wall. Auntie went up to give him some hay and a pat. He bellowed a little more, not eating it at once. In one movement he could have nailed Auntie to the wall with his short, thick horns and his witless strength; he could have ripped her apart with one slash. He did not do it; Auntie was allowed to have her summer.

7

The autumn came. And the day for the slaughtering came just as certainly as did the autumn. The sky always seemed to be gray for the slaughtering, the weather still and frosty. It was not by chance. Father waited until the weather was like that. On that day the ground was always dead and glistening, and the puddles had splinters of ice in them and were covered with a thin film.

Death was in the air.

Per stood at the door of the sheepfold looking in at the sheep in the gray light of early morning. The closely shorn, white bodies were shut in there, ready for the slaughter. Per looked back over a whole series of such days, such mornings. There was a sadness about it, and at the same time peace.

Yesterday they had been shorn, these chosen ones inside the sheepfold. All night long they had been chosen and shorn for the slaughter. They seemed to be floating in there; the fold was in twilight and their bodies gleamed white.

It became lighter. Father crossed the yard carrying the workbench. He took out a club and a knife. Mother and Aunt Anne brought pans and troughs. Everyone was calm; everything was as it should be. There was no alternative for the shorn sheep in the bare autumn sheepfold. Their time had come.

The sheep that were spared and free were still out in the woods.

Father called. He wanted to begin. His earthy voice was as it should be, along with everything else.

Father had strength enough for slaughtering sheep. He did it neatly and quickly. There was nothing horrible about it. One watched with the same expression as one watched other natural events at Bufast: mowing a meadow, harrowing and sowing.

The sheep stood beside the red workbench waiting for the stroke of the club. They hung their heads, no more. The air was sharp against their naked skins. Then the blow fell. Then the sheep lay alongside the others on the frosty ground.

The slaughtering continued. Father asked Per whether he was watching.

"Yes."

Are you watching?— There was emphasis in the question. To be at Bufast, it meant. To be a farmer. To be the master of animals and take their lives when the time came. . . .

There was no sunshine. Small splinters of ice had formed in the puddles. There was a stiffness, a silence over the whole of Bufast.

At dinner time Per went into the stable to give Goldie some hay. He had washed himself thoroughly but knew very well what would happen. When he approached the horse with an armful of fragrant hay, the horse snorted and pawed his stall. He could smell the slaughter on Per's hands and clothes, and it was past bearing. What was the yellow horse thinking? How much did he understand?

"Here you are," said Per, but Goldie simply shivered and tramped with his hooves.

By and by juniper smoke hung in the air. It came from the smokehouse where the meat was being cured. There was an acrid smell from the juniper smoke over the frosty autumn yard. Something flashed through Per: joy in being at Bufast. Then it was gone again, evading his grasp.

Per did the plowing with Goldie. The grass was all pale and withered. The sheep in the woods were rounded up and brought in. Father stood on the cleared land like a broken man.

Per did the plowing.

Joy in being at Bufast? Yes. No. He did not know. Olav Bringa, he thought. Åsne Bakken, Signe Moen, Randi Bratterud, Aunt Anne, girls.

He worked hard through the autumn. He went to the woods and piled up logs. He had to be big enough now. Father came with him: he had never mended; he could only come with him. He had injured himself in the stomach and was reminded of it daily.

They piled up the heavy, wet logs that were lying crisscross on the bare hillsides. Goldie dragged them; the men levered them into position. The logs were fragrant. Sometimes Father would go and sit down on a stone; then he came back again. He could not give up. Far ahead it seemed as if the end could be sighted, sighted and then pushed quickly aside.

Then the snow came, and Per drove the wood home. Towards Christmas there was a severe frost and the ice hardened. On the third Sunday in Advent Per went skating.

He did not seem to be aware of what he was doing until he got there.

The lake was like steel. All around were the woods. Children were yelling, standing upright straddling their legs or falling down. Their mittens were tied together with string and slung around their necks. They were red-cheeked and snotty-nosed.

The older ones were skating in big arcs in the inlets. They circled past each other and saw how young they all were; looked momentarily into the shy eyes of another and saw how unhappy and inquiring they were.

Per took a few turns and looked into some of the eyes. He was almost a stranger to them. What's to become of us now? asked all the eyes.

Åsne Bakken was not on the ice.

Olav Bringa was there, but not Åsne. Olav was laughing and chattering a little way off. It was strange, knowing you were his only friend. Per *was* the only one. Olav's laughter was cold and empty. Why couldn't he accost Olav and ask why Åsne was not there?

Per tripped over a snotty child and went flying. There was a mocking laugh. He realized he was a stranger to them, a subject of indifference. It didn't matter.

He came to a stop beside Olav. Their eyes met and looked away again. Suddenly they were skating together down the lake. Neither of them *did* it; it just happened.

"How are you doing?" asked Olav.

"All right," said Per. "How's everyone at Bringa?" he asked.

"As usual. Nothing's changed."

"Yes, it has."

"No, it hasn't!"

Olav was pale, and his face unrecognizable, Per noticed now: a pale and inquiring face. Per saw his own face in front of him, pale and inquiring. Olav's reply hurt him. Anxiety, anger, hope were on the point of storming out, but were held in check.

"It's been a long time since you came to Bufast."

"Yes."

Now they were in an inlet where no one could see them. A wooded spit of land hid them.

"What have you done?" shouted Per.

"Done?"

"Yes, you've hurt Åsne!"

Olav colored, and he looked at Per in terror.

"Yes, I have hurt Åsne," he replied like an echo.

"You look like it. You can take that!"

And Per hit him. He knew it was childish, but he could not help himself. His anger rolled itself into a hard ball inside him. Olav hit back at once. It was good that he did so. They were furious, both of them, and fighting savagely, in savage longing for each other—a longing to be together with nothing between them, as before.

You're a child, he told himself as he punched and wrestled. Per was knocked down and Olav sat on him. They were out of breath and white around the eyes,

"*You* would have hurt her too!" groaned Olav when he got his voice back.

"Why didn't she come skating?"

"Don't know."

"Is it your fault she didn't come?"

"Don't know."

"What have you done?"

Per's voice was tortured. Olav replied: "I don't know that either. It's impossible to understand her."

A tremendous clamor made them jump to their feet. The children had come out from behind the promontory, had seen the fight, and were bearing down on them at full speed, hungry to see what would happen. Per and Olav escaped, shamefaced. The twilight was coming on fast. The days were short now; an afternoon was nothing.

Some of them were going home: the little ones. They were forbidden to stay longer and left enviously and sadly. Per and Olav began measuring out the ice, each in his own part of the lake. In the twilight a couple of new arrivals came, skates in hand. Åsne Bakken had come. Olav and Per noticed it and did not leave.

At once two or three of the others were standing around Åsne, and there was laughter and happy chatter. Everyone livened up because a happy young girl had come out on the ice. The inquiring faces of the boys lit up. They were eighteen years old.

Each time Åsne laughed Per was cut to the quick. Couldn't they hear how unhappily she laughed? How little her heart was in it?

The gray twilight deepened. Night was coming. Åsne skated across to Per.

"Good evening, Per."

"Good evening."

He wanted to say more, but at once there were several others around them. They were all trying to be happy. Kids so small that they were still in school and barely escaped the order to get home before it was dark—they too were caught up in the happy atmosphere and jumped and played about beyond the bigger ones surrounding Åsne.

It became darker. You no longer saw how shy and inquiring the eyes were.

Somebody had found a small fir tree that had blown down on the bank. They dragged it out onto the lake. It was still green, and the branches were supple. The boys shouted, "Sit on it!" and a whole row of girls climbed on. Then the boys each seized a branch on either side and drew it along so that the ice flew from under their skates. Olav Bringa had one branch, Per another. Suddenly they were there. This was a good idea! thought Per. Nothing more was necessary on such a regrettable evening: just dragging the tree at top speed over the ice made the blood tingle. A fir tree full of girls. It was enough to bring a lump to the throat. It was an experience one would not have missed for anything. The fir tree was fragrant, and there were girls sitting in the branches. They seemed fragrant too. It was dark; you couldn't see them, but it didn't matter; you knew what they looked like.

They skated in wide circles, wild circles. Some of them shouted and laughed. Some of them made no noise but simply rushed along in silence. The skates squeaked. Far away on the ice a red bonfire flamed up.

"Look at the fire!" said one of the girls.

The bonfire turned into a pillar of flame. There was no wind, and they were probably burning dry twigs. Somebody shouted, "Come on!" The black ice beneath them, the red bonfire, all that they knew about each other and never talked about—Come on! said the voice. To what?

Åsne was sitting so quietly she might not have been there at all. But you knew she was. You knew Randi Bratterud was there and Signe Moen. The boys who were pulling the tree fell silent. Some of the girls were noisy.

What's to become of us now? Åsne had asked on that bitter Confirmation Day. Per had been asking the same question ever since. Come on! called a voice inside. The ride was over.

They fell silent. Gloom spread through the group. One of the girls could stand it no longer.

"Come on! Let's go!" she said.

It was Randi Bratterud. Per knew how slender and elegant she was in the daylight. Somebody was climbing down from the branches. Åsne's voice came thickly: "Randi?"

"Yes, I'm going."

"No, *stay*—"

"No, I'm going."

She was out of sight at once, as if swallowed up by the darkness. What was the matter with *her?* There was a gust of something ominous. They looked about them for guidance, for peace. Those who were happy stopped being happy for a moment. Come on! beckoned the bonfire, and they braced themselves again and sailed across to it.

They were greeted with wild clamor. The flames colored their faces copper. The girls could be seen among the fir branches, their eyes wide from staring out into the darkness. The boys were sweating. It seemed as if something was about to happen. They all shivered. They took hold of the fir tree and swept into the darkness again with an avalanche of children after them. They rushed farther and farther away from the warm fire, faster and wilder; soon none of the children were following them any more. Their speed was terrifying. With clamor and laughter. It was past bearing. Purposely or by accident they ran aground so that they stopped with a jerk and all tumbled into a heap. They staggered about and caught hold of each other, caught hold of strange bodies, aware of weak, strange scents. Per was holding somebody. It was Åsne. He was holding her. An unknown hand tried to snatch this tantalizing warmth that was Åsne. Per threw off the hand, and it was gone. It was so dark they could see nothing. Many of them were laughing riotously.

"Let's go now," said a thick voice. It must have been Signe Moen.

Åsne, beside Per, did not answer. Another girl replied, "Yes, let's go."

Her voice was tired and empty. You heard disappointment in it. Emptiness and thistle fields. You heard yourself and were afraid. And meanwhile some of them were laughing as happily as if nothing could ever be painful. Far off the bonfire glowed like a red star that had fallen from the sky.

A boy's voice said wildly, "No, you're not going."

"We'll do as we like."

"No!"

Per could not see his face, but it was Olav. A tortured, unrecognizable Olav.

"Come on, Åsne," said Signe.

Åsne did not reply. Per was holding her hand.

"Good-bye; thanks for the ride," said Signe. She disappeared into the darkness. The others made up their minds too and ran into the dark, leaving the fir tree where it was. "Stay there, then!" said a voice full of hatred to Per and Åsne. It was Olav.

"Åsne," begged Per. She did not answer. He put his arm around her and could not understand why nothing happened.

"Let go; you have no right to do that," she said.

He let go, hearing from her voice that it was what she wanted. He sensed it, and let go. He was extremely frightened. What would come of this? He was extremely happy.

"Shall I see you home?" he said.

"Yes, if you like."

They crossed the lake, making for the land where Bringa lay in the darkness. They held hands and skated in step. There was a rushing noise in Per's head. Was this happiness?

They reached the bank.

"How are you, Åsne?"

How had he said it? Suddenly her arms were around him. Is this happiness? he thought. She was trembling.

"Per—"

"Yes, what is it?"

"Are you the same?" she asked, trembling.

"As what?"

"As all the others. No, I'm *not* afraid of you," she said. He stood collecting his wits.

"What has Olav done to you?"

He regretted it the moment the question was blurted out. Her arms squeezed him in painful memory.

"I don't know. He frightens me. There's so much that's painful that—"

His arms were strong and hard and fierce. He pulled her towards him and kissed her. At once he thought of Auntie. In the middle of his delirium he thought of Auntie. But this was a different fragrance. This was earth too. For an instant she stood still and let him kiss her. He felt her body curve towards him. This is happiness, this is—and then her body was suddenly hard and unyielding as wood; she was hard and cold and unyielding as wood and tore herself free. He heard a deep, bitter sob.

"Åsne—"

"Everything's painful," she said, and started to go. "You're just the same."

He followed her dumbly up the slope.

"I want to go by myself," she said harshly.

He stopped and let her do so, let the darkness have her. Then he went home. His head felt as if it were too big for his neck; it was a curious feeling. His heart was too big for his body too. Only his feet knew what they were doing; they went uphill towards Bufast. He always came back there. To Bufast. Everything ended up there.

He arrived home. They had all gone to bed; he came in to a sleeping house. Now it was good. He relived what had happened and felt it was only good. His heart laughed. He tiptoed in. There in the bedroom lay Father and Mother, who had begotten him. It was good that they had done so. He too would beget children, he thought, and a fine trembling seized him from head to foot. Åsne would have cried when she was alone in the darkness. It didn't mean anything; it would be all right.

The clock struck the hour. He could not sleep. The clock struck again.

Upstairs Auntie was asleep. In the spring she would marry and beget children.

You're just the same, Åsne had said, freeing herself from him.

He would take her hand and lead her as he had once led her through the river. She had always been his.

8

In the morning he had to get up early and feed Goldie. Aunt Anne made his breakfast.

"Sleep badly?"

"No."

"Oh, poof, I know all about young boys," she said.

His heart laughed again. If only she knew how much of a young boy he was.

Mother and Father had not come in yet. Åsmund was sleeping so deeply that he shook. Per and Auntie sat at the table. Auntie sat looking at him for a long time. What business was it of hers to see it on him? He could tell she did so.

"Was it Åsne?" she asked suddenly in a low voice. Low, so that it could not be heard beyond the table; kind too. He was grateful to her for mentioning that blessed name so quietly and kindly.

"No!" he said.

She laughed and went to look for her pails. Mother arrived.

"What is it, Per?" she asked.

"Nothing."

She paid little attention and began preparing a new day for the whole of Bufast. Father came in. Father never asked about anything. Per harnessed Goldie and went far into the woods to haul logs.

Would he see Åsne on the fourth Sunday in Advent? Would she come to the lake then? And afterwards it was Christmas, when much could happen.

The image of Olav rose up. He pushed it aside; there was no room for it in even the smallest corner.

She did not come to the lake the next Sunday. Per stayed there until late in the evening. Olav did not come either. It was a long, boring Sunday. Åsne would wait until Christmas.

Christmas came. Christmas Eve with steam from the bath and the scent of clean shirts. Clean shirts never seemed to smell as nice on Sunday mornings the rest of the year as they did on Christmas Eve. Per drew his over his head. Åsne is doing this too, he thought.

Afterwards they sat quietly in the kitchen. Aunt Anne and Mother finished their chores and sat quietly. Åsne is doing this too.

On Christmas Day some of them drove to church, some of them stayed at home. Today was not the day for visiting other farms.

The second day of Christmas Per went down to the lake with his curiously enlarged heart. There was a crowd of young people. Åsne was not there. He waited for her until it was pitch dark. Then he went home. He remembered how large his heart had been that morning.

He could not understand it. He looked at Aunt Anne. How calm and unafraid and complete and rich *she* was. How unlike his companions among the girls. They were uncertain and embarrassed; there seemed to be no peace in their lives, only empty laughter and noise to hide their searching.

They were not grown-up. The knowledge suddenly struck him. That was what made him and Åsne and Randi and Olav and the others so helplessly different from Aunt Anne: they were not grown-up.

On the third day he went to the lake again. Åsne was not there. Was she sick? No, he was certain she was not sick.

The Christmas party was held on the evening of the third day. Per was there. The party hummed. The lights, the tree, the angels, the young people—it all hummed with festivity. The adults sat watching with eyes like children.

Åsne was not there. Olav was not there. Per sat staring at a trampled piece of orange peel.

"Come on, Per," said a voice.

He looked up. A hand was stretched out towards him. It was Randi Bratterud. He stood up like a sleepwalker and took the hand. It grasped his tightly. His other hand was taken by another girl, Kari Tveit. He knew her; she had been particularly lazy at confirmation class. She was singing with a wide-open, pouting mouth. He went around the tree between them. The lights and the angels and the tree were humming.

"You're not around much?" said Randi to the back of his neck as she sang.

The carol came to an end. They stood still. He turned to Randi.

"What do you mean?"

"Nothing, only that you're not around much."

She said it as if deprived. Her eyes reflected something he recognized in himself. He was lonely. He was like a scared animal; that was what it was. Look, over there on the benches sat the upright adults, staring at the tree like children. He belonged nowhere.

"How's life treating you, Per?" said a voice behind him as he stood turned towards Randi. It was Kari Tveit. She was big and plump and showed white teeth when she smiled. He did not trust that smile. She, too, was eighteen. He gave her some answer.

"Have you seen Åsne?" he asked Randi. He could hold it in no longer.

Randi became distant. She took her hand away, suddenly preoccupied.

"Åsne?" she asked unwillingly. Then she shook her head.

Per stood feeling like a fool. But Kari had heard his question. She opened her pouting mouth and said, "Åsne and Olav Bringa drove to a party in the next district. They left yesterday morning."

He stared at the pouting mouth that gave him such news. This was Kari Tveit. She had never learned her lessons, but that was of no account now. She was like one of the others, just as amazed and perplexed as they.

He had to get out. Behind him hummed the party.

Outside, snow was falling thickly and silently. The ice would be snowed under. It seemed as if a great sin was being committed out here in the darkness: the ice was being snowed under.

It was all the same to him.

She had gone to the one she feared. The one who had frightened her had got her.

Why had she done it?

He would spare himself the trouble of wondering about it. He hated them! No, he didn't, and yet. . . .

9

He felt *light*. Light and empty. His clothes felt light and thin against his body. It seemed always to be windy, and the wind blew through his thin clothes.

That was to begin with. January and February. Nothing happened and nobody came. He drove the timber as soon as the snow had fallen thickly enough. He had a man with him to clear the tracks and help load the biggest logs. The logs were wet and heavy.

Father sat at home. Sometimes he walked along the timber tracks. It was uncomfortable meeting him there. He came wandering along, tall and square; you thought you were meeting a giant, and then it turned out to be a broken man. He stood aside to make way for the creaking load, and they looked into each other's eyes as the load slid past

Otherwise driving timber was cheerful work. The tree-trunks were fragrant, large, and easy to handle. The work was enjoyable. When the track was hard, the ends of the tree-trunks sang as they dragged along the ground. It was a pleasant song.

One could not be killed.

Sometimes this flickered up like a gleam of light, the knowledge that one could not be killed.

He was in the barn threshing barley. He saw nothing and heard nothing, simply threshed and threshed. Father came to the door and burrowed his hands into the unwinnowed grain.

"Splendid grain," he said.

Per stood with his back to him and threshed. These days in the barn were more trying than those in the woods. He had no idea why. He wished he could make himself small and helpless.

"The grain's splendid this year," said Father again behind him. "Round and white."

Per did not turn around. It was impossible for him to turn and say, Yes, it's splendid. He threshed. Threshed.

What am I made of?

Father left him. The barn door gaped. Then Per could turn around. Now the barn door was empty, gaping over emptiness.

March came round.

Mother was kept busier than usual this winter. Aunt Anne had to find time to prepare for her wedding. She was going to get married in the spring, and reflected it in everything she did. She was such an important part of Bufast that the whole of Bufast reflected it too. Auntie was weaving and sewing. Per fell into the habit of sitting beside her in the evenings after his work was done, watching her hands as she worked with piles of clean, white homespun and linen.

Auntie had been scorched and dry in the throat. Per had

listened while pain had knocked her words to pieces. Now she was sitting here full of vitality and strength once more. It was a comfort to be near her.

Over in the corner Åsmund was doing his homework. Mother was sitting by the lamp patching Per's jacket. Father was just sitting. But Aunt Anne was sewing her linen. She touched it, held it. Per sat with the latest book he had borrowed from the library, feeling his fatigue creep over him. He put the book down in his lap and watched Auntie. Auntie was more comfort now than all the books. She must not leave Bufast.

Perhaps she would not leave either. Bjørn Moen would not inherit the Moen farm; someone else would have it. Bjørn had no farm of his own. So perhaps he would come here and live at Bufast. If only he would! Aunt Anne had not yet told them what they intended to do. She only touched her linen. That, too, was part of her happiness.

Mother was patching old clothes. How unjust it was to watch with less joy Mother patching an old jacket than Aunt Anne sewing fine new linen. He tried to exchange his feelings, but it was a poor attempt and made him feel guilty.

Father sat turned towards the spring, in great impatience. It was the end of March.

He brought earth indoors with him still. His clothes were clean of soil, but there seemed to be a whiff of earth about them. There was earth in the house.

"Bjørn's cutting timber for the house!" Aunt Anne told him. She and Per were alone.

"Suppose our house were to be built at Bufast, Per; would you like it?"

Yes, he thought.

"Why do you ask *me* about it?" he said.

"Oh, you'll be the one in charge of Bufast soon."

He started in surprise. The thought had probably occurred to him, but still, it was hard to have it straight in his face. The old reluctance was there too. It had been pushed aside for a long time. All at once the possibility was there, within sight: acceptance of Bufast.

The farm had not changed because Eilev Bufast sat disabled and would die. It simply went on revolving. Trees were felled in the woods. There was lowing in the barn. Goldie stamped in his stall. The magpies that went with the farm sat on the gable end of the barn. The river whispered beneath the spring ice. Nothing changed because a man would soon be gone. Many lives ended on this farm all the year round, but *the farm remained.*

Per knew quite well what he longed for most. It was not Åsne, but Olav Bringa. He wanted Olav beside him again, Olav right in front of him so that he could see his gray eyes; he wanted to be able to sit silent beside him, to swim in the river with him, and lie in the sun on the flat stones.

And Olav would be bound to come back.

Why should he, when he has Åsne?

Even so, thought Per, Olav will come back.

He imagined their meeting.

Good day, Per.

Good day, Olav.

I've come back.

Yes, I knew you would.

The starlings arrived. Three of them came and said vree-vree! and po-o-o-ie!

"The starlings are here," said Father. He was consumed with longing. He would burn up and wither now that he was forced to sit still with it.

10

Father harnessed Goldie intending to work in the fields. It was May. Per let him do it. Nothing came of it. In a short while Father was sitting down to rest.

"I can't understand it," he said when Per came over to him. "I can't manage anything."

Father was burning with the desire to drive the plow, to harrow, to clatter with the implements of the spring sowing, yet here he was, sitting because he could not keep up the pace. He went home. The earth had given him a reminder that he was small. His furious toil had had its revenge.

Per, Aunt Anne, and Åsmund did the spring sowing. Goldie drew the plow. In the black furrows lay upturned grubs and small snails. Aunt Anne had drowned eyes. She would soon be married.

Åsmund's eyes were clear. He and Per were strangers. They never really met. There were many years between them, and they were different in temperament. A boy with a slender body and a birdlike face often came to the farm. It was Knut Prikken. Åsmund and he stuck to each other faithfully. Per was never with them. Now Olav must come soon.

Per harnessed Goldie to go to the field.

Father came out and hovered about. He stood as if waiting for something, for Per to finish harnessing the horse perhaps. Per felt his eyes on his back. Goldie was tired and sulky. He was inclined to sulk when the work was hard, and the spring plowing could never be other than hard. Plow and harrow had to cut through the field, and Goldie had to see to it. He sighed and shifted a hoof. Eilev Bufast was standing there, but Goldie was sulky and did not turn to him for a kind gesture. Per busied himself with the harness and then led Goldie away, right past Father. Past Father, who was waiting for a kind gesture.

Later Per remembered that Father's eyes had seemed more consumed than ever. He had not bothered to look, merely pushed past. And Goldie had pushed past. Father had stood asking for kindness. All this occurred to Per afterwards. At the time he had only thought about getting to the field together with Aunt Anne and Åsmund. He did not notice what became of Father, who had been deprived of any kind gesture.

A couple of hours passed; Per and the others worked in the field. The spring sowing had an incitement about it. You felt an urge to quicken the pace. To clatter, to shout, to watch the soil spurting in front of the implements. But it was no use trying to do more than think about it. Goldie set the pace and would not let himself be tempted beyond it.

"Look at Father!" called Åsmund. "He's starting to work again."

Åsmund's voice was unrecognizably happy and relieved. He must have been longing to see this.

Auntie straightened her back. "Yes, look at your father."

Then she gave a start. "Something will happen. You must go to him, Per!"

Per looked up too. Over in the cleared land stood Father, in the deep, black furrow where his field ended and the uncultivated grass began. He was standing there working, tall and very much in his rightful element. They heard the clinking of stones. They did not know how long he had been working there; they had been too busy to notice and down in a hollow in the field so that they could not see around them.

"Go over, Per. Quickly!"

"No!" said Åsmund. Clearly Åsmund had had a burning wish fulfilled: that of seeing Father in his rightful place again. They realized they had all been longing to see this. They could not drive him away.

"But he'll destroy himself this time," said Auntie. "He's been forbidden to do any work."

Per remembered Father's devouring eyes a while ago. Something had broken out.

The spade clanged against a stone. Father, who couldn't manage anything, was digging. Was it a miracle? Now they could hear the mattock, the satisfied, thick sound of a mattock in gravel and sand.

Åsmund and Per were standing close together as they had seldom stood before. The boy Åsmund was in no doubt: a miracle had happened. And his belief infected Per. Per believed with Åsmund. Only Aunt Anne did not let herself be deceived.

"We must get him away from there," she said, and hurried across. They did not call out to stop her. They only looked to see if Mother was in sight; it would make her happy.

Father stood swinging the mattock. The sound reached them, satisfied and staccato. Aunt Anne had come up to him now. They heard her speaking in a high, frightened voice. They did not hear the earthy voice answer. Goldie turned his head towards the fright in Auntie's voice.

She was gesticulating. "Come here!"

They ran, seized with sudden dread.

Father went on striking with the mattock in stubborn rhythm, red in the face with obstinacy. Where did he find the strength, he who had none? He had probably been there for a couple of hours. He swung the mattock, crumbling the light gray subsoil. Small stones that lay as if cast into the hard rind of the gravel were loosened. A larger stone was lying beside them. Father seized the crowbar and pitched into the big stone. The heavy, steel crowbar. Now Father was working with a strength he did not own, and it would be bound to take its toll.

Aunt Anne stood helpless. Åsmund turned white and trembled. Per flew at his father: "Hey there!"

Father took no notice, simply went on working.

"Hey there! Get away from here!"

"Leave me alone!" shouted his father back. "You're not going to destroy me any longer!" he added. "Just you try."

He talked as if addressing a crowd of enemies and continued with what he was doing. He was clearly in pain, but he went on.

"Run home and get your mother!" said Auntie, and Åsmund ran.

Per shook his father by the arm. "You'll kill yourself doing this! Don't you remember? If you work you'll kill yourself."

Father paused and fumbled a little. His face was close to Per's; it was large, heavy, and ravaged with impatience. His eyes were staring and wide with defiance and futile longing. Then the gleam in them altered; they saw Per and recognized him.

"This is where *you* belong, Per," he said. "You can never leave it."

It sounded like a command.

Per did not reply. His father insisted: "Did you hear what I said?"

"Yes. And now come home."

Per felt grown-up. He drew Father away. He felt strong. He got Father half out of the furrow, but then Father found a spark of his borrowed strength again and shoved Per aside.

"Is it you or I who's the boy?" asked that rough, rusty voice. He seized the spade and began shovelling the loose gravel.

Aunt Anne had collected herself and came forward.

"You're being unkind to us now, Eilev."

"I'm only showing you that I can still work, I'm—"

"Eilev, come now before Ingjerd has to come and get you home. It's much better."

"Stop plaguing me!" he shouted. "What do you know about it all?"

He went on with it, digging, breaking stones. Everything was done with great skill. He attacked the stone in the right way, his mattock bit into the gravel, his movements with the spade were easy and assured. Every exertion pained his shattered body; you saw how he winced with each stab.

There were Mother and Åsmund. Mother looked calm.

Father began to resist before she had even reached him. "Yes, I can see you!" he began. "Just you come along and try!"

He bent over the stones and the soil again. It was alarming. All around them was the spring day, the earth open and raw. Over there stood Goldie. Farther downhill the river churned. The air was singing. But here Father's own people were gathered about him to take him by storm, as if he were a dangerous force that had to be destroyed—and *he* saw them all as enemies on the attack.

"Let him alone," said Per quickly to his mother. "You won't get anywhere."

"Oh, I expect I will."

She stepped down into the earth to him and stood, all gentleness, in the newly dug soil. There she put her arm around his shoulders as he bent over digging. She had been his woman for a long time. He knew those arms from better times, more beautiful moments.

"Eilev, when you know you shouldn't—"

"Be quiet! What do you know about this?"

She did not let go, but said, unable to hide her fear any more: "No, I don't know anything about this. But you must live and stay with us!"

"I'll die if I go on as I have been doing, let me tell you."

He managed to shake off her arm and gesticulated to give himself room. His defiance increased; he grasped the mattock and swung it around him to make the space greater.

Per was about to jump on him all the same, but Aunt Anne screamed "No!" so sharply that he paused.

Mother stood deathly pale, hurt and insulted. "You'll have to learn your lesson when it comes, then, Eilev," she said bitterly.

"Let him alone, Per," she added. "He shall have his own way."

Her voice was bitter. She spoke with such sudden authority that none of them tried to oppose Father any more. He should have his own way. They knew what would happen, but he should have his own way.

He must have felt as if he was in a fight. He stood there breaking up the stones, digging, back in his old breakneck

167

rhythm. But he seemed to be fighting an enemy. He did not look as if he loved earth this time, but was tortured and persecuted by her. And his people there on the slope around him were also his enemies. He was ringed about by enemies.

They stood in a half-circle, waiting for him to collapse. It was dreadful to watch, and Per was on the point of going forward, and Aunt Anne was on the point of going forward —but Mother was the one to decide now; she was the closest to him.

"Leave Eilev in peace," she said. "You can go away if you want. It has nothing to do with you."

But they stayed. The sight of him toiling in senseless defiance held them there. They knew he would lose pitifully against the forces he was defying. It was horrible. He did not even see them now, only toiled in delirium, moaning each time he felt a stab of pain in his body.

Behind them they heard a high whinny. It made them all start: there was a wildness about it. Goldie was standing far away in the field wondering why they did not come back. He whinnied, and they all started and saw death before their eyes. Death. Strange that a horse's whinny should remind them of death. Father did not even notice.

Mother stood still. Per thought with a shudder that this was most likely a settlement of accounts; that this thing ravaging Father, this defiance and fury, had burned and ravaged secretly when Father and Mother were alone together. One could only guess, but Mother was standing as if it were so. It has nothing to do with you, she had said, and so they stood knowing themselves to be ignorant and small.

"Oh—" said someone.

It was finished.

He was finished. His swollen, defiant face turned gray, and he crumpled up over his stomach, then sat down on the edge of the furrow to steady himself. His head hung nodding, unable to carry itself upright.

Mother went to him quickly. They all went to him. Per held his breath: would Mother spare him a rap because he had lost? Would she say: There you are, what did I say, Eilev? Or would she *not* say it? She bent over him; she took hold of his head and righted it— Dear God, don't let her say it—

"Come home, Eilev," she said. "You've finished with this now."

She simply *spoke,* not with authority nor as a victor. He was too exhausted to answer.

Joy flooded Per, in spite of everything. If Mother had taken advantage of Father's stupidity, it would have been worse than all the rest. She had not done so.

They got Father to his feet and helped him home, supporting him on three sides, while Åsmund went in front of the procession as if showing the way. It was a strange thing for Åsmund to do; Per remembered it long afterwards without understanding.

11

The doctor could not do much about Father, except tell him to lie still.

"I'm finished now," said Father.

"We don't know about that," said the doctor.

"Yes, *I* know."

"Oh, no," said the doctor, "we don't know about that."

So Father lay still. And got better little by little. At least enough so that he could sit up.

Per was working at the local sawmill with Bjørn Moen. They were sawing Bjørn's timber. It was pleasant work: Aunt Anne and Bjørn were going to live at Bufast; their house would stand in the yard. As soon as the grain had been sown, they decided where the house would be built.

Per had been called indoors one day. There sat Father and Mother, and Aunt Anne and Bjørn Moen.

"Per, what do you think of Bjørn Moen building his house here at the farm?"

Father himself asked him from where he sat tied to his chair.

"I—?" said Per in confusion. His first thought was, Auntie will be staying here. His first feeling was peace. The next was a curious awe—awe of the farm. Here sat four adults asking what he, Per, thought about building a new house in the yard, about making a small change in the farm. Everything that happened to the farm was important.

It was at that moment that Per seemed to *take over the farm*. He was afraid! There sat Father saying in so many words that he was no longer the man in charge.

Bjørn Moen was staring in front of him. Aunt Anne was looking at Per with expectancy. Peace and joy came to Per. He said of course they could build their house here.

He went out again, feeling a little dizzy, a sensation in his eyes like the smarting of the river water in them when he went swimming.

So now Per and Bjørn were working at the sawmill. The cleared land was being given a rest this year. Father could not move, and he had not asked Per to clear it. He must have had the shock he needed and saw that it was not wise to embark on too much at a time.

Sawing timber for the walls of a house was work you could not help liking. The river was in flood, and the sawblade was greedy and strong. Sawdust spurted up in your face. Bjørn laughed at the slightest thing these days. He lifted the raw, white walls and built them up in layers. Per carried the other end of the planks. Bjørn was carrying his house. Within these brand-new, white walls he and Aunt Anne would live.

In the Bufast yard two men were digging the foundations of the house and building the stone walls of the cellar. There was a clatter and the sound of staccato sledgehammer blows.

Goldie began driving the planking up from the sawmill to Bufast.

Bjørn and Per sawed the rest of the timber. The wood was good to handle. Bjørn touched the wood of the wall in the same way as Aunt Anne had touched her linen. Bjørn carried the walls. Within these walls he and Aunt Anne would beget children. Into this house Aunt Anne would come from the barn with foaming buckets of milk.

Bjørn and Aunt Anne were married in the middle of all the turmoil of building the house. For the time being they lived upstairs in the old Bufast farmhouse, and Auntie helped Mother just as before.

On the building site all was noise and confusion. The foundations were almost ready. In the middle of the day, when the sheep were in the pen, Åsmund and Knut Prikken would be there, enthusiastic and eager to lend a hand with the building. Then the clock would strike and their faces fall, and off they went to the woods. Per had herded the sheep alone when he was Åsmund's age. But Åsmund had to have Knut with him; the two of them were inseparable. Knut Prikken with his birdlike face was just as certain to be found at Bufast as on his own people's farm.

Now Olav must come.

Per did not seek the friendship of anyone during this time. He simply waited. Sooner or later Olav would have to come back. On Sundays he sometimes went to the old meeting-place at the river. Olav was not there.

On one such day Åsne came there to look for him. He had not expected that. He saw her coming and had a strange urge to be indifferent to her. This was important, but he forced himself to sit feigning indifference. She came quickly, looking embarrassed. There was not the slightest affectation about her; she came as she was.

"I thought you might be here sometimes," she said. "Olav has told me you used to meet here."

"Yes. Have you been here before?"

"Yes. But this is the first time I've found you."

This was important, but it was unlikely to change anything. He seemed to know this.

"What do you want with me, then?" he asked.

"Oh—I rushed off so strangely."

"Yes. I hadn't frightened you enough, I suppose. But Olav had."

"What nonsense you talk! It's not easy to be a girl."

"Isn't it?"

"You don't know what it's like for us," she said helplessly.

"You manage to hurt us, at any rate," he said, and let his voice sound harsh.

"You're the one I like best," she said.

He thought he must be turning pale.

"Am I?"

"Yes, I think so."

"Why come here and talk like that?"

She had taken Olav away from him; she could go hang. He didn't want her. Yes, he did want her, but Olav had meant more.

"I came to tell you," she said.

"You'd best stay where you are!" he replied, losing control.

Åsne uncoiled like a spring at the tone of his voice. Her cheeks were flushed.

"I hadn't thought of doing anything else. Oh, you're just a couple of boys, both of you."

"Yes—and what are you, may I ask?"

Her head drooped forwards, as if it was too heavy.

"It's no use trying to get you to understand. You're a boy. It's all so painful."

He did not reply.

"Are you angry with me, Per?"

Oh! *That* question! He had been waiting for it all along. There it came. Angry with me—why did Åsne say things like that? Such a stupid question.

"No," he replied, sick and tired of it all.

Suddenly she was crying into the grass. He could not see her face, but her shoulders were shaking. He should have had his arms around those shoulders. She was sobbing bitterly. Åsne was tall; she shuddered from top to toe.

Well, she would have to go on crying; there was nothing to be done about it, he thought. He got up to go. Nothing happened. He turned after he had gone seven or eight paces. She was lying just as before. Well, let her; *he* couldn't offer any help. He would not have been man enough to go over to her and comfort her if they had stood over him with a whip. He could not understand it: not himself, not her, not anyone.

—But how tall she was. And beautifully made. He had seen it once more.

Now Olav would have to come soon.

12

Ivar came for the haying as usual.

"This will be my last year at Bufast, I suppose," he said the first time they rested.

"I suppose so," said Per.

He felt sorry about Ivar. Sullen and cross as he was, still he had always been there for the haying. And Ivar had a sister at home to support. But now Bjørn was coming, and there would be enough hands, even though they could no longer count on Father. There was nothing to be done about it. You couldn't follow your heart; it was the farm that decided and laid down its own strict rules. Ivar too must have known that the farm laid down rules that had to be followed. You were part of a great cycle of many creatures and many forces when you belonged to a farm. And you yourself were small when you belonged to a farm.

Aunt Anne helped with the raking as before. This was yet another summer among her good ones. A truer and more rightful summer. Her eyes reflected her anticipation of next year, of a summer even more true and rightful. She looked after the red-flanked, white-backed cows; she milked them and carried in the milk.

There was a great deal of unrest that summer. Bjørn and his two helpers were building in the yard. There were the sounds of sawing, chopping, and hammering, and the smell of fresh pine. From the carpenter's shed came the noise of planing. The white shape of the new house rose out of the piles of shavings and chippings. Sweating haymakers came hungry home to the farmyard. There was the clatter of hay-loads and the bellowing of the bull shut up in the barn. All this at once. This was the summer when Aunt Anne got married.

Mother was behind it all. Per could never really understand how she was behind everything; he knew it was so. She did not have Aunt Anne's radiance. But whatever was done started with her. Everything had to pass through her hands. Per was very aware of it and was silent in wordless veneration.

Father sat like a statue, radiating impatience. He could not come to terms with his situation. The others went out to work and he sat. *He—!* It consumed him rapidly. Father was not yet fifty and was marked down to be felled.

And now the farm took a hold on Åsmund too. He was helping with the mowing this year. Åsmund did it as a matter of course; he did not say whether he liked or disliked it. On Sundays Knut came, thin and lightweight, his eyes looking in all directions at once. He and Åsmund would disappear. Nobody asked what they were up to. Mother went out when it was time and called, "Come in and eat!" Then they would reappear, from the attic or the wagon shed, or from the strip between the fields. Food was good. Afterwards they would vanish again.

Sometimes Åsmund would be summoned to Mother for

cross-examination: "Does Knut Prikken teach you wickedness?"

"What do you mean?"

"What does he teach you?"

"He can't teach *me* anything," boasted Åsmund.

Mother was too astonished to reply.

Per decided to tell Åsmund off as soon as they were alone. He really gave it to him. Then he paused: Åsmund was simply standing letting the scolding pour over him, standing without listening to a word. Per was furious: "Get out."

"All right. I'm not afraid of you," said Åsmund. "I haven't done anything."

His eyes were cold and blue. Per felt ashamed of himself.

There was a chasm between them. And out of it rose Botolv, it seemed to Per. This empty chasm that he could not cross over to Åsmund, this chasm was Botolv. He could not understand why, but Botolv sat there and prevented him from passing. . . .

The long Sundays. The long Sunday afternoons. Bjørn's new house stood dead and silent. Ivar lay in the shade. Mother slept with one of Per's library books in her lap. The door of the hayloft was a mouth that had yawned its jaws stuck. Up along the road rushed the Sunday drivers. He felt uncomfortable in Sunday clothes. A hen cackled. A fly buzzed. There was not a cloud in the sky. He longed for Monday.

Monday mornings were good. Then everything came alive. He wore his old clothes and his work shirt faded by the rain and the sunshine. Then he could thresh until he forgot the things he didn't want to think about. Then he was tired and looked forward to the next Sunday. Then the clouds came and rained on the Sunday-dried hay.

August.

Another warm Sunday. The quiet! Per called out aimlessly: "Åsmund!"

Åsmund popped up from between the grain fields. Knut's birdlike head popped up at the same time.

"Want to come down to the river for a swim?" asked Per. He meant it as a friendly gesture, an offer of comradeship.

There was a hasty parley. The birdlike head swayed and then shook. Finally Åsmund called, "No!"

The birdlike head was moving excitedly. Per could see the eyes looking in all directions. Åsmund steeled himself and called again, "You never wanted us to come with you before, so—"

Per left with an uneasy conscience. There was a good deal of truth in what Knut Prikken put into Åsmund's mouth.

But it was because Åsmund and Knut had no memories of Botolv. To them Botolv was only the name of a little boy who was alive when they were very small. They did not know what Per knew about Botolv. They did not understand that Per felt so bound to him because of what had happened that he had only *one* brother, and that was Botolv.

13

Per went down to the swimming hole at the river. He followed a path that ran parallel to the main road, but farther down the slope. Up on the road a cart trundled. Going to the store, he thought automatically. Nonsense, it was Sunday; the store would be closed. For Per the road was closely bound up with the storekeeper. It was there in order to get to the storekeeper. Yesterday he had been driving along up there himself. You always had to drive to the store. It was tiring. You drove there and gave away all the produce the farm could do without. You stood at the counter. Everyone stood at the counter.

He was surprised out of his thoughts. In front of him on the narrow path stood two town girls. They were lightly dressed. Brown skin. Flowers in their hands. Flowers in their belts.

They were standing right in front of him, laughing a little, about nothing, and he smiled unwillingly back. They made it natural and easy to smile.

They asked if he had been startled?

"No."

"Neither were we," said they, and disappeared into the copse that lined the narrow path.

Flowers in their hands, flowers in their belts. Life was easy.

They did not understand his temperament and mentality. They did not know what it was to be a part of the seasons. He tried to compare them with Aunt Anne and with Åsne, but gave up. Aunt Anne and Åsne and he himself shared in the great cycle all year round, and because of this they had a different mentality from those who spent only a few brief summer weeks here. The earth demanded work and serious purpose, and was insatiable in her demands. These strangers did not understand that. They could stand feeling insulted because country people did not have the time to notice them when the harvest was in full swing. They had other laws. Sometimes you watched them enviously as they passed; sometimes you felt grateful because you knew hundreds of things they would never see or learn. They could not share in the great cycle of the earth and the seasons.

He came to the old swimming hole at the river. There was Olav. He was lying on the flat stone drying off after a swim. He was tall and well-developed and was lying naked on a flat stone.

This was incredibly good—and at the same time incredibly casual after such longing. Olav had come. He saw Per and half rose. His body was light brown. He waited until Per had come down to the bank. Then he said, "Is that you?"

"Yes."

"The water's good today."

Per took off his clothes. The river was low and the stones baking hot. Baking hot sand. Per plunged into the narrow channel. Olav lay on the stone.

The water filtered past his sides. It was incredibly good to be there. There on the stone lay Olav, naked and friendless.

He must have been in the sun a good deal that summer; his body gleamed. He was tremendously handsome. In a little while he would talk about Åsne. He must have lost her by now.

Per swam. Beneath him he could see the clean pebbles on the river bed. The water was crystal clear. The Tvinna was wonderful.

The wave of warmth that had rushed through Per when he saw Olav subsided in the cool water. He was calm and could go ashore. Olav made room for him on the stone, and then they sat for a long time in silence.

"Have you been here before this summer?" asked Per uncertainly.

"Yes. Last Sunday."

"Åsne came once when I was here." He spoke her name as indifferently as he could. But that name had to be spoken. He had to talk about her.

"Oh, did she?" said Olav. "Yes, it had started by then."

"What in the world had started?" asked Per, taken aback.

"Oh, nothing. I know it started to be embarrassing and impossible, at any rate. Nothing else. But that's *enough,* isn't it —that it should be impossible?"

"Isn't there any more to it?" Per dared to ask directly now.

"I don't know. We're as bad as we can be to each other."

"Has she left Bringa?"

"No, are you crazy—in the middle of the harvest!"

"Then I suppose she'll go in October?"

"I suppose so."

"Where to?" said Per, so calmly that it hurt.

"To Bufast, surely?"

"Oh, indeed?" said Per. "That's what *you* say, and you don't mean a word of it."

"No."

"Does she want to go home?"

"Yes."

"Will she come back and marry you?"

"Yes. In two years' time. Perhaps. We disagree about everything."

It seemed to Per that the river was murmuring a little more loudly. That was the only unusual thing he noticed outside himself. It was not the same Olav who had come back. He had come, but he was different. They sat in silence, without any desire to say more. They were full of questions. They had made a mistake; they had thought they could speak out about everything close to their hearts—and they could not. But they could keep silent.

Olav did not expect to be upbraided for his behavior; that was clear. He did not say that he had behaved badly. He had simply come. Per was full of gratitude because Olav had come like this. Had he come like a sinner, Per would have left him at once.

In two years' time Åsne would come back to Bringa. Then all three of them would be twenty-one. When Olav had gotten this settled, he would come back again. But he would not come with downcast eyes because he had won the girl Per loved—and thank heaven for the person who has such confidence in you.

They lay still on the stone. They could smell the slight fragrance from their bodies, and from the warm stone too.

"You ought to come and see all the changes at Bufast."

"Yes, I should."

They went home to Bufast together.

14

That year it was heavy work reaping the grain. The sun felt hot. The work periods felt long. The stubble rustled about their feet, dry and prickly. Drier and more prickly than usual. Don't you feel it too? he felt like asking the others.

The carpenters hammered in the yard. The house for Aunt

Anne and Bjørn began to take shape. It would not be ready for the move until autumn.

Father sat indoors. But nothing happened that was not supposed to, in the fields or in the pasture. The man in the kitchen had the whole farm spread out in front of him, as if in a mirror, and knew all about it. He opened his mouth when things had to be done. He did not bother about any introduction but sat in his corner like a figure of wood and clay, suddenly opening his mouth to say something: "It's time to do so-and-so." It made Per start sometimes before he realized what was happening. Afterwards he went out into the meadow and the fields and did what the mouth had ordered. He did so with confidence: it was never mistaken.

Father sat there and could expect death daily. Something in him was about to crumble. They were all aware of it, he himself as well as the others. All the same he sat running his farm.

The grain was golden and ripe. But the sun had never burned as it did now during the harvest. Sweat glued up Per's eyes. It made him think of slaughter on the battlefield. The stubble rustled. Didn't the others hear how it rustled, prickly and reminiscent of death?

Per did not ask them out loud. The others went on reaping: Aunt Anne, Ivar, Åsmund.

They walked home across the prickly stubble. Death and parting seemed near. It was because of the prickly straw. They entered the house.

Father's mouth opened and asked, "What's the grain like at Brattåker now that it's in the sheaf?"

Ivar answered, "It's golden and ripe."

The potato harvest was like the reaping. The soil was heavy to walk in this year, heavier to dig in this year.

The potatoes lay in a friendly clump in the earth just beneath the leaves, like a family, stock still. Then they were torn up by the stem and shaken off the roots and lay shining and smooth in the daylight.

Doesn't one person feel that it's worse to be alive this autumn?

One day Aunt Anne said, "The potatoes have never been so easy as this year."

Knut Prikken was there to help. He and Åsmund dug side by side. Per struggled with the heavy sacks, drove them home, and tipped the potatoes into the cellar. They thudded and bumped against each other in a curious way. Father sat listening to the thuds and bumps in the cellar. He had plenty of time to calculate how many half-bushels had been emptied. He sat waiting for death.

Bjørn and the carpenters continued with the new house. The roof was on now. For the first time they could watch the house disappear into the thick autumn darkness. It seemed like a baptism for the house.

Per groped his way in through the gaping doorway one evening, attracted by the scent of pine. He caught sight of something in a corner. He went closer. It was a person. It was Aunt Anne.

"Auntie?"

"Yes. I just thought I'd come in for a little."

He turned to go. She sat as if hallowing her house. He ought not to disturb her or interfere. But she stopped him.

"I'm glad you came," she said.

"Why?"

Suddenly she lost control and tugged at him. "So that I can tell somebody! Something's going to happen to me, Per! In April."

He felt a stab of warmth. Auntie was going to have a child. He felt he ought not to be there, and went out again. She stayed. Outside there was a smell of rotted potato plants. A light was shining from the kitchen window.

Father opened his mouth and said, "The big bull will have to be slaughtered. He's too old."

This was early one morning. Father was sitting in his corner, waiting. In the meantime he condemned the big bull to death. At once the big bull had only a few hours left in which to live.

A cold draught of autumn and finality blew through the kitchen. You knew nothing about it, and then Father suddenly spoke the death sentence over the most powerful animal on the farm.

They made hurried preparations. Ivar had left by now, but Bjørn and the two carpenters were there to help. They found rope, and then looked at each other: who was going to dispatch the bull? There was only one person who ought to do it, and he sat crippled and helpless.

Åsmund came out and called to Per. Per hurried in. "Father's asking for you," said Åsmund.

"*You'll* have to slaughter the bull in my place," said Father. Per took a step backwards. "No—"

"No?" said Father.

"All right. I'll do it," said Per quickly.

Ice-cold autumn in the kitchen, he thought. Frost-hardened earth. He pictured it: the bull standing right in front of him. Himself with the rifle in his hand. It fired. The great beast collapsed. About him the ground was encrusted with ice.

He saw it all once more as he took the rifle down from the wall. The bull's eyes pursued him. Father sat destroyed, unable to do as much as a child. All the same, Father merely opened his mouth, and the big bull had to bite the dust.

The others stared when Per arrived with the rifle. He did not pay much attention. He was in the grip of an extraordinary sensation. There was a film of ice on the puddles. The faded grass was stiff. It was cold, as it should be. The bull should fall on hard ground.

A fever seized him. No, it was gone at once. He saw clearly, and his hands were steady again.

Bjørn and the two carpenters came out with the enormous beast. The bull walked forward slowly, his heavy head swaying a little, carried powerfully on his neck. His horns were erect. He did not *look* old, but his master, sitting quietly here on the farm, had said he was. He had stood in the barn for many summers, bellowing and butting the wall. The neighboring districts were full of his progeny. As the result of his virility, hundreds of cows had been bred who stood in the farms, being milked. If it were all put together a stream of white milk would flow from morning till night. That was why the bull was not being sent away alive; he must be allowed to die on the farm.

The bull strode forward. It was a long time since he had been out under the open sky. It was difficult to know whether to call him terrible or splendid. He stopped and sniffed the air. The air was thin and tasteless. He lifted a hoof and pawed the frozen ground with deliberation.

The moment had come. Per went forward. There was Aunt Anne standing with her back to them, unwilling to watch the bull fall. Two heads peeped out from behind the corner of a building: Åsmund and the birdlike head of Knut Prikken. Naturally Knut Prikken was there. Per saw and thought it all in an instant, then raised the rifle. The bull was looking straight at him. He must have known what it was all about. Why didn't he try to break loose? To gore them? He stood looking straight in front of him. It was true that Father was the one to have done this. He alone. Per saw this clearly as he raised the weapon between those staring eyes and pulled the trigger.

The big animal lost its footing and crumpled up. The ground was hard. The bull's hooves stretched stiffly up in the air.

Per was in the woods stacking firewood. The weather was mild again: rain and bare, cold branches. The entrails of the bull were lying out on the field with the magpies pecking and pulling at them. At home there was hammering and joining going on in the new house. Was Per the only one who knew how Aunt Anne had hallowed it that evening? Bjørn Moen must have known.

"Per," said Auntie, "is it true that Olav Bringa is going to marry Åsne?"

"Yes, it's true. In two years."

"Then you must find someone else!" said Auntie bluntly. "There are plenty who are willing. I think all of them would be."

He was grateful to her for saying so but pushed the thought away from him and went in to his father.

Father said, "Send for Skrim."

Skrim came the very next morning.

"Have you a lively young bull for me, Skrim?"

"Yes, I do know of one," said Skrim.

He brought the bull a couple of days later. The magpies in the field fluttered up from what they were worrying, and settled again as soon as Skrim and the bull had gone past. The bull was young and lightweight. He bellowed when he came into the yard, and it was almost a calf's bellow. Father caught a glimpse of him through the window, and looked satisfied. Shortly, the bull was standing tied in the old bull's stall. This one would stand there too and grow big and father hundreds of trembling calves. Milk would flow in the farms.

There was life here! Blind and fertile, with sap for the thirsty.

In the spring Aunt Anne would have a child. In a couple of years Åsne would marry and have children. What was he to do with himself in all this? He was drawn by the sap now just as when he was small. He was thirsty.

15

Timber had to be felled in the Bufast woods to pay off debts. Bjørn left the two carpenters to their own devices and came to the woods. Per gradually piled up the timber. The logs lay glimmering inside the dark piles of fir needles. In a few years the branches would harden and lie with the bark flaked off, and thickets of raspberry canes would spring up.

Goldie pulled the logs.

"How old is Goldie?" Bjørn happened to ask.

Per did not answer. Bjørn needn't have asked about that, he felt.

No snow fell before Christmas. During Christmas Per stayed at home. During Christmas Åsne was at Bringa; Olav came one day and told him so. "Åsne has been to see us," he said. "Yes, I suppose she has," said Per.

Life was no longer so painful. Olav often came to Bufast. Per went to Bringa less often. Åsne had gone home in October, as arranged.

Father sat through the whole of the Christmas holiday. He did not die, but embarked on a new year.

After the New Year came heavy snowfalls, and Per and Goldie were in the woods from morning till night.

How old is Goldie . . . ?

It was too bad that Bjørn had brought up that question, and in *that* tone of voice. Would Goldie soon have to be led away behind the wall of the barn, without harness, sway-backed and pot-bellied? Of course not. Goldie was as strong as ever. But perhaps Bjørn saw things more clearly, coming from outside the farm? No!

March.

At home windowpanes were shining in the new house, and a stove had been put in so that the carpenters would have a little warmth indoors and could boil glue. They were working on the floors and moldings and furniture. Aunt Anne, who was heavy with her child, spent long hours there watching. Then the carpenters would whistle quietly and strangely, each to himself.

It was not until April that they got the house sufficiently in order for the move. Bjørn Moen and Aunt Anne moved in. Signe Moen, Bjørn's much younger half-sister, was there too on moving day. And Bjørn's old mother and the brother who was to inherit the Moen farm. His father was dead.

They moved into a house of scented wood and gave a meal there for all the people on the farm except the farmer himself. He stared straight in front of him and remained sitting in his corner.

"Go on over, all of you," he ordered.

They went. And he was still alive when they returned.

Two weeks later Aunt Anne's child was born. That day Per laughed inwardly with relief. Now that too had happened to Auntie. It was the best thing that could have happened to her, the way she was. Now she was full of milk, as Mother had been once.

It was a raw, windy day. There was rain in the wind, and the remaining patches of snow shrank and disappeared. There was a strong scent of earth. Per went out of doors and wandered about.

This was how it should be! *Children* ought to be born here, rows of children, he thought. A kind of wildness. Rows of children, like the swallows that sit on the telegraph wires.

The ground was steaming. Wild desires seemed to rise up out of the earth, as imperceptibly as when the grass and leaves grow.

Now Aunt Anne was full of milk. And the air full of rain. He went back into the new house and told Auntie about the rain, managing to make a whole speech about it. Bjørn stared at him in amazement, as if he saw a different Per from the one he was used to. Auntie did not listen to him; she was lying waiting for the child to be old enough so that she could give him suck.

Åsmund was torturing himself about something. He looked as if he were walking about with wet feet all day, or something of the sort. Per noticed it very soon, and noticed in particular that Knut Prikken was no longer about. His skinny birdface did not pop up and disappear among the farm buildings any more.

"Where's Knut Prikken?" asked Per.

"He's at home."

"What's the matter?"

"None of your business," said Åsmund. "You all keep picking on me so."

But Åsmund seemed to want to confide in him all the same. Per was chopping wood. The field was too sodden to start plowing. One day when Per went across to the woodshed a piece of paper was lying on the chopping-block. The writing was in Åsmund's childish hand, and the note contained the answer to Per's question.

"It's God," it said. Not a word more.

For the rest of the day Åsmund avoided Per. He was embarrassed. It was God. Åsmund was old enough to prepare for confirmation that year. Per could well remember himself and all the frightened thoughts he had had at that time.

If Åsmund did not want to confide in anyone but himself, he must accept it, thought Per. He was grateful for it. And no sooner was he grateful than Åsmund understood this and came to him of his own accord.

"Knut's so odd these days," he began.

"Oh?"

"He says we shall go to hell because we're sinners," said Åsmund in a frightened voice.

"Who told Knut that?"

"He's read it. He won't ever come here again."

Per did not reply.

"We haven't done anything terribly wrong either. But we're sinners just the same."

Åsmund's eyes were scared. Long, bottled-up brooding was at last coming out.

"God has seen everything we've done," he said.

"Well, what have you done?" asked Per, knowing that it was a stupid question.

"Mmm, it's not very easy to explain. But it's enough to send us to hell, Knut says."

"I think you'd better talk to Mother about this," said Per. Åsmund's scared eyes worried him.

"No!"

"Somebody else, then?"

"No."

Per stood at a loss. There was nothing he could do about this. All he felt was his own brooding at the time of his confirmation.

"We've followed people and seen everything," Åsmund burst out.

"Well—"

"What shall we do, then?"

Per was silent.

"Shall we pray to God?"

"Yes, I think you'd better," muttered Per. He left him. Åsmund must be in bitter need to come to him like this, worse than himself, for he had managed to keep it in.

Over in his poverty-stricken home Knut Prikken, too, was torturing himself.

Per kept an eye on Åsmund but did not learn much. Åsmund did not come to him a second time with his fears. It was rather a relief that he did not do so. Per was still possessed by his old dread: you should not talk about God.

Knut Prikken was never around. They almost missed him. They were used to seeing his head peeping and gesticulating around the farm. But Knut stayed at home, suffering for his sins.

"Isn't Knut ever coming back?"

"Don't know," answered Åsmund.

Per could do nothing—just as no one had been able to do anything for him at that age. There's worse to come, he might have said.

"The grain must be sown today," said Father suddenly.

"Yes," said Per and Bjørn.

An agreement had been made with Bjørn about his work. He was to work on the farm and have a share in the crops and cattle. They had finished with the cleared land for the time being; it was more than enough work getting it into good condition. It was as if Father's eyes had cleared so that he could see this.

Aunt Anne had no time to help with any of the work out-doors. She was busy raising her child.

Per sowed the field with grain. He was taking the farmer's place. They say grain looks like a golden spray when it leaves the hand of the sower—and it was so.

16

Whitsunday.

That morning Per and Åsmund met in the yard. Åsmund was on his way to the woods with the sheep. This year he ran off alone with them.

Åsmund looked at Per contemptuously. He was not being given the day off and therefore looked at his brother with scorn. Per was forced to look away and somehow feel ashamed of himself. Åsmund said nothing; he was simply full of cold, wordless mockery of one who was free and in his Sunday best. He knew very well that Per had worked hard enough all week, but that didn't help today. It was a relief when he finally had to go.

Per had a difficult day in front of him, which was why he was doubly hurt by Åsmund's mockery.

"Come over to Bringa on Whitsunday," Olav had said last week.

"What for?"

"Åsne will be there."

"All right, I'll have to see," he had replied. He wondered why Olav wanted to hurt him. He would go after dinner to see why Olav wanted to hurt him.

The sky was blue. Blue smoke from the chimneys, and air that told you it was going to be hot.

Åsmund came home again with the sheep, his face swollen with crying. With crying in bitter loneliness, anger, and the sulks. Everyone noticed it, but not a word was said in comment. He would have to herd the sheep. Someone *had* to herd them, Whitsunday or no. They looked at Åsmund with calm eyes as if everything was as it should be. He was contemptuous of them all at this moment, and behind their calm expressions they were afraid of him.

Dinner time came. Whitsun was late that year; it was almost summer. The sun made them lazy. The air was full of the buzzing of bees.

Åsmund looked at them all coldly and scornfully and went off to his afternoon in the woods. This was his last spring with the sheep. Next year he would be confirmed. Per watched him go: next spring he would know what it was like to be out in earnest in the thistle fields.

Per got ready and walked to Bringa. He arrived before Åsne. It was Whitsun, and Whitsun weather. Leaves that had not been there before hung from the trees. Olav was very calm.

"She's bound to come when she promised," he said, wanting to be kind to Per.

"Yes, I expect she will," replied Per, wondering all the time why he should be tortured with this, why Olav was doing it.

There she was. You could tell from far away that it was Åsne. She nodded to Per. Then she went across and put her arms around Olav's neck. Unhesitatingly and frankly, as one might expect of her.

A bell was ringing; Per could hear it. No, it wasn't; what nonsense. But a bell was ringing and ringing.

The three of them spent the day together. An endlessly long Whitsunday afternoon. Åsne laughed. Åsne was fragrant. Per looked dizzily for a sign: a sign from her, signs and wonders. No. Nothing. She was big and tall—magnificent, it seemed to him. But the hand he took in farewell said nothing. Something he feared began growing in him.

Olav was very calm. He and Åsne were left together when Per went.

When Per was on the way home, it suddenly occurred to him that Olav had meant well in everything he had done. He laughed aloud bitterly and strangely at the idea.

He did not get home as soon as he had expected.

Halfway along the short-cut between Bringa and Bufast he met somebody. When he came nearer he saw it was Randi Bratterud.

No! he said quickly to himself.

He did not want her. He wanted to go away. He wanted to be left in peace. He would drown himself. He wanted to be left in peace by girls. The day with Olav and Åsne had tortured him to the marrow. He had very little control of himself now.

There was Randi coming to meet him. He did not love her. She must not come like that, must not lie in wait for him like that. She had clearly been waiting for him. When he first saw her, she was sitting down. When she saw him, she got to her feet and came to meet him. He watched her with fear.

But what a beautiful curve there was to her cheeks, and she had never wanted desperately to be the best in school, but had given clear, sensible answers. He could not run away now. He went towards her. She was a beautiful, full-grown girl coming to meet him.

"Good evening, Per."

"Good evening," he replied. He stood in front of her and knew that Randi wanted him. A kind of wild hope was flickering in her eyes. She had embarked on a daring gamble that evening.

He did not love her. He wanted to go. But instead he asked her whether they should find a big warm stone to sit on. He knew of one down by the river, he said. He wondered why he said such things, when he did not really want to at all.

"Yes, let's," she said. The hope in her eyes flickered up.

He was aware of the slight fragrance about a girl: of thin, clean clothes and hair. The scent of hair was like the earth. But there were other kinds of scents. He sensed it acutely and with terror. Something was going to happen that he would regret.

They went down to the flat stone where he and Olav Bringa used to lie to get dry after swimming. The river was swollen; the water lapped against the stone.

"Is that the big warm stone you know about?"

Her voice sounded quiet and a little thick. It was quiet and thick with waiting for what was going to happen.

The water flowed past. There was yellow sand on the bottom. Per would have given much to have had Olav beside him on the stone now. Then they would have had a quick swim in the chilly water, and afterwards lain naked and secure on the stone, enjoying the sun's warmth that the stone had soaked up. He would see the map of England in the small of Olav's back. They say it's a big country, Olav had said the very first time. It was precious, the memory of when he and Olav had met, and Olav had let him see England.

"You don't talk much, Per."

He gave a start. They had been sitting there for a long time. She was not as tall as Åsne. She made a movement and called all her fragrance to life. Did she know that? That she brought it to life and that it was dangerous for him? This would be a shameful and painful memory.

She was looking out over the water. Her cheek curved gently. She sat gently. She was a gentle girl.

He stretched out his right arm and drew her to him. He put his arm around her. It felt good to his hands. A large bell was ringing.

"What does this mean, Per?" she said.

He answered by finding her mouth.

It was shameful. He did not love her. But he could not bring himself to say that now. If only she had asked him: do you love me? Then perhaps he would have managed to say no, and saved them both. But she did not ask. She only kissed him.

"Per," she said. There was liberation and peace in her voice, peace as if after a long walk on a desolate, marshy heath. But she was deceiving herself, and he had not the will to tell her so. He behaved as if he loved her.

"Per," she said.

He understood her well enough. She wanted him. She had loved him for many years. In a flash he remembered many small things he had wondered about. Now he understood them. And now she was here, and she was going to stake everything on it. He saw she would stake everything she had this evening, and he hated her for it. He had not asked for this. At the same time as he was full of reluctance and anxiety, he was stroking her cautiously. His hands could not stop themselves.

"How I've longed for you, Per."

"Have you?"

"Have you been longing for me, Per?"

This was the moment in which to say *no* as hard as stone and quench this fire. Then she would tear herself away from him and stand there, curt and insulted, and say good night. But the words did not cross his lips. Her fragrance, the sight of her, his hands which thought this was good and right, bound them. They bound his words. He was a prisoner. Deep down inside he was angry.

"You don't answer?"

"Yes."

"Have you been longing for me?"

"Don't know," he said. "You don't do anything else but long for things, for everything," he said. One moment he was angry and cold, the next eager and dazed. This was a shameful day. Whitsunday. The Holy Spirit. The Holy Spirit, about Whom he had dreamed almost more than about anything else— He should have been present at an encounter such as this, or so he had thought.

She caressed him. "You didn't say no," she said. "I was so afraid of that!"

She had staked everything. She did not demand more words or promises. She was in a daze now. The cold, angry resistance deep inside Per was muffled.

"Come on, let's go," he said.

They jumped down from the stone. Whitsunday evening, still and warm. The air limpid, sounds carrying a long way. Not spring, not summer—a *becoming*.

They walked into the birch woods. The new leaves were shining.

Now there was no salvation. The resistance had gone entirely. Per scarcely knew what he was doing. He had no idea what *she* did.

Was she crying? She was sitting hunched up on a tussock of grass. He could hear no sound, but he knew she was crying. It was all miserable and spoiled. And what an enormous disappointment. What had he dreamed it could be? It was like crossing a frontier, and there on the other side you began with a great disappointment.

"You don't love me, Per?"

"No, I don't," he replied honestly. He could say it so easily now. He might have said so first, he thought.

"You might have said so first," she said.

In any case the words had the effect on her that he had expected. She got to her feet, her face dry and hard. She would not ask for pity. She had lost her gamble, but she still held her head high.

"No, I should have known you can't get anything by bullying," she said bitterly. "Good-bye then, Per."

She went. She had always carried herself proudly, and now she was herself again.

Per smiled sourly after she had disappeared among the

birches: the Holy Spirit had not been *here*. It had only been torment, and disappointment, and shame.

A cold thought came creeping in: am I going to be the father of a child? What shall I do?

How topsy-turvy everything was: a child that one ought to be so happy about. He thought of Bjørn and Aunt Anne.

Suddenly he saw more clearly what had happened: saw himself, saw Randi. But it did not alter the memory. The memory would be a memory of a disappointment. And shame, because it had not been right or true.

At last he went home to Bufast. It would soon be midnight, yet it was still light. From now on there would be a shadow over the long, light Whitsundays.

17

He was not going to be the father of Randi Bratterud's child.

He and Bjørn were digging the garden of the new house in the Bufast yard. Many weeks had passed since that ruined Whitsunday. It was past St. John's Day* and full summer. The cows were in the home pasture. The new bull was standing in the barn with lonely, empty days in front of him. He tried to see whether he could turn up the whites of his eyes and bellow. And he could.

In the evening Bjørn went into the house to look after the child, and Aunt Anne went to fetch the cows home. Auntie breathed fully and deeply. She was living fully and deeply now. You could see she was rich.

Inside the old house sat Father, still alive. Mother prepared the days for him. The farm kept running; it would not come to a stop even if Father were to die.

* Midsummer Day.

Some weeks after Whitsun Per got a letter from Randi Bratterud. "Can I talk to you?" it said. Nothing more. He trembled and wrote back to tell her where she could find him. Now he would be told that he could expect a child. What shall I do—?

They arrived at the meeting place almost at the same time.

"I'm glad you came," she said. "I couldn't be sure you would."

She looked the same as before, but that should not fool anyone.

"I did rush off so strangely," she said, looking directly at him.

He did not answer.

"Were you never the slightest bit in love with me, Per?"

"No."

"Nothing came of it either," she said in a strange voice.

An avalanche slid off his chest. How topsy-turvy it was. An avalanche lightened his chest because a great miracle had not happened to Randi.

"Was that good news?" she asked searchingly.

"Yes," he said.

"Yes, I suppose it was," she replied bitterly. "But it won't be a very pleasant memory all the same."

"Are you going already, Randi?"

"Yes. Good-bye. I've learned something now."

"Good-bye, Randi."

He scarcely knew which of them had lost. There she was, walking away.

I must go elsewhere, he thought. And he went home.

At home Father was sitting in the kitchen. He looked as if he knew all about it. Oh, no, it was only imagination, but he sat amazingly wide awake to everything that concerned Bufast. And this concerned Bufast. Into the middle of his preoccupation with Randi's sad words came the thought: this concerns Bufast. Everything I do concerns Bufast. All the young girls around concern Bufast. One of them is destined to be the housewife here. I won't—

Father was on guard.

Per could see it from his appearance. He sat still, but every little thing was noticed and considered. Father sat knowing more than they realized. It concerned Bufast.

This year Ivar did not take part in the haying for the first time as long as Per could remember.

Olav Bringa came on Sundays, and it made Sundays pleasant. It was good that Olav came as if nothing was the matter. He was not told about Randi Bratterud.

"I'm going to the agricultural school in the autumn," said Olav.

He was going to be married in the spring.

"Why don't you come too, Per?"

"No—"

But afterwards he thought it over. The idea stayed with him through the reaping and the potato digging. *I'm going to get away from here,* was what he thought.

Finally he talked to Mother about it—Mother, who prepared the days at Bufast.

"Yes, I've been thinking about it too," she said.

"But what about the money?" he said.

"Yes, that's the problem—I'll talk to your father."

A few hours later Father said abruptly, "Have to sell a cow to get money for school." You could hear from his voice that the cow was already sold.

At once it did not mean getting away after all. Bufast had an iron hand and held those who wanted to leave. Father had decided that this concerned Bufast. So a cow would have to go.

Per was not happy about it. He made his preparations. Olav came and was glad to have someone he knew at school with him. But Per was not in the least bit happy. A knot lay in his breast. He watched Skrim taking the cow out of the barn. One of the best ones, so that there would be money in it.

When he was ready to leave, Aunt Anne said it would be

strange to be without him, even though it was only for six months. *That* was comforting to take with him.

They were not to spend more than six months at the agricultural school. They could not afford to be there longer.

Father said little in farewell, simply stared in front of him. It was dreadful to leave him. He was unlikely to live until Per came home again. Mother packed him food for the journey. She gave him no advice, and he blessed her for it silently.

There was Åsmund. He would be going to confirmation class this winter. He stood there feeling that life was difficult and miserable, Per knew. He was growing fast and looked ungainly; he would be big and tall. He was lonely in the cold, harsh springtime he stood in. Knut Prikken was not here, but he did still come to Bufast now and then. Åsmund gave Per a curiously sad look; Per could not figure it out. Goldie took Per and Olav off to the boat. It was the middle of October.

18

So Per and Olav went back to school. A few things reminded them of school when they were boys, but not many. Now they were grown-up. There were no girls there either; only big, grown boys with strong hands.

They bought books and read about earth and animals and trees. They knew about these things already, and knew some things that were not written about in the books. But there were a lot of things they did not know, too. They went into big cowbarns and watched and learned. But Per could not help thinking of Aunt Anne, and then this cowbarn was no longer the best, however new and fine and large it was. Here, nobody got up early in the morning to make beestings pancakes when a cow had calved in the night.

Out in the fields and meadows there was not much to be done at this time of year. They had to sit reading and learn from the books. The weeks passed quickly and pleasantly. One could watch the great cycle which is a farm, see it with the eyes of others, and compare it with what one had seen oneself. It was best when you noticed that you knew about many small, hidden things that the books were unable to describe. All that mass of scents that one knew about, and all kinds of lights and sounds in the pageant.

Several of them were in the same position as Olav Bringa in that they were going to get married and take over a farm as soon as they returned home. They talked about their girls. Some of them told the others nothing. Pictures of girls were brought out of wallets and shown with a certain amount of embarrassment. Girls were discussed, and daring stories told about them. Everything had a background of earth. Earth and trees and farmyards were always a part of what the boys were talking about.

Bufast came close sometimes. How are things there now?

Tonight Father will die, Per might think in the evening when he went to bed. Åsmund wrote brief letters and told him dryly what was happening at home. Mother wrote longer letters and told him the same things. Aunt Anne wrote, but only about her baby. Bjørn and Father did not write.

Olav got splendid, long letters. The letters occasionally lay on the table waiting when Per came back first to the room he and Olav were sharing. There Åsne seemed to be lying. He would pick up the letter and hold it. Perhaps she had kept it at her breast before sending it.

Olav arrived.

"Åsne sends greetings," he threw out quickly as he read. How thoughtlessly and casually he said it!

The school was not far from the town, and they went in often. They would just wander around. Now and then they sat about in cafés, but the majority did so seldom. Most of them had no money. They only had strong hands that had been used to wielding farm implements since their childhood.

Tonight Father will die, thought Per as he undressed. He expected it in every letter. He began to feel something that was new to someone who had always lived at home and in the same place: homesickness.

They went home for Christmas.

When Per came in, he found Father sitting facing him. "Look, here he is!" he said loudly.

Per was deeply affected. Father had been waiting.

Everything was the same at Bufast. But as soon as Per arrived, Åsmund came and stood in front of him with frightened eyes. "This business of Knut Prikken—" he said, and failed to get out any more.

"What's happened to Knut?"

"But didn't you know—he's dead. Now, just before Christmas. He got a splinter in his finger, and it festered, and—"

"He's dead? And you never wrote to tell me?"

"It happened just before you came, I tell you! The funeral's on Holy Innocents' Day."

That strange birdlike face. Those eyes rolling around, everywhere at once. Now Knut was dead.

Dead. It was an oppressive word. It reminded you of dry stubble in the field after the harvest. It was brief, sharp, and comfortless.

"I watched—" said Åsmund tensely.

Per shuddered. He realized that Åsmund had watched something terrible. Åsmund had more to say—in defiance, or whatever it might be.

"*I'll* be invited to the funeral on Holy Innocents' Day too, even though it will be in a different parish."

"Yes."

"Nobody else will be invited from Bufast, let me tell you. Nobody at all from our parish."

"No."

Åsmund stood like a barrier of defiance and sorrow. It would not be crossed for a long time. I've never done anything to Knut Prikken, Per was about to say. But he stopped himself, uncertain, and went to the others.

200

"Hasn't he grown?" asked Auntie, showing him the baby.

He saw at first glance that Mother was tired. How was it with her and Father now?

"Åsne does nothing but sew," reported Olav. Per pictured her hands resting on small piles of homespun and linen; how her hand would pause for a little and remain there.

They were at a party together, at one of those familiar, dear Christmas parties. Per held Åsne's hand at that party; Olav held the other. Then they circled round the tree. On the other side of the ring was Randi Bratterud, and at another spot, Signe Moen. And there was Kari Tveit. Everything was the same. There was Åsmund, in the smaller ring between the adults and the crowd of youngsters nearest the fir branches. Knut Prikken was not at Åsmund's side this year; he lay dead in the neighboring parish.

Per was silent as they circled round. The tree was marvellous. It stood there, the focus of it all, as if sowing a new tree in every heart.

The ring halted and broke up. The party was not yet over, but Per left. Would he always have to leave the bright Christmas party in sadness? It was snowing silently. He could not see it. But he felt it when he tilted his head backwards. Snow falling through great tracts of darkness, down onto a face.

He and Olav travelled back to school at Twelfth Night.

Knut Prikken had then lain in the earth nine days. Per could not help thinking about Knut every once in a while. Knut had meant more than he had realized at the time when he went slipping between the buildings, nodding his head like a bird. He felt his absence strongly. Åsmund had come home from the funeral with his face stiff and tense. They had not been able to bring themselves to ask him about the wake. They had felt guilty.

Per and Olav went back to their books about earth and trees and animals. They learned to see it all as a whole, all of the rich cycle. Father had not been to a school like this, but

Per was certain that no one there knew what Father knew about the earth and the seasons.

A girls' class had been started at the school. Young girls learned how to look after the farmhouse and the cows. The boys watched the girls in their large blue aprons. It was like watching Mother during this period when they were unable to do so. They were like young mothers. They rolled up their sleeves to do the washing. They had flour on their aprons after baking bread. They came from the cowbarn with plump arms washed clean. The boys watched it all and said many thoughtless, rough things to hide it.

Once a week the boys and girls met socially. But then the girls were no longer pleasant young mothers. They were dressed up and were abrupt young girls with whom you felt a stranger. You longed to see them as they were every day among pleasant things, like flour and milk.

One day Olav said to Per, "Knut Prikken has lain in the earth two months now."

"Yes," said Per with a start of surprise.

Olav, too, was evidently burdened with something that had to do with Knut Prikken. Why did everyone feel guilty about Knut? Nobody had done him any harm.

Tonight Father will die.

Per put out the light.

But the letter saying that Father had died did not come. He longed to go home.

Spring was coming. They went out into the meadows to do early spring chores. Boys and girls met and went for walks in the evenings. Per had no desire to do so.

But I want to go home. That thought was clear enough. I want to go home; there's nothing there to frighten me any more. I'm not afraid of Father any more.

Olav was looking forward to going home with impatience.

"Are you in love with Åsne?" Per asked him.

Olav merely stared at him.

Per had not meant to say it like that; he had meant to ask,

Is Åsne in love with you? But it would have been wrong to have asked that. Olav had no doubt that she was.

One day school was finished, and they left. Now it was spring. Now Olav was going to get married.

On the way home Olav asked, half afraid, "Will you come to my wedding?"

No! no! was what Per wanted to answer. Olav knew that too.

"Do you think I should?" said Per.

"Yes."

"Yes, I think I should too."

19

Åsmund was confirmed. They all went to church from Bufast, all of them except Father. There was Åsmund, standing as if holding open an empty space beside him. It was where Knut Prikken ought to have been.

What would become of Åsmund? Would *he* take over Bufast, and marry and have children? He stood there in church, tall and withdrawn. After this he would bring his hurts and difficulties to Per no longer. He was too big now, and would suffer in silence.

In the congregation a year-old child was crying. It was Aunt Anne's boy. It was some time since he had been christened and given the name Helge.

The service was exactly the same: the confirmation candidates standing stiffly in two solemn rows, and silent, worn parents sitting in the chairs around them.

The Bufast people hurried home, home to the member of the family left behind alone. They had not intended that all of them should go, but he had told them sharply to do so.

Nobody said anything solemn to Åsmund, and Per knew

he was grateful for it. It was good to feel that Åsmund was grateful for once.

What will become of me, Åsmund was probably thinking. At home everything was just as when they had left. No calf had arrived and was lying on the floor as on Per's Confirmation Day.

All the same Father's eyes rested on Åsmund more than usual. Another son was grown-up and confirmed.

They sat at the table. "Well, well," said Father as they ate.

It sounded like the end of a task. It meant that Åsmund's childhood had been struggled through. Åsmund probably had a bitter taste in his mouth after making promises today that he could not keep.

After the spring plowing Olav Bringa sent out the invitations to his wedding. Many people were gathered there. Per was there from early morning until the evening. He kept Olav company among the crowds of people in the farmyard and farmhouse at Bringa. They were together all day.

So Åsne was married. She might well be satisfied.

It was easier after the wedding. Per felt as if he had rid himself of a burden. Åsne had become a burden, since he could not stop thinking about her, knowing at the same time that she belonged to Olav. Now he was rid of it.

The haying season went briskly. Åsmund's scything had improved greatly since the previous year. And Per realized that his own body was strong and fully-grown when he lay down in the field to rest. He used it until his limbs ached.

Aunt Anne did the raking. The child lay crawling and babbling. Auntie raked with her face turned towards the child.

Father sat just as before, and the whole of the summer passed. The carriages rumbled along the road above. Per stayed in the same place. Towards autumn Olav Bringa came and told him that Åsne was going to have a child at such and such a time. He told him with pride. Then the carriages rumbled again, and the river murmured again. Per stayed in the same place.

One day Åsmund announced that he wanted to go to school. It came almost as abruptly as the pronouncements Father made as he ran the farm without moving from the spot.

"I suppose I'll be going to school this autumn, won't I?" said Åsmund.

Per felt at once that Bufast was teetering between Åsmund and himself. Perhaps it was Bufast Åsmund wanted. Per's place. Had he *said* school, but meant that he ought to be offered Bufast?

Åsmund was an unknown quantity. He was on the far side of Botolv. There, beyond Botolv, he stood with Knut Prikken of the birdlike face. Per wanted to say to Åsmund: Why don't you stay here too? But he did not say it. He noted that he was reluctant to give up his place here. He was astonished to feel it; he had seldom thought of the farm with warmth, and perhaps never with affection—but now he realized that he *wanted* to stay there all the same. Father's eyes rested on him like a great weight.

There was a tense silence.

"Aren't you going to send *me* to school?" asked Åsmund once more.

"Do you want to go?" asked Mother.

Åsmund did not reply.

"Why don't you answer?" said Father. He had sat in silence.

"I don't know if I want to," said Åsmund dejectedly. Per felt how lonely he was, wandering about in the empty, painful fields of thistles.

"You said it as if you wanted to," said Mother.

"Yes, I do want to," answered Åsmund sharply, in defiance of something inside himself. "Can I go, then?"

Now Per was certain Åsmund wanted to take over Bufast.

"We've thought about this, and talked about it together,

long before the idea entered *your* head," said Mother calmly. "As long as we can manage to pay for it, you can go to school. It will mean mortgaging Bufast, you know."

"Yes," said Father.

"Because I suppose Per will be the one who'll take over the farm soon," she continued.

"Yes," said Father.

Åsmund said, "I hadn't thought of standing in anyone's way."

He went out. Per was left feeling guilty about Åsmund. What would he have preferred? All of a sudden it was obvious that Åsmund loved Bufast.

The mortgage was arranged, and Åsmund left. It was a bad day when he went. He was Bufast's flesh and blood, and belonged there. He had been a stranger, and this was curious, considering how devoted his mother had been to him; but now he would become doubly a stranger, an outsider to the whole cycle.

Short letters arrived from him, saying that he was well, and so on.

Now I shall stay here whether I want to or not, thought Per. But I do want to. I want to, even if it means that Åsmund will have to leave against his will.

20

The day for the slaughtering came late in October. Per had thought about the slaughtering at night before he fell asleep. He slept in the attic now, where Aunt Anne had lived for many years. Auntie's gentle, deep breathing had laid a film over the room.

This year Per had to be in charge of the autumn slaughtering. He had to get accustomed to it, he who would be master of the farm. The master of the farm was the one to slaughter the animals that belonged there.

After it was over Per lay up in his room thinking about the animals' eyes: staring animals' eyes beside the workbench; the icy fields of late autumn round about. The animals had stood with bent head waiting for the blow. He had had to take many lives.

These were night thoughts. They did not bother him during the day.

"Your father hasn't much time left to him," said Mother. "He scarcely eats anything."

But there was nothing they could do about it. And the farm did not stop running, but went calmly on.

"Do you ever think about Botolv, Per?" said Mother.

Per started in surprise. Yes, yes! He never forgot him.

"No," he said. "It was such a long time ago."

Her face cleared. "Yes, it was a long time ago," she said, and turned to her chores. Per saw that she was tired and worn.

Was it *not* hidden from her after all, the secret he had kept like the grave, of how Botolv had died?

This happened just before Christmas. Åsmund was not coming home. The school he went to was far away; it was too expensive to travel home just for those few days.

They seemed to hurry over celebrating Christmas. After the New Year Per and Goldie began working in the woods. Father sat in his usual place. Father is no different, thought Per; it's just this waiting that's so exhausting.

One evening when he was on his way upstairs to bed, Mother came after him and called him down. "Your father's asking for you."

He found Father sitting tall and upright. He turned to Per.

"I've been sitting here, and it seems to me I have no sons," he said in that rusty voice of his, and with a strange rumble that was disturbing and full of power. Father was not at all weak, sitting there. He was powerful.

Per did not reply. Something in his father's tone annoyed him, so that he had a sharp reply ready on his tongue, but stifled it in time.

The whole weight of Father's face was on Per. "You were the one who wanted to leave us, weren't you?"

"Yes, I—"

"Do you still want to leave?"

"No, not now."

The threatening rumble in the voice disappeared, and his face expressed relief and trust.

"You're going to stay at Bufast, then?"

"Yes," said Per.

"Well, Bufast will give you all you need."

This was uttered like a calm assertion. It was simply stated. "All right, you can go, Per."

Per went.

"I'm going to have another child," said Aunt Anne. "What do you think of that, Per?"

"I don't think anything."

But the news made him happy. Helge was old enough to run about on his own. Now another child was coming. And over at Bringa Åsne was waiting for her child to be born. It was a strange place to be: children came, a frightening unseen force that drove men and women together without asking whether the life that was tossed in would be a happy or unhappy one. He both hated and liked it.

In April Bjørn said, "Goldie will have to be shot soon. Can't you see how old he is?"

Per was hurt. "Is he old?"

"Surely you can see that? No, I suppose you notice it less since you see him all the time."

Don't say old plug, wished Per, and Bjørn did not say it. Goldie stood stamping in his stall.

They did not mention this conversation to anyone. But Father noticed everything that happened on the farm, even though he sat increasingly silent.

"No use keeping Goldie any longer," he said suddenly one day, as suddenly as when a cup is shattered. Everyone gave a start of surprise.

They waited for more. Father sat pale and withered, and condemned Goldie to death. Mother was standing ladling out water; she paused, holding the full dipper out in front of her. They waited for more, and it came.

"Do you hear? Goldie must be shot."

"Yes," said Per. "We heard you."

"You'll have to do it, Per."

"Yes," said Per.

Mother poured the water into the washtub; there was nothing more to come. Goldie was finished.

Father kept to his chair. The animals out there never saw him now, but they fell dead when he opened his feeble mouth and said they should. There ought to have been something horrible about it, but there was not. It ought to have produced cold hatred on the part of the animals for this half-dead man who still had authority to take life from animals full of wild vitality. But animals could not hate. They merely stood, puzzled, waiting passively for the blow or the bullet.

Per ambled about for a while. Down in the stall he could hear a stamping against wood. He found his hat and dragged out the cart. The ground was bare early that year; it was possible to drive the cart in April. Per harnessed Goldie and drove over to the store; the eternal road to the store.

Mild damp air, black muddy fields, and grayish-white dead meadows. Birds were singing somewhere on the naked boughs. Goldie pulled the cart, and his belly and his hooves told Per that he was old. When he drew up beside the worn hitching post outside the store, he would stand hanging his lower lip.

They came to the hitching post. Goldie was given a wisp of hay but was not particularly hungry. He stood hanging his lip. Per went inside to the counter and bought something. He had no errand to the store today. He simply put what he had bought in his pocket and went out again. Tomorrow he would aim his rifle at Goldie, and that would be the end of it.

Outside, a man was standing looking at Goldie.

"Goldie's getting old now, Per."

"Is he?"

Goldie stood hanging his lip.

Another man wandered by, stopped beside Per and the first man, and said, "Goldie's getting old now, Per."

Per did not reply. Goldie hung his lip. Per freed him from the post and drove home. He was annoyed. What a stupid idea of his, to drive to the store! Suddenly he remembered that he ought to take home a sack of flour now before they were without a horse. He turned Goldie again and drove back to the post. A man with a rucksack came out of the store with a new spade in his hand. He stopped and looked at Goldie hanging his lip. Hold your tongue, wished Per. But the man said, "You'll be needing a new horse at Bufast soon."

"No!" said Per.

He was given a sack of flour and drove home for the second time.

The next morning was cloudy and thick with large, wet snowflakes that melted as soon as they fell. The ground stayed bare.

No one at Bufast felt like eating. Aunt Anne was in the barn. "I'm not going to be there," she had said. She was heavy with her child. Father was in his usual place. His eyes followed the rest of them as they got ready to carry out his order. Mother and Per and Bjørn made themselves ready.

When Per went to the stall, Goldie was standing hanging his lip as usual. Per put the bridle on him and led him out, across the yard and behind the barn. If there had been a little boy of suitable age in the Bufast kitchen now, he would have been peeping to see what Per had once seen: an oddly naked horse being led quietly behind the barn to be shot. But Helge was too small.

Bjørn took the bridle. Per fetched the small rifle. Goldie was stooping a little. His eyes were black. He did not move a muscle. Goldie, who had snorted and stamped when he smelled slaughter, must have known what *this* was. But he stood still.

Then the bullet hit him. Bjørn took out his knife and used it. Mother was with them for a while; then she went in.

It was mild and still; the snowflakes had stopped falling. The roar of the river stressed how still it was, how sounds carried a long way.

Goldie lay in front of Per and Bjørn; they stood upright. Bjørn went to get something. Per was left close beside Goldie, who was now nothing but a large, dead animal.

At that moment something mysterious happened. Per thought he sensed the earth around him in a different way from before. The wet, awakening earth had mild, cloudy air above it. A slight haze, a thin mist, lay over the meadow. And here, in front of him, on this earth, lay Goldie asleep forever. Per stood trembling and saw it all. He felt that he loved earth. It awoke in his consciousness. He was completely bound to it. To earth. His eyes had become clearer and his ears more sensitive and his heart more open, it seemed to him. He stood in front of the shot horse filled with one single emotion: he loved earth—and air and water, and changes in the weather. It was *right* for him to stay here to the end of his days.

How strange that it should be Goldie who had made it clear to him at this moment. Goldie, who was dead, and who did not spread fear around him because of it, but seemed to be lying in the only place where he could lie so peacefully: the place where he had worked so long.

Per took in an enormous landscape: the horizon of blue mountains, the wooded hillsides, the river, the meadow and the fields, and the gray, damp air. And the big, dead body of the yellow horse.

Bjørn coughed behind Per's back. Per started out of his

thoughts. Had Bjørn been standing there long? Bjørn said nothing. They began to work.

Per suddenly felt he must go in to see Father. Father might die any minute. There he sat, weak as a blade of grass. He did not know what Per knew: that what he had once sown in Per had sprung out today.

"I hear it went well," he said.

"Yes," said Per. He went out again. He did not go over to Father and say: I have come to love earth.

The horse lay as before. The air was just as mild, the earth just as wet and awakening. What he had felt was no illusion; it was reality.

21

"Send for Skrim."

Skrim came. Skrim was much older than Father, but still vigorous.

"You're poorly these days, Eilev," he said.

"That's so."

"I suppose you're looking for a horse?" said Skrim.

"Yes. If you know of one that'll be of use to me, you can buy it."

He said: that'll be of use to me, even though he knew he would never set a finger on the reins.

Skrim said he knew of one. He knew about all the horses and cattle for many miles in all directions. But he could never be good to animals.

So Skrim came back with a gray yearling. Bjørn and Per and Aunt Anne stood around him. Auntie was heavy with her child. She drank in the sight of the splendid animal. Father was unable to come out. The gray horse was led in front of the window.

Skrim said, "You can trust me when I tell you he's a good all-round horse, Eilev. Have I ever lied to you?"

"No, not that I've ever found out."

The spring plowing was different this year. It seemed to Per that he saw the earth as it really was. It was good. In the future he would be close to it.

It was a wild spring of waiting. Auntie gave birth to her child; it was another boy. He floated in milk. At Bringa Åsne's child was born; it was a girl. Olav came bursting with the news.

A wild spring.

"Isn't Åsmund coming home soon?" tumbled out of Father in his eternal sitting.

"Not yet. He'll come after midsummer."

"But I'm dying, you see—"

Per and Mother sprang over to him. He had collapsed in his chair, and lay trying to say more but could not get it out. He struggled wildly with his arms but could not speak. The light gradually went out of him.

They called his name: "Eilev!" "Father!"

His eyes merely widened. He probably saw his farm Bufast more clearly than ever before: fences, wide meadows, cattle.

Per ran across to the other house to find Bjørn. Bjørn ran for the doctor. Aunt Anne went back with Per.

"Eilev, my dear!" said Auntie.

He did not see her. And Bjørn was too late with the doctor. Eilev Bufast was dead before they came.

There was nothing frightening about him. He was laid in his coffin and put in his own barn while they were busy with the arrangements for the funeral.

Åsmund was sent for, was excused from his lessons, and arrived at Bufast the day before the funeral.

When Åsmund stood in the doorway, they all noticed that there was something new and strange about him, a different kind of strangeness from before. Mother went in with him to his father.

Per was at once made aware that Mother was a widow. He could not point to anything in particular, and yet he was aware of it. People fell quiet in her presence.

When all the hubbub of the wake was over, late in the evening, they sat in the house very silent, tired, and forlorn.

Mother was the first to move.

"Well," she said, "I suppose we'd better get some sleep. It's late." She got to her feet. The others made no move. The house was empty and cold that night.

"Go to bed," she repeated. "It's late."

"Yes," they said.

It was a great loss. They looked around for the gaping emptiness that was there. They could not see it. It was behind their backs all the time. They felt unbearable longing for that rusty voice. Sometimes it had sounded like gravel thrown from a shovel, scattering, falling, and then silence.

Per, curt and gruff, confronted Åsmund. "Do you like it where you are?"

"It's all right."

"When are you going back?"

"Tomorrow. I'm in the way here at Bufast."

"*I've* never said so."

They stopped in time and went their separate ways to bed. They had an urge to sling out the most cutting words they knew. It was because Father was dead and Mother was a widow. They pulled themselves together and realized that they were savage with sorrow.

Before Åsmund left, he and Per had a brief talk. Per could not rest until he had a clear statement from Åsmund about himself and Bufast.

"Would you prefer to leave school and stay at Bufast?"

"Yes," said Åsmund.

"Then why not do it?" said Per as indifferently as he could. But Åsmund only laughed a cold little laugh.

"Oh, no. We can't hit it off together. I'd better stick to it now that I've begun."

"But you'll be a complete stranger soon."

"Yes, I suppose I will."

"Why don't you *stay* then!" Per almost shouted, dread sneaking in.

Åsmund was caught by the same sneaking dread, but he hardened himself defiantly.

"I'm sticking to it now that I've begun, I told you."

The spring merely sparkled on. Per was the one to run the farm, and he did so. He and Bjørn stood side by side; Bjørn was much the older, but Per ran it. You learned quickly how to do it, he found. He should not have been fooled by the early weakness in his knees. It soon disappeared.

What was this? Images began piling up in him once more: Goldie with hooves outstretched.

Father dead in his chair, his lower lip hanging and passive.

Aunt Anne nursing her new baby so that the milk spurted.

A wild spring.

On.

22

An avalanche fell in the darkness: the sense of loss after Father.

Life did not move on for *everyone* after Father's death— for Mother it looked as if it would come to a halt. She alone entered into a new period so clearly that everyone noticed it.

A widow.

The word attached itself to her in spite of one's wishes and intentions. This was what she *was*. The word was reminiscent of scythed stubble in the field.

There was no time to sit still with their sorrow. Bufast demanded that they all play their part. Per's hands were full; there was a long list of chores to be done every day. It was a blessing. Only once or twice did he start and listen, as if hearing an avalanche on a slope far away.

It was the loss. You pushed it away from you.

On! About them lived earth and trees, indifferent and rich. The farm must go on as before, and it did so. Mother, for her part, could barely cope with it.

Mother. A widow. The two names tussled for validity. The one was dear, the other oppressive.

Mother! Per wanted to call across the yard when he saw her going from house to house.

She would stop and listen, and you knew an avalanche was falling.

She stood in the farmyard like the half of a cleft tree after the wind has felled the other half. The tree has branches on the one side only, and will soon be blown down in its turn.

Per could see how the shadow of Eilev Bufast rose up and grew vast before her. Perhaps she thought she saw him as he was now.

The shadow of a mountain.

"Your father—" she said to Per in a new tone of voice, saying it with veneration as if speaking about great things, great mountains. It was getting dark. She got to her feet. "Good night, Per."

She went to her room, through the kitchen and into the bedroom. It seemed immodest to watch her.

A widow.

She lay down and listened.

No one saw her come in again in the morning. She was always up first. But you imagined she came in noiselessly. Things that had belonged to Father appeared quietly from their hiding places and were collected in a cupboard on their own. It was done when nobody was looking, and made a strong impression. If anyone had opened the cupboard, it would have seemed like opening a grave, because of the shut-in smell of earth from the worn, soiled work clothes lying inside.

The days at Bufast had to pass through her care now as before, but they did not come quite as whole and complete and were not her work only; they seemed to live a life of their own. She was about to lose control of them. The farm passed very slightly into other hands.

She would look about her in astonishment: did no one care that Eilev Bufast was dead?

"I don't understand it," she said to Per when she was alone with him.

"What?"

"Did his death mean nothing to you? To you and Åsmund and the others?"

"Yes, of course."

"No," she said.

"That's an unkind thing to say."

"No," she said, like a blind person, "I'm the only one who remembers, it seems to me."

He replied that she must think as she pleased. He could do nothing but let the unjust accusation stand.

"Well, I'd never have believed it," she said.

He saw that Mother had grown old, old too soon. But it was incredible that she should not understand that not one blade of grass stops growing because a person dies. She seemed offended because Bufast did not stand still and listen like herself. Eilev Bufast had meant more to her than she had realized when he had filled the kitchen with his rusty voice.

"I see now," she said again one day. "When it's too late, you see a great deal."

Per did not want to hear; he did not want to witness Mother's confession.

But Mother had to confess.

"Once your father was quite—"

"It has nothing to do with me!" broke in Per. "I don't

want to hear about things when it's too late—as you said."

"Yes, it's too late," she said. "One day it will be too late for us all."

She paused, and seemed to listen.

Per listened.

An avalanche fell somewhere. There was no other name for it. Mother shivered and said, "I'll hold my tongue, Per."

23

This year Aunt Anne was so busy with her children that she had to find help. They did not hire a girl; it was too difficult to find the money to pay her, but Bjørn went home to Moen and got his sister, Signe, to come and help for the summer.

Åsmund had come home for summer vacation. He worked with them that summer but still did not seem one of them. He would move away from them gradually, and showed that he intended to do so.

Mother prepared the days. She kept her word and was silent about her loss.

Olav Bringa came less often. And when he came he talked mostly about the child. If Per went to Bringa on a Sunday, the child was the center of conversation there.

He was about to lose Olav again. And things could never be the same as they used to be between them anyway. Now he could contemplate more calmly the prospect of losing him.

Åsmund hung about during the vacation and still seemed to be grieving for Knut Prikken. Per thought that his friendship with Olav must have been a poorer sort by comparison.

Later on this became Signe Moen's summer in his memory. She was much younger than her half-brother Bjørn—the same age as Per—and Bjørn treated her and talked to her as if she were still a young girl. Bjørn did not see that Signe was grown-up. Per did. He saw her mostly in brief glimpses; then he did not see her at all. But he had seen her.

She was beautiful. But there was much else besides. She was quiet, he saw, and capable. Signe and Mother, and Signe and Aunt Anne together wove Bufast into a triple weave of womanly concern. The men merely went through and under the weave like a rough warp.

Later that summer he came to believe he had thought about her always. Ever since the day when Åsne had come wading down the river, naked and small, and had spoken the name Signe Moen for the first time.

One could not be killed. He had been dead inside since Åsne went to Olav. But it had been a delusion. He felt now that he was full of strength. He remembered Aunt Anne and how she had righted herself again like a patch of meadow after a hailstorm. Only when one lay on the earth sprawling and stiff like Goldie and like Father, only then was one killed.

Signe Moen went to the pasture to fetch home the cows. She brought them as Auntie used to do: walking in the middle of the herd of white backs and red flanks, with a greedy cloud of horseflies and midges buzzing above them. She pushed up the sleeves of her dress and did the milking, and came out of the doorway carrying foaming buckets.

Per saw it all.

Was this right?

Here, at any rate, was richness.

That summer the big, horse-drawn, four-wheeled carriages bringing the tourists along the post roads disappeared. The new vehicle, the automobile, came instead. The horses started and shied sometimes when they saw this absurd animal. It went terribly fast.

From the yard at Bufast they watched the dust clouds rising into the air from this new, unimagined speed up on the road. The way people rushed about! Up on the road a new epoch was roaring, but here on the farm they stayed in the same place. Rain would fall on the same fields, and the cows would yield bristling, warm jets of milk. The working day here would be just as hard.

One morning they were hanging the hay on the drying fences, on a strip of field shaped like a long tongue. Bufast was gradually acquiring many fields and meadows.

The grass on the tongue of land was thick, so the drying fences had to stand close together. The weather was changeable, with showers and lengthy spells of hot sun alternating as the days went by. There was a fragrance from the growing grass and the newly mown ground. Up on the road an automobile roared and was gone. Bluebottles sat on small heaps of horse dung, glittering like steel.

Per had scythed a section of the thick grass late the previous evening. The grass was lying as fresh as if newly mown. It had rained in the night, and the grass was heavy.

Per, Bjørn, Åsmund, and Signe were hanging the hay on the drying fence. When it hung there on the wire, the dew and moisture began dripping from the ends of the stalks. The whole fence was full of it; it poured off.

Their clothes were wet from hanging up the hay. But it was warm, so they did not feel chilled. Per saw that Signe was wearing a light blue dress. Strangely fascinated, he noticed how two darker patches of moisture appeared on her breast where she had pressed the armful of hay against her body.

He thought she was goodness itself.

He thought something would have to happen, but it did not. They went on hanging up the hay as fast as they could through the morning. The sun burned, then hid itself again. Bjørn and Åsmund went to rake the green hay into heaps on another patch. Now Per and Signe were alone. He knew her;

he had seen her all his life. Suddenly he remembered innumerable things about her. He looked at her, but she looked away.

They were raking near the end of one of the fences. Something brown moved in the pile of grass. It was a frog, half dead; it had been cut by the scythe and was dragging itself along. It was Signe who found it.

"Ugh! Come here!"

He came quickly.

"Look at this."

The frog was injured horribly and lay struggling. Per shuddered. Then he said all of a sudden, "What shall we do with it? You, who are such a kind, kind person, shall we kill it?"

"Yes," she said seriously.

Afterwards he wondered why he had said such a thing. Calling her a kind, kind person. It sounded so odd, but it had simply rolled off the tip of his tongue.

He found a fence post to hit the frog. Signe turned away and bent to pick up another armful of hay. Per struck. The frog screamed a tiny scream the instant it felt the blow. Per heard Signe give a little moan when she heard the frog scream. It sounded strange. It was full of sympathy and sorrow for the frog, or for whatever lives and feels. It cut Per to the quick.

She did not look up.

He dropped the frog into an empty posthole. Quickly. As if it were important to free his hands as quickly as he could and go over and take hold of Signe Moen, who had to be his girl. It lay before him so clearly that he was startled.

The frog disappeared into the darkness of the hole. Per stood up, eager and trembling. Signe was there in front of him. Her arms were wet, and a little red where the wet grass had rubbed them. Her lap and her breast were wet.

"Signe," he said abruptly, "I'm in love with you!"

"Yes?"

She said it expectantly and yet as if she had known it all

along. She stood there and said yes as if they were at last talking about something that had been ready and waiting all summer.

"I'm in love with you," he repeated. They were heavy words, difficult to say, but he wanted to say them. Thin, cold voices that denied it were stifled.

"I'm glad," she said straightforwardly.

Suddenly he was afraid of her. He *didn't* know her after all. He had not expected that answer. He was scared. No. This was right. This one would be able to prepare the days on a farm.

He took her in his arms and held her close. She was fragrant with the earth and the moisture that had attached itself to her, and with her own youth. He felt her body rest against him. Her body was calm, as if arrived at its goal. A wry thought flashed through him: that she felt she had arrived at a goal of her own planning. No. He pushed it aside. She radiated calm and peace. But she could not blind him; he had gone through a hard apprenticeship in what work really is. He saw shadows in front of him: hard work, debt, anxieties.

But this is what I want.

Meanwhile he sat and kissed her. He was giddy. Great waves like the sea seemed to be rising inside him. Before long he would go to her in all solemnity—and whatever happened that meeting would be better than the painful encounter with Randi Bratterud on Whitsunday.

"Let me go. Bjørn and Åsmund are coming back!" she said.

"Let them come," he said indifferently, and kept his arms around her. At last he had found something certain to hold onto. He felt a fleeting peace. This was no goal, but a great turning-point.

"Let them see," he said.

So he had said that he meant it. That this was no game, but bitter earnest. And that was how she accepted it. Her body was heavier against him because of his words.

222

He asked her if she had been sure it would turn out this way?

"No, and yet—"

He was close to the earth now, pressed close to it by the weight of a woman. He was intensely one with the great cycle.

Suddenly he remembered the dead figure of Goldie and how, close to that stiffened body, he had had his eyes opened to the chain of being. There was peace in pausing at the memory of Goldie lying on the trampled earth.

Published in the
Nordic Translation Series

FROM DENMARK

H. C. Branner, *Two Minutes of Silence*. Selected short stories, translated by Vera Lindholm Vance, with an introduction by Richard B. Vowles. 1966.

Jacob Paludan, *Jørgen Stein*. Translated by Carl Malmberg, with an introduction by P. M. Mitchell. 1966.

FROM FINLAND

Hagar Olsson, *The Woodcarver and Death*. *Träsnidaren och döden*, translated by George C. Schoolfield. 1965.

Toivo Pekkanen, *My Childhood*. *Lapsuuteni*, translated by Alan Blair, with an introduction by Thomas Warburton. 1966.

F. E. Sillanpää, *People in the Summer Night*. *Ihmiset suviyössä*, translated by Alan Blair, with an introduction by Thomas Warburton. 1966.

FROM ICELAND

Fire and Ice: Three Icelandic Plays, with introductions by Einar Haugen. Jóhann Sigurjónsson, *The Wish* (*Galdra-Loftur*), translated by Einar Haugen. Davið Stefánsson, *The Golden Gate* (*Gullna hliðið*), translated by G. M. Gathorne-Hardy. Agnar Thórðarson, *Atoms and Madams* (*Kjarnorka og kvenhylli*), translated by Einar Haugen. 1967.

Gunnar Gunnarsson, *The Black Cliffs*. *Svartfugl*, translated by Cecil Wood, with an introduction by Richard N. Ringler. 1967.

FROM NORWAY

Aksel Sandemose, *The Werewolf. Varulven,* translated by Gustaf Lannestock, with an introduction by Harald S. Næss. 1966.

Tarjei Vesaas, *The Great Cycle. Det store spelet,* translated by Elizabeth Rokkan, with an introduction by Harald S. Næss. 1967.

FROM SWEDEN

Karin Boye, *Kallocain.* Translated by Gustaf Lannestock, with an introduction by Richard B. Vowles. 1966.

Peder Sjögren, *Bread of Love. Kärlekens bröd,* translated by Richard B. Vowles. 1965

Other translations to come.